UNINTENDED
HERO

ENDORSEMENTS

Becky Van Vleet's *Unintended Hero* offers readers a chance to live the World War II experience in a very unique way—through the thoughts, prayers, and experiences of one individual. In great and precise detail, Becky paints a picture of the daily life of a teenage sailor, fully revealing his insecurities, dreams, passions, and fears. With each chapter set against the backdrop of unparalleled events, we examine Walter Troyan's growth from boy to man. Through this sailor's eyes, we view the unparalleled horrors of war alongside the essential bonds of love, faith, and friendship. With its intimate point of view, *Unintended Hero* asks us to reexamine history in a way that is personal and moving while also helping us realize that the narrative of World War II is most clearly understood in the combined and powerful stories of millions of individuals thrown together to mend a world torn apart. Thanks to reading *Unintended Hero*, I know my late grandfather, who served in the Navy during World War II, so much better, and I more deeply appreciate his service and the service of millions of others.

—Ace Collins, bestselling author and Christy Award winner

As a reader who enjoys biography, this book satisfied thoroughly. The story line moves through Pearl Harbor to the end of WWII by following Walter Troyan as he decides to leave his junior year of high school to join the Navy. The book describes his family's reaction, the school's position, and the tenor of the country at large. Each step of boot camp, deployment, friendships, and challenges during four years of war is shown from Walter's viewpoint. The reader experiences WWII up close and personal, leaving little to the imagination. Most poignant is his difficulty at the end of the war to come to terms with what he had experienced and his concern for his new bride. It is Walter's faith that strengthens him to face the future and cope with the memories. This is a story of courage, resolution, and overcoming challenges. There are several appendixes at the end which describe military terms, specs on ships, and lots of photos. An easy read with a strong message, written by Walter's daughter, who researched very meticulously.

—**Cleo Lampos**, BEd; MEd. Coauthor of two WWII books: *The Food That Held the World Together*, and *WWII Christmas Scrapbook*. Mr Lampos is a storyteller who brings lesser-known accounts of WWII to audiences.

UNINTENDED HERO

BECKY VAN VLEET

ELK LAKE PUBLISHING INC

PUBLISHING THE POSITIVE
Plymouth, Massachusetts

COPYRIGHT NOTICE

Cover and Interior Design: Jeff Gifford, Derinda Babcock
Editor(s): Steve Mathisen, Deb Haggerty

PUBLISHED BY: Elk Lake Publishing, Inc., 35 Dogwood Drive, Plymouth, MA 02360, 2022

Library Cataloging Data

Names: Van Vleet, Becky (Becky Van Vleet)

Unintended Hero / Becky Van Vleet

p. 23cm × 15cm (9in × 6 in.)

ISBN-13: 978-1-64949-690-4 (paperback) | 978-1-64949-691-1 (trade hardcover) | 978-1-64949-692-8 (trade paperback) | 978-1-64949-693-5 (e-book)

Key Words: World War II, US Navy, sailors, Pacific Theater, naval battles, family, Christian

Library of Congress Control Number: 2022944321 Fiction

DEDICATIONS

This book is dedicated to my father, Walter Troyan, and the other sixteen million Americans who answered the call to defend our country in World War II, sacrificing school, jobs, families, homes, personal aspirations, and their very lives.

LETTER TO MY READERS

Walter Troyan answered the call of duty to fight for his country in World War II at the young age of sixteen. I have answered my own call to write his story. Growing up with parents from the Greatest Generation as Walter's third daughter, I heard his recollections about the stock market crashing in 1929, followed by the Great Depression. I listened to my father's stories about World War II with a rapt ear, and I was especially fascinated with his life aboard the *USS Denver*. In 1990, I pulled out two chairs at my kitchen table with my dated cassette recorder, and I asked my father to tell me all his war recollections.

For the next two hours, his stories tumbled out with pride and a remarkable remembrance. I sat spellbound, taking it all in. At the time, my plan was to simply save the two cassettes as historical keepsakes for my family. But more than thirty years later, the call to write a book to preserve these stories came loud and clear.

I have intentionally included colloquialisms to create a sense of the US Navy and the period. Military times are used as they were recorded in the ship's deck logs. A glossary of Navy terminology, shipboard terms, and colloquial expressions of the day is provided at the back of the book. Nonfiction and fiction come together to create a story about my father's adventures and experiences aboard the *USS Denver*. This light cruiser becomes, in her own right, a pivotal character. I hope that Walter's story will honor him and all the young Americans, including the Japanese Americans, who stopped what they were doing to enlist in the military to fight for our country in the spirit of patriotism and loyalty like no other.

To that end, Walter's story would not be complete without mentioning the 33,000 Japanese Americans who served in our country's military in World War II. This valiant group of people fought against their own race to demonstrate their allegiance to America—their true and actual home. The hostility and resentment from the *Denver* sailors against the Japanese nation I portray clearly in this story were very true to the time. It is a part of our country's history. This in no way reflects our nation's relationship with Japan in current times. Today our country is blessed with citizens from many cultural and ethnic backgrounds, including Japanese, all of whom have made our America a richer nation.

"All ships have souls, and all the sailors know it."
—Edward L. Beach, Jr.

PART ONE: WALTER'S DECISION

CHAPTER ONE

"Walter, quick!" His mother grabbed his elbow and pulled him away from his friends gathered outside after worship—her face white and cold as snow.

"We have to get home right now," she said, her voice wavering. "We have to get the radio on."

Walter pulled his elbow back. "What's going on?"

Mom waved at Arthur on the other side of the walkway to catch his attention and motioned him over.

"I'll tell you, but let's get out of the church crowd and get to the car."

Pop walked by and whipped out his handkerchief, wiping his brow. "Come on, boys. The word is spreading fast."

Before the family reached their green 1936 Plymouth, Walter heard moans and gasps from the church parishioners and turned around. Many had started huddling into groups with embraces and tears.

"Mom, Pop, c'mon. I asked what's going on?"

"We just heard there's been an announcement about an attack on Pearl Harbor. Sounds like the whole base has been struck down by Japanese planes."

The family jumped into their car seats as Pop started the engine, sputtering at first.

Walter removed his tie. "If the whole base has been struck, how will we find out about Chester?"

Pop looked sideways from the front seat. "I don't know, boys, but we've got to get home and turn the radio on." Clutching the steering wheel, he uttered, "Oh, please God, not Chester."

Mom panted her own prayer, struggling for breath as she removed her hatpin. "Oh, dear God, watch over my son."

Walter's heart beat faster with each turn, fear controlled him, and nausea set in. Finally, Arthur, his older brother, placed his elbows on his knees and balled up his fists.

All in a hurry, other drivers honked their horns in frustration with even a little traffic. Mothers and fathers shouted and corralled their children on the sidewalks to keep their families together. The world around the Troyan family was suddenly in upheaval with the news of the Japanese attack.

When the four scrambled out of the car, Jacky, the family dog, barked and ran to greet them as usual. He chased Walter, who was running like a madman, to the front door. Then, dashing into the living room ahead of the others, he clicked the radio on, turned the volume dial almost as far as it could go, and fidgeted while the old set warmed up.

"... the USS Arizona is ablaze. Riddled with bombs and torpedoes, the USS West Virginia appears to be on the verge of capsizing. The USS Oklahoma has rolled completely over. The USS California has been torpedoed and ordered abandoned. It is sinking along with the USS Utah. Ladies and gentlemen, Pearl Harbor is under attack in the worst possible way. We have reports that the battleship USS Pennsylvania is on fire, and two destroyers close by her have been reduced to twisted wrecks. Word has just come in that the USS Shaw was split in two."

"What about the *San Francisco? What about the *San Francisco*?" Mom screamed in a frenzy, not even sitting down.

Walter swiped his watery eyes and wrapped his arms around his mother's shoulders. Fury and fear gripped him as he fought the urge to out scream his mother.

Pop paced the floor like a tiger in a cage. "Elizabeth, I'm going over to the Adams to see what they know." He rushed out the door without saying another word.

Arthur ordered, "Walter, you watch Mom. I'm going over to the neighbors with Pop." He ran out the door faster than Pop, leaving a draft to fan the room.

"Mom, quit pacing. Come here. We can at least pray. Maybe Chester's ship is okay."

"Well, this news sounds like the whole base is on fire," Mom said in a ragged, grief-soaked voice.

Walter and his mother prayed, paced, and listened for updates on the radio until Pop and Arthur returned.

Arthur said, "The Adams don't know any more than we do. And there's a bunch of neighbors talking in front of our street. They don't know what's going on either."

The Majestic mahogany radio blared all day about the attack upon Pearl Harbor American Naval Base and the impending impacts on the United States. Still, it offered no specific news about the *USS San Francisco*, Chester's ship, stationed at Pearl Harbor. So the family went through the rest of the day like wooden soldiers, eating, cleaning up, pacing, praying, and waiting.

When the night grew late, Walter walked over to his parents where they sat on the red sofa, heads bowed, Mom clutching the almost finished Afghan she'd been working on. He hugged his parents and kissed his mother's cheek. Words escaped him.

Turning back the orange and brown quilt on his twin bed, he looked over at Arthur, head buried in his bunched-up pillow. He appeared to be sleeping, but he thought he heard a soft sniffle. His own stomach wrenched like a rusty axle as he twisted and turned all night, brooding about the possible loss of his older brother.

December 8, 1941

Walter awoke earlier than normal on Monday morning to the background noise of commentary on the radio. Arthur was already out of bed. He threw on his clothes and headed to the living room.

"They're repeating it again."

"What, Mom?"

"It's President Roosevelt. He's declared war."

Walter sat on the sofa next to Arthur, sinking down with the partially broken springs. Rubbing his eyes, he ran his fingers through his thick black hair.

Yesterday, December 7th, 1941—a date which will live in infamy—the United States of America was suddenly and deliberately attacked by naval and air forces of the Empire of Japan. With confidence in our armed forces, with the unbounding determination of our people, we will gain the inevitable triumph—so help us God. I ask that the Congress declare that since the unprovoked and dastardly attack by Japan on Sunday, December 7th, 1941, a state of war has existed between the United States and the Japanese empire.

Walter stood, fists clenched. "Well, our president has declared war, and I declare I'm going to fight in this war."

Arthur yanked Walter's back pocket to make him sit again, surprised at his brother's assertion.

"Don't be so impulsive."

"Aye yi yi yi yi." Mom broke off into her Polish prattle and wrung her hands. "Son, everyone's up in arms over this. But you're only sixteen."

"I know, I know, but my mind's made up. I'll join the Navy just like Chester."

He paced the small living room and said, "Mom, I don't feel like going to school today. Do I—"

"I don't either," Arthur interrupted. "No one will feel like having lessons. Even the teachers won't."

"Boys, you need to go. School is the best place to get your mind off this thing, although you'll probably hear more news about it. You're apt to learn more about what's going on than me or your father."

Pop leaned in from the kitchen with a coffee cup in hand. "Your mother's right, boys."

After breakfast, the brothers trudged to school along the sidewalk like they were wading through glue.

Arthur yawned. "Well, I got no sleep."

"Me neither. You know we won't until we hear about the *San Francisco*. I heard Mom crying all night."

"Well, at least Chester's ship hasn't been specifically named for exploding."

The brothers joined up with other classmates, walking over to the three arched doorways at the entrance of the red-brick school. Walter leaned against one of the white entryway columns, joining in the animated conversations before the first bell rang.

When he made his way to his first class, conversations became more subdued. He walked the hallways in a stupor like everyone else for the rest of the day.

Before his last class, he saw Arthur down the hallway motioning to him.

When he caught up with him, Arthur grabbed his shoulder and said, "C'mon, let's get on home. No one will know we're leaving early. Do you have any homework?"

"Not a bit."

"I don't either."

With no convincing needed, Walter ditched his last class, obeying the internal urge to get home.

For the next three days, Walter attended school, going through the motions like a robot. He practiced his violin, completed homework, did chores, and played with Jacky after school to keep his routine going. But nothing he did slew his despair. Not knowing the fate of the *USS San Francisco* or if Chester was even alive gripped him like claws.

He and Arthur talked privately about Chester and this newly declared war in their bedroom at night.

"I'm gonna do it, I'm telling you, I'm gonna join the Navy and fight in this war myself. You just wait and see."

Arthur pulled the covers back on his bed and clambered in. "Like Mom said, you're only sixteen. I don't think you can."

"Well, my friends are already talking about quitting school and fighting for our country. I bet yours are too. No one's going to bomb one of our Navy bases and get away with it."

DECEMBER 11, 1941

The aroma of cooked sauerkraut filled the kitchen right before supper, then a telegram arrived. Walter's knees wobbled like wet noodles, fearing what he might learn as he stood next to the kitchen sink. Most telegrams meant— *Oh, no, not Chester. He can't be dead. Please God, no, not my brother.* Preparing for the worst news and watching his mother's trembling hands, he held his breath. Finally, his father ripped it open and read:

> Msg Taras Troyan ... I'm okay ... Ship heads out soon ... Chester ... 11 December 1941

Wiping tears of relief, Walter grabbed his mother in a bear hug like no other and let out a whoop for the neighbors to hear. The whole family chatted at once. What about this, what about that. When they finally sat down for supper, Walter ate like a horse.

Before bed that night, he waited for Arthur to come out of the bathroom. As soon as his brother stepped foot in their bedroom, he let loose.

"His ship could have been anywhere else, but no, he had to be at Pearl Harbor when those Japs ... well, what would we do if we'd heard that—" his voice broke. "As soon as I can, I'm enlisting in the Navy. Japan will never do this again."

"You can't. You're only sixteen. You need to stay in school. Mom and Pop would never—"

"I don't care. I mean it. I'm enlisting. My mind's made up."

One week blurred into the next and the next. Walter never spoke aloud again about enlisting, especially not to Arthur. But the urge to fight for his country churned within his soul.

Christmas came and went, and he never lost his resolve to enlist. Rather, it grew as each week passed.

———— ⌘ ————

On Tuesday evening, January 6, 1942, the Troyan family listened to President Roosevelt's State of the Union address on the radio. Walter sat on the floor with his back against the sofa. The president rallied the nation around a common purpose and laid out the goals of the new war. He called for the production of 60,000 aircraft and 1.2 million tons of shipping.

"And we're going to start rationing tires? This war is really happening," Mom stated.

Walter swallowed hard. *Yes, it is. And I intend to fight for America.*

"I can't believe it. This war's bad enough, but why were the Hashimotos whisked away so quickly? What's gonna happen to their house?"

"I don't know, son. But it's wrong, just wrong." Pop pulled up a chair in the kitchen to sit down next to Walter.

Mom, busy at the stove, turned around. "Mrs. Adams said the Hashimotos had no idea where they would be going. They had no time to plan."

"But what have they done wrong? They haven't caused this war." Walter picked up his breakfast dishes and walked to the sink. "I mean, it's the leaders in Japan who are crazy, not our neighbors. They're Americans, just like us. I mean, Mom, you came over from Poland, and Pop, you came from Ukraine. Are we gonna be yanked away?"

Pop muttered in his native language and then said, "None of this makes sense."

Much to the consternation of the Troyan family, President Roosevelt had signed Executive Order 9066 on February 19, 1942, which authorized the evacuation of 120,000 Japanese Americans in light of national security. Their Japanese American neighbors, the Hashimoto family, never had a chance to say their goodbyes when they were mandated without warning to pack up their belongings to live in an internment camp in a far-flung part of the country.

CHAPTER TWO

"Walter!"

Walter jerked upright in his concertmaster's chair and plucked the dangling hair from his violin bow. Rarely did the Santa Rosa High School orchestra conductor single him out.

Mr. Josef frowned. "Watch the eighth notes in measure nineteen."

Walter nodded. Distracted, he dreaded the conversation that would take place with his parents when he got home.

Mr. Josef tapped his stand again, quietly counting one, two, three. The young musicians readied their instruments, eyes on the conductor. Walter tightened his lips and sat erect, playing each eighth note in rhythm with his anxious heartbeat. The orchestra continued to rehearse Mozart's Concerto #3 with gusto.

"Excellent, excellent, keep practicing. Class dismissed."

When he removed his chin rest and placed his violin in its case, Mr. Josef approached him. "Walter, are you losing your focus? You've messed up some simple sections lately. You know, when Chester was in orchestra, he—"

"Mr. Josef, I'm sorry. I have something on my mind today. You can count on me. I'll do better. I promise." He didn't want to hear another word about Chester's musical accomplishments.

Grabbing his books and violin case, he pushed his way through the double doors to the exit. The afternoon sun hit him head on, and he shielded his eyes. He walked by Arthur, who was talking with his friend, Marcia. Hoping to avoid his friends, he quickened his pace, violin case beating against his legs. Not quick enough, Mark Snell and Dennis Drefs hustled to catch up with him.

"Hey, you seemed down in the dumps in algebra class today," Dennis said, catching his breath.

"Can't help it." Walter bit his upper lip, a nervous habit. *I should have walked faster.*

"Spill the beans," Mark chimed in.

"Nah, it's nothing. Talk to ya later. I gotta run." Walter walked away to separate from his buddies.

Kicking a rock along the sidewalk on his way home, he contemplated his decision to enlist in the Navy and how to present his plan to his parents. Was he ready to quit high school and fight for his country? Could he give up his concertmaster chair in the orchestra? Some of his friends had dropped out of school to enlist. Terry and Houston had already joined the Coast Guard, so why not him?

When he got closer to his white bungalow home on Steele Lane, he turned around to see if Arthur was behind him. He wasn't. Probably still talking to Marcia. He watched some kids across the street sifting through trash in a nearby vacant lot, no doubt searching for metal scraps for the war effort.

Watching his mother collect water from the rain barrel, he sauntered up the steps to the front porch. She smiled when he gave her a brief hug. Jacky wagged his tail and jumped on his leg, waiting for an ear rub. He went inside and flung his jacket on the brass hook next to the door, then walked through the living room to his bedroom.

Taking a deep breath, Walter considered how to bring up quitting high school and enlisting in the Navy to his parents. *Will they even listen to me? And what am I going to do about Arthur? Will he be on Mom and Pop's side and sabotage everything?* He raised the roller shade to open the window and pulled out the wooden chair to sit at the table he and Arthur shared. Opening his algebra book, linear equations stared back at him.

An imaginary aroma of his mother's sugar cookies almost reached his senses. But no. No cookies in sight. Would the days ever come back when his mom made cookies and treats every Monday to last the whole week? The cupboards were more empty than full. The Japanese had conquered the Philippines, and the United States had lost a major source of sugar imports. His parents had already received notification they would register at the elementary school for their ration books at the end of the month. Like it or not, he'd have to do his schoolwork on an empty stomach.

Walter, a good math student, whizzed through his homework before Arthur arrived home. Closing his book, he opened his violin case to practice some scales and arpeggios. Escaping from the worries of the world, his fingers ran across the strings in perfect rhythm.

A few minutes later, Arthur walked in and plopped down on his bed.

Not in the mood to engage in talk, Walter meandered to the kitchen.

Jacky, mostly relegated to the outside, followed at his heels and barked.

"How'd you get inside? Come on, fella, out you go."

"What's for supper, Mom?"

"Borscht, can you come stir? Your music sounded good. Is your homework done?"

"Yeah, of course."

Walter stirred the soup with the large wooden spoon, breathing in the tantalizing aroma. He looked at the rooster timer his mother had set. The rooster stared back at him. Then he looked at the bright red beets and the pork sausage, and they made him hungrier.

Pop walked in the door from his bakery job and placed some unsold pumpernickel bread on the countertop. Walter left the soup and picked up a knife to slice it.

"Hello, Taras. How were sales today?" Mom asked as she turned off the burner and removed the soup.

"Better than yesterday," Pop answered, rolling his sleeves to wash up for supper.

Walter sat in his usual place at their round oak table in the corner of their small kitchen. Arthur crowded in next to him. His father blessed the food. He worried about how to start the conversation he'd fretted about all day, so he mentally practiced the points he planned to make.

Trying to act normal, he swallowed a few bites of soup. Then, taking a deep breath, he cleared his throat and blurted, "Mom, Pop, I've decided to enlist in the Navy. A lot of the fellows have already quit school, and I'm ready to fight too. You know I said this when Pearl Harbor got attacked. And I meant every word I said. It's time for me to serve my country like everyone else is. Chester's already fighting. If he can, I can."

Mom tapped her index finger on the table and said, "Walter, look at me. You aren't—"

"What?" Arthur screeched, cutting his mother off. "Are you crazy? I thought you'd forgotten about this foolish idea of yours. You haven't talked about this since before Christmas. I'm older than you, but I'm waiting until I graduate first."

Pop threw down his napkin and started to speak, but Walter kept going with Arthur.

"Well, I'm my own person, and there's a war going on. This is not foolish. And it's what Mom and Pop think that counts, not you. I'm ready to fight for my country."

Walter slurped another bite of soup as if that would ease the tension. He stared at his parents. Their silence drained him of all restraint, and he yelled, "I'm going to enlist, and I'm ready to do it now."

He threw his spoon down, scraped his cane chair back, and stood.

"Not so fast, son. Sit down." Mom frowned and rubbed her temples.

Walter sat, fidgeted with his bread, and stared at his parents while Arthur smirked.

Pop muttered in Ukrainian as he always did when he was angry or nervous. Then, with clenched hands on the table, he spoke.

"Well, Son, don't push the horses. Chester's already gone, and we nearly went out of our minds when we thought he was killed at Pearl Harbor. And who knows when this war will end. I bet the ships are still smoldering at Pearl Harbor. There will be no swift victory against the Japs, I can tell you that. And what about the orchestra? You're the concertmaster, and you're only sixteen. And don't compare yourself to Chester. He's older than you."

Arthur jumped in before Walter could defend himself. "Well, yeah, I'm older too. I want to help the war effort just like you. I'm already making a plan to enlist. But I'm gonna finish high school first."

He didn't know what to say. Words stuck like peanut butter in the back of his throat while he shuffled his feet under the table.

Mom pushed back a stray clump of hair. "Your father's right. Chester's older, and he was ready to take this step. We were not even in a war when he joined the Navy, and he had graduated from school. It made sense for him. Arthur makes a good point to graduate first. But no matter what we say, it seems like your mind is made up."

"Mom, doesn't he have to have one of you sign for him since he's not eighteen?"

"Of course, he does."

"Yeah, I know this." Walter stifled a hiccup from nervousness and swiped his hand across his mouth.

"And what if I don't sign? You know your father's not going to."

He stared at his mother, biting his upper lip, and pushed his soup aside.

Pop scrunched his cloth napkin and wiped the corner of his mouth. "You don't have to do this, you know. You can still be patriotic for our country and help the war effort in other ways. You haven't been drafted yet. You're underage."

Walter watched the pulse throb in his father's temple.

"I know, Pop, but I want to do this. I want to serve. We need to stand up to those Japs. You've said it yourself—we all have to come together for the war effort. Chester's in the thick of the war, and I can do this too. I'll prove myself. You'll see."

Pop abruptly scooted his chair back, leaving half his food untouched.

Losing his own appetite, Walter stared at his borscht that had tasted so delicious only a few minutes ago. *I knew it. They still think of me as the baby of the family. I'll never measure up to my older brothers.*

Distress consumed the Troyan family as more information about the Japanese Americans being sent to internment camps came out, some of whom lived in Santa Rosa. These second-generation American-born Japanese citizens had been whisked away, losing their property and their very lives as they once knew them, after President Roosevelt authorized Executive Order 9066. Even so, Japanese American men and women volunteered to fight for America, demonstrating their allegiance to the country they loved, notwithstanding their service units were segregated.

As a result of the government's order, several of Walter's classmates were no longer attending his high school. When the students asked about this facet of the war, the teachers struggled to come up with answers.

Despite the worries and frustrations of the country's state of affairs, Walter and his family continued listening to the radio every evening for updates about World War II, as the war was now called. They all talked about the possibility of another attack, this time on the United States mainland.

One evening, with the radio newscast dominating the household, Mom picked up her crochet hooks and yarn and said, "I don't even know where Chester is. The *USS San Francisco* is still out there someplace. If we don't get a letter soon, I'll never sleep."

"Mom, at least his ship wasn't destroyed while they were anchored at Pearl Harbor. His last letter said they were headed out to sea. No news is good news, right?"

"Walter, I know, but—"

Pop stood up and turned off the radio. "I've heard enough for today. We can never trust the Japanese again. And now, Walter, you want to head out into this mess?"

Sinking back on his chair, he watched his father amble out of the room, head down.

"Mom, I know this is hard. But I'm telling you, it's going to take all of us to defend our country. Chester is doing his part. And from what we've been hearing, it sounds like the Japanese are going after the whole world. So, how can I stay home and play my violin when the whole world may be attacked?"

CHAPTER THREE

APRIL 9, 1942

Walter decided to move forward with his plans. When he talked about quitting high school again last evening at the supper table, he waited for the arguments, but there weren't any. He waited for his parents to say they wouldn't sign for him, but they didn't. Their silence baffled him.

When he took the first step to meet with the local naval recruiter on Thursday after school, his mother accompanied him, tight-lipped and clutching her pocketbook. Her green shirtwaist dress with half sleeves and a calf-length skirt swirled around her legs when she stepped into the car in her businesslike way. Walter scooted into the front seat next to her, grateful she came with him.

When they met with the recruiter, the man explained that new recruits must meet the physical, academic, and moral standards to serve in the Navy. When Walter disclosed his age, Mom signed the papers without a smile. He understood she was sad, not mad.

"Thank you, Mrs. Troyan. I know this is a sacrifice for mothers everywhere."

The recruiter took the paperwork.

Another appointment was scheduled for the next day after school. He would have his physical exam, find out more details, and if all went well, he would be sworn into the Navy.

The recruiter's eyes roamed Walter's lean frame. "Sonny, I'm not sure if you'll pass the weight requirement. But come back tomorrow anyway. A lot of the boys figure it out. It's wartime."

On their way home, he tried to shake off the recruiter's discouraging comment. *How can I possibly gain more weight by tomorrow?*

Mom turned the steering wheel and chose her words carefully. "Walter, if you don't meet the weight requirement, you must know it was meant to be. It's another week before you turn seventeen. You can try again later."

"I bet I won't meet it. Then you and Pop won't have to worry about anything."

He held onto his crankiness the rest of the day and had trouble sleeping that night. At one point, he awoke after a crazy dream where a dozen weight scales had arms and chased him away.

The next day at school, Walter met up with Dennis and Mark and other friends at lunch. He opened his sack to pull out his sandwich and talked about meeting with the Navy recruiter. Then his buddies took over the conversation. They boasted of their own plans to drop out and enlist.

"Yesterday, the recruiter said I might not pass the weight requirement, but he told me to come back today anyway. Dennis, you're no bigger than me. What about you? Are you worried about the weight requirement?"

"Well, yeah, a little, but I'm also worried about my height. So tell ya what, meet me after school. I have an idea."

Lunch continued, and Walter squirmed in his chair when he watched the girls whispering their own conversations, some wiping their eyes. He understood that his enlistment would add to the vacant seats held by boys who had already dropped out since Pearl Harbor was bombed.

When orchestra class was over, Mr. Josef called his name. Walking over, the director patted him on the back, and in a friendly fashion, said, "Walter, I heard about your plans. Are you sure you want to enlist now? Our orchestra won't be the same without you, son. But I'm proud of your patriotism and eagerness to serve our country. What are you, sixteen, seventeen? This war will make a man out of you pretty quickly."

Walter's bushy black eyebrows shot up. "I'll be seventeen next week. But this is my country. I need to serve."

"You have to promise me one thing."

"What's that?"

"When you return from the war, you must finish high school. Get your diploma and get your violin out and play again, perhaps even some war tunes. I hope Chester will play his violin too. He was so good with the runs and dynamics."

"Yes, siree." Walter grinned.

When the last bell rang, he headed outside to look for Dennis. His physical exam was in a little more than an hour. Would his lesser weight disqualify him? What then? He heard Dennis calling his name and caught up with him.

Dennis grinned and said, "I've thought about this, and I'll tell you what I'm gonna do. When it's time for my physical, I'm slipping some weights into my pockets to add on some pounds, and I'm gonna put some wedges in my shoes to make me taller. I didn't want to tell everybody this at lunch."

Walter grinned. "That's brilliant! Wish I would've thought of it myself."

After he got home, he managed to complete part of his homework before walking to the bus stop. When he arrived in downtown Santa Rosa by himself, he spotted the Navy Recruitment office right away. Striding in a quick pace with hands in his pockets, feeling the weights he'd found, he sidestepped some crows pecking on garbage crumbs at the main entrance. He checked in at the desk and sat down to wait, discreetly eyeing the other boys ahead of him.

They look a lot bigger and stronger than me. Why couldn't I be tall like Chester or muscular like Arthur? Scanning the waiting area, he spotted President Roosevelt's framed photograph on the wall hanging a little crooked, next to the flag stand. More boys walked in as those ahead of him were called back for their exams.

Within a few minutes, the doctor opened the door and said, "Walter Troyan."

Scurrying out of his chair, he checked his posture. He'd barely entered the exam room when the doctor tossed him a white towel and said, "Strip."

Totally caught off guard by this demand, Walter worried. *What about my weights?*

Shaking and embarrassed, he took off his clothes and clutched the towel around his waist, grasping the weights in his hands, hoping not to be caught.

"Step up, young man, for your height and weight."

Walter stepped on the scale and trusted the towel would add a little weight in place of his missing clothes. Without much confidence, he tried to swallow, but his throat constricted.

"Well, you made the weight requirement by barely one pound, Walter. Now sit over here for the rest of your exam."

Walter let out a huge sigh and relaxed. His sweaty palms let up on gripping the weights while the doctor listened to his chest. Right before the eye and ear exam, he slipped the weights under his pile of clothes, undetected, relieved to be rid of them.

"I'm signing your paperwork. Hang on to it." The doctor scribbled his name at the bottom of the papers and handed them to Walter.

Following the doctor's directions, he headed to another room for the final swearing-in. Two commissioned officers stood guard on the black-and-white tiled floor, waiting for all the boys to finish their exams. When one of the officers finally walked to the front, Walter listened as he explained the requirements for boot camp entry and the strict expectations of all the new recruits.

"Expect strenuous work and a regimented schedule. Forget about getting a lot of sleep. You will be up each day before light, and you will work and sweat. Much information will be thrown at you to learn in a short amount of time. You will not question orders. Keep in mind that your training is intended to prepare you for the worst warfare of any kind. I've been through this myself. I know what I'm talking about. Before you leave, go down the hall and turn left where you'll be issued your transportation documents for San Diego boot camp."

Never taking his eyes off the officer for a second, Walter forced his breathing to remain even.

"Arise"

Immediately, he stood erect with the other boys.

The officer said, "Repeat after me, using your own first and last name."

When he raised his right hand for the enlistment oath, an overwhelming sense of patriotism filled his heart.

"I, Walter Troyan, do solemnly swear that I will support and defend the Constitution of the United States against all enemies, foreign and domestic; that I will bear true faith and allegiance to the same; and that I will obey the orders of the president of the United States and the orders of the officers appointed over me, according to regulations and the Uniform Code of Military Justice. So help me God."

Stifling a smile, he embraced his new status as officially inducted into the United States Navy. Before exiting the building, he joined in small talk with the other fellows for a few minutes.

With springs in his feet, Walter climbed the steps of the bus to return home. The smudgy window by his seat made everything outside look blurry, like his present state of mind filled with glad and bad at the same time. *Can I do this? That boot camp stuff sounds scary.*

When he arrived home, his stomach growled when he caught a whiff of chicken cooking.

As soon as he sat down with his family for supper, the questions came at him. Did you pass the weight requirement? How many other recruits were there? Did you talk to any of them? Were you scared? Can we see your papers?

Chowing down on the delicious supper and fielding all the questions displaced any intruding doubts he may have had.

CHAPTER FOUR

APRIL 15, 1942

"Happy birthday, Son! I've been setting aside some sugar so I could make you a little cake. Hard to believe you're seventeen, and I'm glad you're still home."

"Awe, Mom, thanks. We can all share it."

When the family sat down for supper, Pop pulled his napkin to his chin. "You better enjoy your mom's cooking for now. When you go off to boot camp in a couple weeks, you won't be eating like this. When I was in the last war, I remember ..."

Walter didn't totally tune out his father's WWI accounts, but his mind wandered. Everything had changed in his world as he'd known it in such a short time. The shortage of sugar, boys quitting school, the girls acting scared all the time, the worry about Chester.

——— ✎ ———

After supper on April eighteenth, Walter and his parents listened to the latest war news on the radio as they sat down together in the living room.

The Doolittle air raid has struck the Japanese archipelago. Ladies and gentlemen, this is our retaliation for their attack on Pearl Harbor. Sixteen B-25B Mitchell medium bombers were launched from the *USS Hornet* deep in the western Pacific Ocean. Although the damage is negligible, our message is clear. Their own homeland is not safe. The bombing raid killed about fifty people, including civilians, and injured four hundred. The Americans will continue westward to land in China and—

Walter stood. "Mom, I'm going to check on the dog."

Stepping away from the living room abruptly, he headed to his bedroom to break away from the madness of the radio, never checking on Jacky. *Am I ready to fight in this war? What if I'm killed?* He rubbed his sweaty palms on the sides of his pants. Images of carnage buzzed like flies through his head.

When he walked into his room, Arthur shut his book. "Well, it won't be long until you head to San Diego. I'm proud of you, little brother, but I still think you should've waited this thing out. I'm enlisting as soon as I graduate. The Troyan brothers, all in the Navy, all fighting in the war. You know Mom and Pop are gonna worry about us."

Taking a deep breath and gathering his thoughts before replying, he said, "Yeah, they'll worry, that's for sure. And I'm gonna miss your graduation. And what are you gonna do about Marcia? She's got googly eyes for you. I see that all the time."

"Well, don'cha think I know that? Say, I've heard San Diego is huge. And you're going to be right on the water. You'll hafta fill me in. Will you even be able to write letters? You know they're going to be strict on you."

"I know, I know. But no one can stop the mail system. I'll write home for sure."

Fifty people killed? Civilians? Hundreds of injuries?

Walter sat down on his bed, facing the opposite direction of Arthur. The thought of his own possible wounds and even death hit him head on.

Walter fidgeted all day with thoughts of his departure to boot camp. He almost wished he was back at school. Yesterday had been bittersweet, saying goodbye to his friends and teachers when school dismissed. Teasing, well wishes, pats on the back, and even a few hugs disguised the true atmosphere of apprehension all the young students faced with the overhead cloud of a world war.

Placing his duffle bag on the bed, he started packing the necessities for boot camp. At the last minute, he threw in his harmonica. What would San Diego really be like? He'd been no further south in California than San Francisco. Jacky nudged him with his nose and whined a bit.

"Hey, aren't you supposed to be outside? How'd you get in?"

He rubbed Jacky's ears exactly the way he liked, taking in his doggy smell, but the dog whined again.

"Aw, come on, boy, I'm gonna miss you too. Don't make this any harder for me."

The next morning, the smell of bacon and eggs pulled him out of bed and down the stairs into the bright, cheerful kitchen. After eating his fill, he headed to the living room to join his parents, the homey aroma of coffee lingering throughout the house. Arthur walked in, yawning, half ready for school. The brothers embraced.

"Don't do anything I wouldn't do," Arthur teased.

"Son, did you, umm, pack your paperwork?" Mom stammered. "And here's a couple of sandwiches."

"Yeah, I've got everything. I double-checked."

Pop waited tentatively by the door.

When they stepped outside to walk to their car, a mourning dove cooed from the roof to greet the new day. Walter looked back at the front porch to savor the familiar surroundings of his home. The climbing rose bush on the trellis showed signs of many new buds. He picked one now and then and took it to his mother because they were her favorites. She'd always smile at him and find a vase. *So much is going to change.*

Arriving at the bus depot a few minutes later, the three sat on a bench. Other Navy recruits walked around, also waiting for departure. With elbows on his knees and chin resting on his fists, Walter ignored the pigeons who came to visit him. Although the messy pigeons, cigarette butts, and scattered litter did nothing to enhance the scenic view of Santa Rosa, he still took it in. This was home, and he was leaving it behind. He knew he would miss it—all of it.

When the time came to board, he embraced his parents, keeping his emotions in check. But his mother struggled to let go at all. Finally, Walter whispered in her ear. "Mom, everything will be okay."

Pop cleared his throat. "Son, we'll pray for you. Stay tough and strong for boot camp. Chester said it's a killer. Just don't quit, whatever you do. See it through."

"Keep your faith, do what's right," Mom said. "Your father and I love you, and God will watch—" Mom grabbed her handkerchief as her voice trailed off.

Walter inhaled the unpleasant bus fumes, heart beating faster than usual. He set his duffel bag on the sidewalk and stood as straight as possible. Offering a weak smile, he decided to be patriotic and salute his parents. He almost convinced himself that he was going to be okay. Maybe Mom and Pop would believe it too.

PART TWO: BOOT CAMP

CHAPTER FIVE

When the bus doors slapped open, Walter dragged his duffel bag up the bus steps, forging confidence for boot camp. He swallowed, trying to alleviate the persistent lump in his throat.

He chose a window seat. A few other young recruits who had previously boarded leaned back for sleep, and others were right behind him in the narrow aisle. The cracked vinyl seat he scooted into with a ninety-degree back offered little in the way of comfort.

Settling in, he smiled wryly when he thought about the lead weights he'd clutched secretly in his hands to make sure he qualified for the weight requirement. No one knew except Dennis, not even Arthur. But then again, he remembered the recruiter saying, "the boys figure it out."

When the tires squealed as the bus halted at the next stop a couple hours later, Walter awakened from his doze. About a dozen more recruits hopped on, shuffling their way down the aisle.

"Okay to sit here?"

Walter glanced up. "Oh, sure." He scooted over to make room for a handsome fellow with dark wavy hair and brown eyes.

"Eddie's the name. Eddie Page. Where ya from?"

"Santa Rosa. How about you?"

"A little town called Parlier. Ever heard of it?" Eddie stretched his legs.

"Nope."

"I haven't either," Eddie said, throwing back his head to laugh. "So, you're doing what I'm doing, taking the big plunge to join the Navy? How old are you?"

"Just turned seventeen."

"I'm nineteen. Had my birthday in April too. I take it your ma or pa signed for you?"

"Yeah, I quit high school, and so did a lot of my friends. I felt the call to serve after what those Japs did. My older brother was at Pearl Harbor. You know, this is *our* country, and if we have to fight for it, I don't need a lot of convincing."

Eddie opened his mouth wide. "Did your brother survive?"

"Yeah, he did. We don't know the details, but we got a telegram saying he was okay. He's on the *USS San Francisco*, a heavy cruiser, and we've heard he's out on the waters again."

Walter looked Eddie over. He was definitely bigger and taller than him.

When Eddie glanced back at him, he quit staring and grabbed one of the sandwiches his mother had made. In doing so, his finger touched his harmonica. He decided to show it to his new friend. "See what I brought?"

"You play that? Hey, I could use a tune right now. Can you play 'Oh, You Beautiful Doll?' My mom sings that one all the time. Boy, I just got on this bus, and I already miss my mom. And I'm for sure missing my gal, Emma."

Walter brought the harmonica to his lips and tried to figure out the tune for a few minutes but gave up.

Tearing away the wrap from his first sandwich, he asked Eddie, "Hey, I have another sandwich. You hungry?

"Nope, not yet. I'm okay for now. Thanks. My mom packed me a couple of sandwiches too."

Walter bit into the peanut butter on white bread with raspberry jam oozing out the edges, and he closed his eyes momentarily, thinking about his mother. A slight pang of homesickness hit him.

He brought the harmonica to his lips again after finishing his sandwich and figured out the tune after a few tries.

The bus rocked like a cradle down US 101. Walter and Eddie talked awhile, then leaned their heads back on the seat to rest. Walter decided not to tell Eddie he was missing his own mother too.

As the day wore on, whenever the bus made stops, Walter got off to stretch and use the restroom. Almost all the windows were down on the bus—even so, the heat and humidity were stifling. At times, he and Eddie talked and turned around to talk to others. He enjoyed watching the palm trees come into view the further south they traveled.

More recruits hopped on the bus throughout the day. With the first hint of dusk, the full bus finally turned off Stockton Road and pulled into the San Diego Naval Base gate. As the gate opened, Walter stared at the black arch that stretched across the main entrance. The symbolic eagle stared back at him. The driver turned left toward the in-processing parking lot.

Shouts and silliness emerged from the bus due to the boys' repressed energy, and Walter found himself smashed between other boys in the aisle as he tried to get off. With a push from behind, he finally stepped down right after Eddie and looked around to orient himself. Other buses had recently dropped off their own recruits and a couple other buses pulled in.

"Eddie, this place is huge."

"You're not kidding. Hey, if we get split up, maybe I'll still see ya 'round."

Almost immediately, officers with clipboards, stern faces, and loud voices greeted Walter and the hundreds of other recruits and quickly got them organized into smaller groups. Last names were shouted out, and the petty officer's arms motioned in various directions.

Lining up with the hundred recruits of his own motley group, the civilian officer frowned at them and paced back and forth.

He barked, "Welcome, swabbies, welcome to Cal-i-forn-i-a."

Light snickers surfaced when Officer Turner pronounced the state with the emphasis on the last two syllables.

Glaring at two boys at the end of the row, he continued.

"From where I stand, I mostly see swabbies and seagulls, and let me say it, it's mostly swabbies. I know what I'm talkin' about. You swabbies come at me right and left. You're not civilians anymore. You're mine for the next eight weeks. You all are Company 292. I repeat—you are Company 292. I will provide everything you need. I will see to it that you get some new clothes, good enough for modeling. My barbers will whack off your beautiful hair, but I will ask them to be careful with your ears."

Walter stared straight ahead, only blinking as necessary.

"I will see to it that you get a real comfortable bed. If you haven't been making your beds at home, you'll be making them now. And the fun part? Usually, it's the shots in both arms at the same time. Shots, haircuts, new clothes for modeling, three meals a day, and a bed. What more could you ask for?"

Walter swallowed and rubbed his hand across his dry throat. A cold glass of water sounded good to him right about now.

Duffel bag over his shoulder, Walter followed directions for the check-in process, entering two different buildings for the final steps with the entire company. When he finished, he received his assigned barracks number and the location.

After a tiring day, he walked mechanically with the other recruits along the landscaped promenade lined with tulip trees toward the barracks area. As he got closer, the design of the barracks surprised him. He had envisioned small wooden shacks. These Navy barracks were large, two stories high with orange-clay tiled roofs. The black-paned windows, tall and thin, contrasted with the pale, yellow stucco.

He finally entered Barracks Seventeen as the sun was setting. After trudging his feet up the stairs at the end of the long day, the barrage of laughs, jokes, and cuss words assailed him when he walked into his dormitory. Suddenly, a pillow came flying through the air, and he barely ducked in time. When he heard all the talk about girls, he blushed. *I've never had a girlfriend.* Even with windows open and a slight breeze, cigarette smoke clouds hung like fog over the ocean.

"Well, hey, we still have our hair," one of the boys shouted for the whole top floor of the barracks to hear. "Last night for us to feel like we have anything on our heads."

Per instructions, Walter pulled his personal items from his duffel bag, which would need to be mailed home. He found his small locker assigned to him for his Navy-issued clothing as well as his assigned bunk, one on the bottom.

The stocky boy on top got his attention.

"Hey bunkmate, my name's Sam Laughlin. Where're you from? How old are you?"

"I'm seventeen, from Santa Rosa. Name's Walter."

"I'm sixteen. I dropped out of high school, and I'm from Boise, Idaho, right off the farm. Look at that kid over there, three bunks down from the wall. He's only fifteen. Name is Clyde. I just met him."

"Are you kidding?"

"Nope, he told me he lied about his age, and I know others who did too, like me. Elroy's over there, and he's only fifteen and a half. He said his dad forged a new birth date on his birth certificate. He told me when we were in processing. But who cares? Uncle Sam don't care. He wants all of us."

Walter shook his head. Exhausted, he prepared for bed. He scrunched his flat pillow and stared at the exposed conduit running along the wall, welcoming some shut-eye time.

———————

Startled, Walter awakened when a blaring bugle call sounded. Thinking it was still the middle of the night, he ran his hands through his black hair. When the bare overhead light bulbs flickered to life, he momentarily squinted his eyes at the brightness, sat up, and looked around.

"How'd you sleep, Troyan?" Sam hollered down at him with a cracking morning voice.

"I managed. Do you have any idea what's gonna happen today?"

"Probably breakfast first, I guess. Then we just listen to instructions. That's all we'll do here, listen and obey, no questions asked. We better get used to the yelling. They're gonna teach us how to act, what to say, what to do. My pops said if they say shut your mouth, you better shut your mouth."

Walter rushed to the showers. If not already wide-awake, he was now when the cold water blasted his chest.

After a rushed breakfast of oatmeal, sausage, and bananas at the mess hall, Walter gulped his barely warm coffee down in time to follow orders to head to Preble Field. The clear blue waters of the boat channel at the end of the field lured his attention to a new kind of beauty. The hazy San Miguel Mountains came into view in the distance.

Looking in all directions, he watched in awe as the new enlistees throughout the entire naval facility joined up together. He speculated as to how many there were. Thousands? Based on his own company, he believed all the companies consisted of one hundred men each.

Chief petty officers walked around, barking orders, and getting everyone organized into their company groups. Walter found himself lumped into 292 again.

"Come this way, Company 292. Haircuts, inoculations, and more supplies are next on the agenda," Chief Turner yelled.

When the clerks started passing out Navy attire, one of the boots hollered and cussed. "Hey, these are huge—not my size."

"Not my problem, boots." the clerk snapped back at him.

When it came time for shoe distributions, Walter stood in a long line. He finally approached the bench.

"Size?"

"Ten"

"Here you go. Two pairs. One pair of dress shoes, the other work boots. See to it you keep them shined."

He watched the clerk write the size of his new shoes on the tracking chart.

After stowing their new gear in the barracks, Walter and the rest of Company 292 continued orientation with another medical exam which included seven vaccination shots. Hundreds of young boys lined up with him as if in an assembly line for needles.

"Arms at your sides. Right or left?" the medical examiner asked Walter.

"What do you mean, sir?"

"Are you right-handed or left-handed?"

"Right-handed, sir."

"Okay, you'll get three jabs in your right arm and four in your left. Here we go."

Walter steadied himself, looked straight ahead, and swallowed hard.

The dreaded buzz haircut came next. Barbers ran their electric razors over hundreds of heads like race cars, with total disregard to style, creating heaps of hair strewn all over the floor. Someone with a broom and a large dustpan attached to a stick stayed busy cleaning up the heaps.

When he received his Bluejacket's Manual about naval procedures, which was used as a reference for active warfare, he thumbed through it. Setting it aside, he looked forward to some serious reading.

Supply clerks tossed seabags, rope pieces, and sleeping gear around like banana peels.

A tall clerk with a protruding and bobbing Adam's apple yelled orders right and left, walking in circles. When his voice cracked a number of times, Walter got the impression this clerk adjusted the volume and tone of his voice to show off.

"Weave the ropes into your seabags to use as a drawstring. And make sure you stencil your first and last names on the bags. These seabags will represent your lives. They'll stay with you until we hear the enemy surrender, and then they'll go home with you."

Walter opened his bag, fingering the grommets. Before he could finish weaving his rope, more orders came from Adam's Apple.

"Turn to page eighteen in your manuals. You will follow the packing regulations set forth for your seabags. Every detail is for a reason."

Walter gathered his hammock, mattress, two mattress covers, a pillow, two pillow covers, and two blankets. Then he practiced laying out his bedding items on the flattened mattress in the required order. He finally had time to stencil his name on the side of his seabag. Stomach growling, he looked for a clock in anticipation of lunch.

When lunch and then supper were served in the mess hall, the boots stood in regimented lines to get their food trays. Even so, Walter welcomed the food, a nice break from the marching, waiting in line, and training classes.

Later that night in his barracks, sitting on the edge of his bed, which he had learned was called a "rack" in the Navy, Walter ran his fingers over his newly cropped hair and then rubbed both sore arms. Yawning, he opened his Bluejacket's Manual to start some reading. When his eyes could no longer stay open, he prepared for sleep.

Before Sam climbed on the top bunk, he pointed to Walter's seabag and quipped, "Hey, glad we got our fart sacks. That's what I heard they call these things.

"Whaddya mean?"

"Mattress covers."

Walter joked back. "Yep, I guess that's why they gave us two!"

CHAPTER SIX

Within the first week of boot camp, Walter completed more paperwork, learned the chain of command, learned how watch-standing worked, and received instructions in Navy customs and courtesies. He completed a first aid class, practiced knot-making techniques, and learned ship jargon and flag-signaling in the long ten-hour days.

Calisthenics took everything out of him. The heart-thumping push-ups, curl-ups, ten-pound rifle-over-your-head drills, and loading heavy shells into five-inch guns took nearly half a day. Pulling the oars in assigned boats out on the channel of water in front of Preble Field was grueling work, but Walter half liked the water splashes and the exhilaration of it all. At the end of the channel, he could see San Diego Bay.

Petty Officer Turner made it clear. "You swabbies are not just doing this to make you look good in your uniforms. These exercises are intended to make you deadly, to save your lives and those of your shipmates too."

When the time came for the swim skills testing, the boots were divided into two groups: swimmers and non-swimmers. The non-swimmers would start lessons. But the swimmers went right into skills testing.

Walter was confident when he joined the swimmers group. After all, Pop had thrown him and his brothers into the Russian River with a sink or swim order at a very early age.

Hundreds of boots gathered in lines around the pool, all wearing skimpy black swim trunks. They were all too crowded for any thoughts of embarrassment.

"Time for your fifty-yard swim and prone float. I'm timing you, men." Officer Turner held up his stopwatch for his group.

Walter fidgeted in line. He watched a designated Marine guard yelling "dive" as each turn came.

When his time came, he hesitated, a bundle of nerves.

"Hey, son, I said dive, and I mean *now*, not at the end of this war," the Marine barked.

Without warning, someone behind him slapped his back, forcing him to dive.

After he completed his fifty-yard lap and prone float, he waited a moment, treading water, trying to calm his nerves. He frowned when he saw Petty Officer Turner and the Marine not even paying attention. *Well, that's over with.*

Next came marching practice.

Oh, the marching. Could he ever get it? Half step, column right-march, column left-march, right step, left step, right flank, left flank, up and down Preble Field with hundreds of others. His rhythmic skills from orchestra counted as one little advantage, he supposed.

Walter ate like there was no tomorrow, and every night his mattress absorbed his crashes after he massaged his aching feet.

For the next few weeks, Walter attended academic classes in preparation for shipboard life. He learned self-discipline and following orders—no matter what. Still, he stiffened from anxiety when petty officers barked commands.

"Up and at 'em, boots."

"Scrub that floor. I'll be checking with my magnifying glass."

"Clean the latrines like your life depends on it, for in truth, it does."

Right before supper one evening, Walter spotted Eddie not too far away and walked over to him. "I'm surprised those officers have any vocal cords left with all that yelling. If they want to harangue me, they're doing a good job of it. How are you feeling about all this? I mean, sometimes I don't know if I can keep going. My back is killing me. I never get enough sleep. Sometimes I even wonder if I should have—"

"What, joined the Navy? Well, same here. This ain't no picnic in the park. But ya know, we've got to give it our best shot. We can't just up and quit. Remember, there's a war going on."

"I know. My pop told me not to quit—no matter what, but sometimes I wonder."

Before bed that night, Walter wrote a letter home, in part because he was homesick and also to vent to his family.

Dear Mom and Pop and Arthur,

I'm surviving so far. But boot camp is no piece of cake. We exercise, march, drill, scrub clothes, do calisthenics, pull oars in a boat, load shells, more exercise, and clean latrines, and this is just the tip of the iceberg. The training is hard, at least ten hours a day. On most days, I feel like the only thing I see is the back of another boy's head—for hours on end. And there's plenty of heads to stare at, thousands of us.

Boot Camp is equalizing, that's for sure. Some boys here are younger than me. Some are only fifteen. And they've come from all over the country and from all kinds of backgrounds. We all do things in unison, and we work as a team. I've made some new friends, and I especially like Eddie Page. You'd like him too.

I'm following orders, even if they're disagreeable. If we don't, discipline follows in the way of less sleep, less food, humiliation in front of everyone, or anything else they think of is heaped on us. Most days I don't get enough sleep. I don't think I've gained any weight, but I do feel stronger. I passed my swim skills test, and I thought about my Russian River days.

I hope Jacky's doing okay. Arthur, can you stop by the orchestra class and tell Mr. Josef hi for me? I'm sorry I'm missing your graduation. I haven't seen any of San Diego except what's on the base. But the channel of water beyond the field where we march is beautiful. I hope to see all of you in a few weeks.
Love,
Walter

⎯⎯⎯⎯ ⧯ ⎯⎯⎯⎯

A couple of weeks later, Walter was startled in the middle of the night when the petty officer on watch turned on his flashlight. He waved the light around on the other side of the room, going back and forth across the top bunks.

Not sure what was going on, Walter raised himself up on one elbow and saw someone crawling from top bunk to top bunk. *What in the world is that kid doing? Is that Clyde?*

The boy finally got back into his bed, and the petty officer turned off his flashlight. Walter fell back to sleep.

The next evening at check-in time for sleep in his barracks, he noticed the young kid named Clyde was missing.

"Hey Sam, where's Clyde?"

"Haven't you heard? He was sleepwalking across the top bunks last night, and the petty officer on watch had to report it. So, he's gone. Poor kid."

"Gone? Like out of the Navy gone? Just for sleepwalking?"

"Yep, I heard it's not safe to keep sleepwalkers in time of war with battles and all."

Walter was speechless. Surely Clyde could be reassigned to do something else to help with the war effort, he thought. After all, the kid was only fifteen. *He must have enlisted because he really wanted to fight for America.*

———————⊙⁓⁓⊙———————

With only two more weeks left of boot camp training, Chief Petty Officer Turner announced after supper, "Tomorrow at 0800, Company 292 will report to Building C for aptitude testing. We're gonna see what you're made of."

That night, before he went to sleep, Walter asked Sam about the aptitude test and what he'd heard about it.

"I don't think we have too much to worry about. We just take this test, and later they'll tell us what we're good at. I guess for future assignments or something like that. Don't sweat it. We can't fail it."

Walter played a few tunes on his harmonica to relax. He even took a few song requests.

———————⊙⁓⁓⊙———————

The next morning at breakfast, Walter balled his hands into fists, rubbing them nervously against his legs. *What am I made of?* His company marched to Building C for the aptitude test by way of the promenade. The tall palm trees lined up in front of the building swayed in the wind.

After the testing, they lined up outside to wait for the others. He was able to talk with Eddie. "Well, that wasn't so bad."

"Well, I bet they're gonna tell me I'm good at basket weaving."

They both laughed.

Within a few days of the aptitude test, he and Eddie and a number of other boots received summonses to meet with

Chief Petty Officer Mahler at 1300 at the same building. The officer paced at the front of the room as they all entered, everyone removing their hats.

Biting his upper lip, Walter stood at attention.

Chief Mahler addressed the group when he sat down on the corner of his desk, one foot on the floor.

"Men, you have been selected to attend Fire Controlman School, based upon your test results. It's an honor, actually. You will be trained to operate all kinds of guns for the specific ships that you'll be assigned to. Upon graduation from boot camp, you'll have a liberty leave of one week. I know most of you will want to spend some time at your homes. You'll attend Gunner's Mate School right here at the San Diego Naval Training Center for sixteen weeks. After graduation, stop by this same building to pick up your traveling itinerary."

When Walter found Eddie outside Building C after the meeting, they grinned at one another. Eddie said, "Well, get a load of that, Troyan. You can't get rid of me. We're gonna stay together. I'm Navy now. I feel it. I look it. Hey, man, we get to fire those big guns on the Japs. Don't know if I can wait out the sixteen weeks." He rolled his tongue, made a firing noise, and slapped Walter on the back.

"Sure, Eddie, sure. As for me, I'm excited. I didn't expect this. I quit high school, and now I'm going back to school. You know, I feel like I'm a part of something for the good of America, and it's a good feeling. I need to get a letter off to my folks to tell them about the latest and greatest."

—————⟡—————

By the time the final two weeks of boot camp were nearly completed, Walter learned he'd passed the final fitness and skills tests. He doubted he could even survive boot camp, and now here he was, close to graduation. He spent his last days on the training base like a dog with two wagging tails.

The boots practiced marching in preparation for the graduation ceremony, which dignitaries and parents would attend. Walter wished his parents could make the drive down, but the distance prevented their attendance.

Finally, the big day arrived. Shipshape and standing in formation on Preble Field, he participated with the various companies when everyone fell in line for the graduation parade and final review.

Then some dignitary he'd never seen before declared the boots had finished their training, had changed from boys to men, and would get leave to return home and display their uniforms with pride. Walter fingered his black navy neckerchief and looked at the American flag waving in the breeze in front of the Commander Station. He nearly popped a button. Proving himself, bringing honor to his family, and serving his country well ascended before him. He'd started boot camp as a petrified civilian and would depart as a sailor fit for war.

CHAPTER SEVEN

JUNE 25, 1942, SANTA ROSA, CALIFORNIA

After the long ride back to Santa Rosa, Walter eagerly stepped down the steps of the local bus in his sailor uniform to walk home. Although it was dusk, he could see the old oak tree illuminated by the front porch light of his house with dancing branches making shadows. He cleared his throat and quickened his pace in anticipation of seeing his family. *Have I been homesick?* Jacky's friendly bark welcomed him, and the two scuffled a bit on the front porch before his mother opened the door.

"Oh, son, *aye yi yi yi yi yi.*" Mom chattered in Polish as soon as he walked inside. They hugged each other, and he didn't even mind the kisses she planted on his cheeks.

Extending his hand to his father for a manly shake, Pop pulled him in for a hug instead.

"I stuck it out, Pop, just like you told me to."

Arthur clutched Walter's shoulders. "Look at you! Lookin' pretty good in that sailor uniform."

Until bedtime, the four shared stories in the living room and caught up. Walter lost no time in asking, "How's Chester doing?"

Pop rubbed his day-old whiskers. "His ship got to San Francisco in late April, and he was granted liberty leave to come home for a few days."

"I wish you could have been here too. Then I would have had all three of my boys at home." Mom sipped her tea.

"Well, what did he say about the Pearl Harbor attack?"

Mom started to answer, but Arthur jumped ahead of her.

"Well, first he said the *San Francisco* was at Pearl Harbor because the ship needed cleaning really bad or something like that. Since he's a cook, he was down in one of the lower decks, I guess in the galley, minding his own business. And then he felt the ship suddenly shake with horrible vibrations. He made it to one of the upper decks, and he couldn't believe the smoke-filled skies and the explosions right before his eyes. The ships were blowing up all around him. He said the metal pieces rained down on everyone like a rainstorm, and he covered his head because he didn't even have his helmet on. He said the gates of hell opened with the two waves of destruction."

Mom cleared her throat.

"Well, that's what he said."

"Uh, yes, I know. And don't forget the part about him seeing the Japanese planes," Mom interjected.

"Oh, yeah. He said when he looked up, he could see the big red meatballs on the sides of the first planes flying away, you know, the Japanese insignia. And then, the sailors all began to secure the ship for watertightness and began to look for ways to fight back. He crossed over to another ship which was berthed right next to his ship.

"The *New Orleans*," Pop interjected.

"Oh, yeah, and they needed help manning the anti-aircraft batteries and a bunch of other stuff. And then someone told him he could help transfer ammunition to another ship."

"The *USS Tracy*," Pop added.

Arthur stifled a yawn but kept going. "He said it was chaos because everyone was grabbing whatever rifles and machine guns they could find to defend themselves. Everything was on fire with a bunch of the ships burning, and the water was black with oil. He said he shouted continually and that he was hoarse for several days after the attack. Oh, and he said the *USS Arizona* burned for two days. Well, I wish you could have heard him talk about it firsthand."

"Well, Arthur, I think you nearly told it firsthand." Mom grinned with a hint that Arthur had dominated the conversation.

Pop walked over to the kitchen to turn off the light and then turned around and said, "We're so grateful we still have Chester and that his ship didn't take a hit. I still worry about him, Walter, and now you're heading to the dangerous waters. And who knows ..." His voice trailed off.

When Walter told his parents good night, he followed Arthur to their bedroom.

"Hey, how was your graduation? Sorry I wasn't here."

Arthur opened his drawer to retrieve his pajamas. "It was good. Mom made a little cake. Marcia came over and a few other friends. But I have to say, a lot of the boys weren't even around to graduate."

"When are you going to enlist?"

"Soon. I want to do Navy, but I don't want to be on a ship. I want to fly."

"Yeah, I can picture you on a plane already. You'll be good."

Walter raised both windows higher to get some cross ventilation for a night breeze before slipping into bed. He listened to the crickets and a hoot owl nearby as he tossed and turned before sleep pulled him in, thinking about all that stuff Chester went through at Pearl Harbor.

⚬⚬⚬

The vibrations of the church bells stirred Walter's insides when he made his way up the red-brick steps for church the next day. He passed through the carved wooden entrance, removed his cap, pulled his black Navy tie to keep it nice and straight, and followed his parents to the front pew where they liked to sit.

After the service, he talked with many parishioners, answering their questions about the Navy.

How did he like San Diego? What would he be doing next? Oh, Gunner's Mate School? How long was that? When would he go off to fight? How was Chester doing?

He conversed well, proud to be wearing his Navy uniform. His mother had told him that morning how handsome he looked.

The week flew by. Walter relaxed as he settled into the familiar rhythm of home. He visited friends, helped around the house, and talked incessantly about boot camp stories with his parents and Arthur.

One evening he walked into the kitchen and hugged his mother. "Ahh, I'm smelling something delicious. Have you made borscht just for me?" He leaned over the kettle to take a peek, inhaling the rich aroma.

"Yes, of course. Well, it's just good to have you back home, son. Oh, the Adams are coming over this evening."

"Is LaVerne coming?"

"I think so."

When their neighbors arrived, they all sat down in the living room. The Adams's teen daughter, LaVerne, sat down next to Walter. He enjoyed taking the spotlight again when Mr. and Mrs. Adams asked questions about boot camp. But after a few minutes, the adults engaged in their own conversation, and his fuss dwindled.

LaVerne started asking her own questions, and he answered with pride and enthusiasm.

"Were you scared when you got yelled at?"

"Well, sure, at first," he answered. "But we fellows got used to it. You just have to have guts and make the best of things."

"What about the marching? How does everyone learn to do that? I mean, what if you make a mistake and you get out of line with the others?"

"Well, it helped that I was in orchestra, and I was used to counting, and I already understood rhythm. But we all learned pretty quickly what 'forward march' and 'halt' meant. We took thirty-inch steps and placed our heels first. When we practiced the coordinated arm swing, we always cupped our hands with our thumbs pointed down. And get this, the drill instructors would yell at us to keep our arms straight but not too stiff and to have a natural swing. We had to swing nine inches to the front but only six inches to the rear. Boy, that was tough for me. Do you know what 'mark time, march' means?"

Before LaVerne could answer, Walter continued to regale her. "Well, it's basically marching in place without moving forward. We had to learn mark time, half step, column right-march, column left-march, to the rear-march, change step, right step, left step, and, let's see, oh, yeah, right flank, left flank. Here, I'll show you."

Arthur walked into the living room right at that moment and sat on the arm of the sofa.

"Come on, Walter. LaVerne doesn't care to see all that."

But he jumped out of his chair anyway and began to demonstrate some marching maneuvers for his friend. The adults stopped talking, surprised by Walter's sudden demonstration. He looked sideways at LaVerne, hoping he impressed his young friend, but caught her yawning behind her closed fist.

PART THREE: GUNNER'S MATE SCHOOL

CHAPTER EIGHT

When his week of liberty ended, Walter let Jacky inside the house when no one was paying attention and summoned him into his bedroom. He checked his seabag for the long bus ride back to San Diego early the next morning. Jacky watched, tail between his legs. The dog stared up at Walter with his large, limpid eyes, pink tongue lolling out the side of his mouth.

"Yep, Jacky, I'm leaving again. You're in charge." He rubbed his dog's ears for a long time, contemplating the sixteen weeks of Gunner's Mate School. The realization that he wouldn't return home when this second training ended brought a lump to his throat.

Climbing into bed that night, he and Arthur talked longer than usual. When he finally rolled over on his side, a jittery feeling overtook him. He balled up his pillow, but he still couldn't sleep. What kind of ship would he be on? What would his responsibilities be? Would he have the courage to use the guns he'd be trained on to take others' lives? What if he didn't make it back home? What if … He threw the covers off and tossed and turned most of the night with images of dead sailors and exploding ships floating through his mind.

Morning came early. Walter yawned and stretched, and after getting dressed, he set his seabag by the front door. As he walked into the kitchen for his last breakfast at home, the toasted bread popped up smiling. He relished the aroma of fresh scrambled eggs and fried bacon and savored each bite. Before guzzling down his orange juice, he placed his elbows on the table and rested his chin in his hands. He looked around the kitchen, taking mental pictures of the white-painted wooden cabinets, the Wolverine stove with red trim, and the black kit-cat clock on the wall. Swallowing hard, he watched his busy mother drying her hands on the white cloth towel.

In a quiet voice, she said, "Here are your sandwiches for the bus ride, son."

After breakfast, he looked into the mirror when he brushed his teeth, furrowed his thick eyebrows, and stared at himself. *Can I do this? What am I made of?*

He joined his parents in the living room when Arthur walked in half-dressed with messy hair.

"Ya gotta write home and fill us in. And I want to know all that stuff you'll learn about the guns." Arthur cleared his throat and disguised a sniffle.

"Oh, sure, I'll write. If only San Diego wasn't so far away, you could visit. You gotta write, too." Walter swallowed hard.

"I don't know when we'll see each other again, ya know."

Walter nodded. "Yeah, I know. This is the hard part."

The brothers hugged.

Walter and his parents headed out the door to the shed where the car was parked. The warm summer air, chirping birds, and blooming flowers spoke peace to him, not war. He breathed deeply, appreciating the tranquility of home.

When they arrived at the bus depot, Mom grabbed her handkerchief and wiped her eyes.

"Always do what's right, son. Keep your faith no matter what. We'll pray every day. And please write whenever you get the chance. We'll be glued to the radio to hear any news."

"Your mother's right, son. Think about what we've taught you. We'll be praying for you and Chester constantly. And we're praying for President Roosevelt too. It's a tough time for our country. You haven't even left, and already I want this war to be over."

Mom added, "You know your father and I didn't even come to America until we were a little older than you. But we're Americans now. Fight for America, son. I know you'll make us proud."

He hugged both his parents, lingering. He didn't care if anyone saw him.

When the bus doors swung open, Walter's foot hit the first step, but he turned around to wave goodbye to his parents one last time. He found a seat on the side where his parents stood. He waved again through the open window, memorized the looks on their faces, and settled into his seat with a lump in his throat that threatened to explode.

———— ⚬✯✯⚬ ————

Walter prepared himself for the long bus ride back to the base. He wondered if Eddie would step on his bus. When the driver made periodic stops, more new recruits and enlisted sailors like him boarded, but Eddie did not.

Finally arriving at the Recruit Training Center in San Diego, the driver dropped off the new enlistees first for the boot camp. Walter remained seated with his wrinkled uniform smelling his own sweat. He could see the officers with clipboards calling out names. He recalled his own first few days of training. New city, scared feelings, no friends, doubts about his decision, and homesickness.

After a few more miles of twists and turns, the driver made his second stop at the Gunner's Mate School entrance at Point Loma. He rubbed his stiff legs as soon as he stepped off the bus. Looking around, the layout of the walkways, buildings, streetlights, and barracks in the distance appeared the same as the boot camp training grounds on the other side. The evening dusk still offered light for early summer, and he caught a glimpse of the now-familiar sight of the boat channel waters opening into the bay.

Officers stood by with clipboards in hand, providing directions to the registration point. Slinging his seabag over his right shoulder, Walter joined in light conversations as his group walked together.

Upon check-in, he received the number and location of his new barracks. Along with a few other sailors, he figured out which way to walk.

As soon as he walked into the first floor, a familiar voice yelled. "Hey, Walt, over here." Eddie got his attention right away.

Walter walked over to claim a bunk close to his friend. They slapped each other across the backs.

"Hey, look, it's Troyan. What's buzzin', cousin?" Some of the other familiar boys from boot camp paid their own greetings.

Setting his seabag on his new bed, the familiar street language, smoking, girl talk, and dirty joking greeted him again. Although he didn't like it, he expected it all the same.

"I just got here yesterday," Eddie said. "I thought we'd be on the same bus."

"Yeah, I thought so too, but, well, here we are. Are you ready for this?"

"You bet I am." He held his hands up in a shooting gun position.

"Then I'm ready too."

CHAPTER NINE

For the next few days, Walter attended more in-processing meetings and endured another medical exam. His schedule was similar to boot camp with early rising, showers, breakfast, and off to daily marching and calisthenics.

Although boot camp had toughened him to some degree, the yelling and barking of orders still got under his skin.

"Those push-ups look like sissies."

"You're off by an inch. Watch your steps, or we'll be marching until midnight."

"Don't look left until I say so."

When he heard that the actual academic classes for firearms skills would start the next day, he was ready.

"Finally, this is what I've been waiting for."

"Hold on," Eddie said. "You know everything is just going to get harder."

"I know, I know, but this is what our aptitude tests showed we could do. I like math and configurations. I'm ready to do more than just exercise and march."

After an exhausting day in the hot sun, Walter shuffled his feet mechanically as he headed back to his barracks with Eddie after supper. He fell on his bunk, dog-tired.

"My head is killing me."

"Not as much as mine," Eddie said.

"Oh yeah?" Walter grabbed his pillow and flung it at him.

Eddie threw the pillow back and flexed his arm muscles, squinting his eyes. "Well, let's see, how many more weeks of this stuff do we have? I'm ready to go meet up with some Japs now. Forget the classes."

Walter raised himself up on one elbow. "Settle down, Page. I've got a joke for you. What month do all troops hate?"

"Heck if I know."

"March."

When Walter sat down in his chair for the assembly with the entire group for the first day of classes, he watched an officer walk to the front of the room. A tall man with a receding hairline, standing sentinel, he waited for all the new recruits to be seated. He introduced himself as Lieutenant Beebe.

"You and you and you over there, and the guy sitting next to you, you must want to be gunners. If not, you shouldn't be here. Every young man must want to get into this fight and win it. You'll be assigned to smaller groups, and your instructor will stay with you for the duration of this training. His job is to teach you and teach you well. He'll want you to be first-class gunners, second to none. All instructors will report on each man's progress for every hour of training."

The lieutenant turned around and pointed to a large chart on the wall.

"See this? All of you will have a daily progress sheet like this for a report of your work for every hour. You may be wondering what kind of work you'll be doing. First, you'll meet your new friends, the guns. They will need to be your intimate friends. You'll learn each part of the guns, their functions, and call these guns by their first names."

Walter rubbed his knee and glanced sideways, taking a deep breath.

"Men, you'll be learning the types of guns, artillery, cannons, and specifications and ranges for each gun and shell. You'll learn how to break down the guns for cleaning and reassembling, which will demand repetitive practice. It's critical you know the right kind of ammo for each gun, as well as the speedy stocking and resupplying. You'll have to figure out what is wrong when your gun jams, and they will unexpectedly jam. During a real battle, you'll have no downtime to figure this out like you do in class. Get used to this."

Lieutenant Beebe continued for the next hour with his part of the orientation, explaining what the next sixteen weeks would entail. When he finished talking, Walter waited his turn to find out which smaller group he'd be assigned to and his instructor's name.

Eating their hot dogs and salads at lunch, Walter and other new gunner recruits talked like firecrackers about what the next few months would hold for them.

He poked his fork in his salad and stabbed a piece of tomato. "My instructor is Chief Cotaling. I heard someone say he's pretty intense. Who's yours, Eddie?"

"I got Chief Daigre. I heard he's a tough old coot. I guess I'll find out. Too bad we're not in the same group."

After lunch, Walter walked to his assigned classroom and found a table and chair next to the gray wall. He looked around and wished the open windows would provide some ventilation to ward off the heat.

Chief Cotaling, an indisputably imposing figure, introduced himself without a smile and bellowed out expectations for his group. After some general remarks, Walter could tell he was a no-nonsense instructor when he headed right into hammering out ballistic calculations.

"Boys, you'll need to memorize these formulas like nobody's business. The ballistic coefficient of a body is a measure of its ability to overcome air resistance in flight. We refer to this as the BC. It is inversely proportional to the ..."

As Chief Cotaling droned on, Walter took notes furiously. He watched chalk dust poofs float in the air as the instructor wrote all the formulas on the front board.

That night in his barracks, Walter took out his notebook and made some notations. Oblivious to everyone around him, he recited his new knowledge aloud. "Okay, maintenance schedules, keeping the guns lubricated and firing properly, the ballistic coefficient is figured by—"

"Troyan, what are you yammering about? For crying out loud, I'm trying to concentrate and make my own notes." Lloyd Mankin, always giving orders in the barracks as if he was the captain, grabbed a straw and aimed a spitball in Walter's direction.

"Shut up, Lloyd. You're a rack hound." Eddie said.

Albert Thomas paced in a circle in the main aisle. "I don't know how to calculate the elevation of the guns based on the ammunition used. Who gets this?"

"I can help." Walter sat down with Albert to review for the rest of the evening.

Before going to sleep, he quietly played "When the Saints Go Marching In" on his harmonica, trying to let go of tension.

The next day in class, Chief Cotaling prepped his recruits with more details for specific areas of training.

"Boys, the most important thing you'll learn at this school is range estimation. You are expected to receive a perfect score for the international Morse Code. A little later on, you'll practice shooting at moving targets in a darkened projection room on a screen with a trainer at your side. At the end of the course, you'll learn gunnery control and tactics."

He wiped his brow with a handkerchief and continued his lecture.

"This gunnery school is only for practice. But when you have learned your academic work, when you score high on your practice targets, when you pass your final examinations, then it will no longer be practice. You'll have to be good, darn good, in the real action of the war. You'll have to be a gunner who wins. It's up to you in these next few weeks."

Lieutenant Beebe calls us men. Chief Cotaling calls us boys. What are we?

When the class dismissed, Walter stood, stretched his neck, and headed outside to walk to the mess hall for lunch. He chatted with his classmates and watched two yellow-hooded orioles playing tag and squawking in a nearby tulip tree. Looking at the boat channel in the distance, he half-wished he could jump in a boat for more oar training.

———————⊙⊙⊙———————

Each day blended into the next with classes and intense training. Walter's confidence in his math and mechanical skills increased, and now he was putting those skills to work, even helping other classmates. Day after day, he took notes and committed terminologies and commands to memory.

One morning in class, everyone found their seats quickly when Chief Cotaling looked around the room and said, "Close your eyes."

He paused, and Walter closed his eyes.

"Okay, you can't see a thing, right? And this is why we have radar, a brand-new technology, I might add. Radar will be your eyes and will win battles and save lives by intercepting coordinated attacks before the enemy can say cheese. Now open your eyes."

Chief Cotaling talked while he drew illustrations of the mechanisms and functions of radar utilized by ships.

Taking in a deep breath, Walter studied the blackboard, took notes, and tried to absorb all the new information that bombarded him like never-ending cannon shells.

When he sat down for supper later that day, he rubbed his forehead after every swallow of his mashed potatoes. His pounding temples needed relief.

"Are you okay?" Albert asked.

"Yeah, I need to get some coffee or aspirin or something. My head is killing me."

I wonder if anyone knows if there are ballistic calculations for how full my brain can get before it explodes?"

A couple of weeks after classes started, Chief Cotaling informed his group that target practice in the projection room would begin for the afternoon session. Walter nearly skipped to lunch in his excitement to hear this.

After eating, he headed to Building F, which contained a large projection room designed to simulate target hitting. Using ear protection, Walter started his first firing practice. Although the practice guns were small, he visualized large canons on a battleship.

Chief Cotaling walked around the room, saying, "Practice and patience, practice and patience." And then, he made notations on their individual progress sheets.

Next came a training film for the forty-millimeter guns, followed by the instructor exhibiting different calibers of shells with demonstrations for loading.

"Time for the real thing." Chief Cotaling instructed Walter's group to line up for more training outside with a real model.

Walter squinted in the bright sun, raising his right hand to shield the glare.

"Okay, these simulation guns, canons, and equipment will provide you an education in the fundamentals of shipboard drills and procedures. Hang on for the ride. You'll need to know the firing terms and commands like the back of your hands."

Chief Cotaling pointed out each part of the forty-millimeter model gun with dummy controls.

"You'll be taught and trained by rote repetition for the next few weeks to shoot your guns in the projection room with the utmost precision. We'll have target practice on the grounds with live firing of your rifles. You'll learn to adjust the oil buffer of a fifty-caliber Browning machine gun, replace the interlock carrier spring from a twenty-millimeter gun, and replace the extractor plunger on a 538 anti-aircraft gun. Then, in times of battle, you'll be on the hot seat to detect, maneuver, and fire to sink the enemy. Let me make this clear. You'll fire, or you will be fired upon. You'll kill, or you will be killed."

Walter shuffled his feet and stared at his instructor. *I kill, or I'll be killed?* Then it hit him. *This is not just about me. It's about everyone else who will be on my ship. It's about everyone else on the other American ships, too.*

CHAPTER TEN

NOVEMBER 1942

As the sixteen-week school session drew to a close, the shorter autumn days and cooler air prepared Walter mentally that his next assignment was around the corner, this time to fight as a full-fledged United States Navy sailor. He studied for his last pass at mechanical aptitude and mechanical knowledge exams.

When he learned that not only had he passed his exams but had received top-notch scores, he asked Eddie how he did.

"My scores were great. So glad the exams are over. We need to celebrate or something."

"Let's head to the recreation center and the basketball courts."

Strolling down the sidewalk, the two chatted and joked all the way, spirits high. The palm trees swayed in the breeze, and the cumulus clouds congregated above their heads with a few seagulls circling.

"I have to tell ya something," Eddie said.

"What's that?"

"Well, ya see, I'm crazy about my gal, Emma. And well, I'm thinking about asking her to marry me. You know, before I go off to war and all. I hinted about this when we were together after boot camp. I even hinted to my mom."

Walter stopped walking. He grabbed Eddie's shoulder. "Whoa, back it up. Really? You know we're going off to war, right? Are you sure about this?"

"Yep, I'm sure. I hope she says yes when I pop the question."

"Well, I can't think about marriage. I don't even have a gal."

When they walked into the gymnasium, Walter claimed an empty court, and they both grabbed a couple of basketballs to practice shooting. In moments, the two were into their own one-on-one game.

"Okay, let's see if you can get by me to make it to the hoop." Eddie dribbled the ball between his legs.

"Well, who says I need to make it to the hoop? I can score on you from anywhere." Walter stole the ball away and sent it flying to the hoop for the first points. "You really think you might get married?"

<hr />

When the out-processing steps began, each member of the division received their orders. Walter and Eddie learned they would be ordered to the *USS Denver*, a light cruiser that would have engagements in the Pacific.

"Eddie, looks like we got our marching orders. Strike that. I don't want to think about marching." Walter laughed. "How is the *Denver* so lucky to get both of us?"

"As far as I'm concerned, if we have to fight this nasty war, at least I'll have my friend."

Walter walked away to find a telephone to call his parents with his news. Fingers shaking from nervous excitement, he dialed the operator.

<hr />

When it came time to leave the Gunner's Mate School, Walter finalized every step. He received a train ticket for the long ride across the country to the Philadelphia Naval Yard. Baffled, he questioned why Eddie, also assigned to the *Denver*, didn't have a reservation for the same train departure. The two parted ways, assuring one another they'd meet up again soon.

Ignoring sniffles and fatigue, he prepared his seabag again, packing according to regulation. First, he rolled his clothes so they would wrinkle less. He had been given trousers, handkerchiefs, a neckerchief, gym shoes and dress shoes, a pea coat, underwear, four pairs of socks, and a rain jacket. He placed his harmonica inside one of his shoes. *You're still going with me.*

Grabbing his shaving equipment, toiletries, towels, pens, pillow, two blankets, pillowcase, and his Bluejacket's Manual, he placed everything in the right order and stuffed them inside.

Next, he formed his rolled mattress around the outside of the seabag and securely tied it, knowing it would be among the masses of hundreds of others. But with his stenciled name on the outside, he understood it would stay with him for the duration of the war and become a part of his identity as a young sailor.

He assumed he'd be required to take his hammock as well, but when he got word that his ship assignment was the *USS Denver*, he learned the brand-new ship's berths contained bunk beds.

With a heave, he slung the heavy seabag over his shoulder and trooped off with all he owned to catch the base bus which would take him to the San Diego train station.

He thought about his phone call to his parents and brother last night, knowing they were sharing the earpiece to listen at the same time. Arthur relayed he'd also enlisted in the Navy and was awaiting paperwork to attend the Farragut Naval Training Station in Idaho.

"Arthur, write me about Farragut. I hope you get to fly. Mom, Pop, well, I guess this is it. I don't know when I'll see you again."

"I know, I know," his mother said. "Write home when you can. Always do what's right, son. You know we love you and …" his mother sniffled.

Pop broke in when Mom couldn't continue. "We'll constantly be praying for you and Chester. You'll be the best gunner there is. Keep your faith."

When Walter walked up to the boarding gate at the train station, ticket in hand, he shivered as a slight wind hit his face and made it hard to breathe through his stuffy nose.

"Blast this nasty cold," he muttered to himself.

The running diesel engine roared like thunder as Walter handed his ticket to the gateman. Scooting into a cold seat with cracked vinyl, he squinted out the dirt-stained window and decided to look for another seat. He jumped when the train jolted.

When the train chugged and picked up momentum as it wound its way along the tracks, heading for Los Angeles, his heart picked up speed too. He tried to rest. Once it halted at the Los Angeles station, he stretched, walked around a bit in his car, and looked through the windows at the large train station. Street dogs and chubby pigeons roamed around, looking for handouts. Through the window, he could see a young newsboy hawking his newspapers on the street corner, shouting World War II headlines. He immediately recalled his own boyhood days in downtown San Francisco when he had the same job.

When the train started up again, he tried to allow the rhythmical chug and clang to relax him and overcome feelings of homesickness.

All went dark as the train whizzed through a tunnel before arriving at Flagstaff. He eased out of his rigid metal seat for a walk-through to other cars, wrinkling his nose when the tobacco-tinged air hit him.

By the time the train rolled through Albuquerque, evening had descended across the landscape.

When Walter got up again to stretch his legs, he accidentally bumped into the porter.

"Watch out!" the man exclaimed.

"Oh, I beg your pardon, sir."

He watched the balding man with a missing tooth systematically convert seats to berths for sleep.

Settling in for the night, images of his parents, brothers, Jacky, and the school orchestra floated through his mind like a movie reel. He reminisced his childhood days when his mother would dress him and his brothers in look-alike sailor clothes when they lived in Hamtramck, Michigan, years ago. *Did she have a premonition that all her sons would later enlist in the Navy?*

Before falling asleep on the top berth, he hummed "Amazing Grace," the last hymn he remembered singing at his church in Santa Rosa.

Walter woke up the next morning to gloomy rain. Feeling stiff, he stretched his weary body. As the train traveled through hills and valleys, the ever-changing scenery reminded him that every minute, every mile, was taking him further away from home and life as he once knew it. He watched out the window as he rode through hills with farmhouses, barns, and cattle eating wild grasses.

When the train made stops in Dodge City, Kansas City, and St. Louis, Walter always watched to see who was leaving and who was boarding. He overcame his initial shyness and talked with other passengers in the dining and observation cars, mostly about the war.

A crusty old man, rather heavy, flicked his cigar and read the headline of the paper he was holding.

"'Hitler Sends Air Troops to Tunisia.' Well of course he does. He wants his Nazis in France and everywhere."

"Frank, just turn the page," another passenger said. "You gotta read about the Allies from the North Africa headquarters smashing into Oran with tanks to occupy the French Naval base."

Walter listened. He would soon be participating in the Pacific Theater, fighting Japan, but he knew the European war was spreading like wildfire under Hitler's regime. He asked the gentlemen if he could borrow their papers to read when they finished.

On the fourth day of traveling, one middle-aged gentleman in a rumpled suit and checkered tie asked him about boot camp and Gunner's Mate school with genuine interest.

"Well, just so you know, young man, I served in World War One. And let me tell you, war is no piece of cake. It will make a man out of you. How old are you anyway?" he asked.

Mr. Josef said the same thing. "I'm seventeen, sir."

"By the way, I'm Reeder, Norbert Reeder. I was in the army, and I had my fill of death and destruction. And here we are again, another world war. You boys shouldn't have to go through what my generation did."

"I wish we didn't either, but I heard the call from my country to fight and defend America. Especially after Pearl Harbor. My older brother was at Pearl Harbor when it was attacked."

"Oh, sonny, I'm sorry." Mr. Reeder hung his head.

"Well, our family is thankful he survived. And I have another brother who just enlisted. Uncle Sam said it's my turn to serve now."

"Where're you headed?"

"I'm assigned to the *USS Denver,* a light cruiser, which is at the Philadelphia Naval Yard. One of my buddies I met at boot camp will be on the same ship. But I'd be lying if I said I wasn't a little anxious."

Mr. Reeder patted Walter's shoulder. "That's to be expected, son. When I finished my training, I wasn't ready to fight anything. But my training taught our platoon to stick together and make the most of whatever situation might arise. You'll do okay, my boy, if you remember that."

"Thank you, sir, I will."

When the locomotive whistle blared upon arrival at Pittsburgh, the porter announced, "This is our last stop before Philadelphia. We'll be there in eight hours."

Walter looked at Mr. Reeder. "Eight more hours? I hope I can make it. It feels like this train ride will never end." He yawned, feeling his hot forehead. His cold had worsened each day.

"You better take care of that cold, sonny. The ship will have a sickbay."

Walter returned to his seat and closed his eyes. He jerked from his doze when the train brakes screeched for its final stop. The dark cab with dimmed lights revealed that night had come while he was napping. *Now I'm almost 3,000 miles away from home.*

PART FOUR: ON THE *USS DENVER*

CHAPTER ELEVEN

NOVEMBER 11, 1942, PHILADELPHIA NAVAL YARD

Walter tugged on his seabag and had his order papers in hand when he finally deboarded the train. The cold November night air, so different from San Diego, provided some relief for his congested head at first. His warm breath formed a cloud before his face. He flung his seabag over his shoulder and squinted as all the flashing lights of the shipyard danced across the sky. The smell of salt permeated the air.

He looked around for the main gate and spotted a line of sailors about the length of a football field. Sneezing and yawning, he trudged to the line to wait it out.

About forty minutes later, he finally reached the front of the line, and the cantankerous shore patrol attendant, cigar protruding, barked, "Orders!"

"Here, sir." Walter handed over his papers, hoping the man's dangling cigar wouldn't fall on them as he did so.

"The *Denver*'s over there. Next."

Walter took his papers back and walked in the direction the man had pointed. A gust of wind sent shivers down his neck and arms. He saw a number of ships in the far distance, but he had no idea which one was the *Denver*.

Am I supposed to just walk? What kind of outfit is the Navy if they don't have jeeps for pick up?

Coughing and rubbing his hot forehead, he began the trek, his seabag over his right shoulder weighing him down. His breaths formed miniature clouds to walk through as he strode toward the *Denver*.

The loading and unloading of hundreds of pallets to the Quonset huts fascinated him. *This place is huge.* The electric fork trucks buzzing about their business, even late at night, signaled the immediacy of a war in progress.

As Walter got closer to the ships, the movement of the massive cranes produced deafening noise. He couldn't decide which was louder, the bellowing of orders or the noise of the equipment. All of it created a racket. The chilly air tingled his cheeks, and he cupped his hands to blow warm breath upon them.

Walking faster, he met up with a group of sailors going the same direction.

"Are any of you headed for the *Denver*?" he asked.

"Nope, but follow us. It's over there somewhere. We have to find our ships too."

A scrappy young boy added, "With all this walking, I'm gonna be dang tired before I even step foot on my ship."

The icy air zapped all of Walter's strength as he tried to keep up. He cupped his hands again and blew into them before shifting his seabag to his left shoulder.

Another young sailor said, "Come on, just follow. We'll all get there soon enough. If we're lucky, maybe we'll even get a little shut-eye tonight."

After a two-mile walk and lagging behind the small group, he focused on a number of ships docked at the piers. Boot camp and Gunner's Mate school had not prepared him for this magnificent sight of illuminated ships ready for war duties. Walter stood frozen in place for a moment, studying the landscape of ships before his eyes. He took a deep breath, staring with weary eyes, lips quivering in the cold air.

As he walked closer to Pier 4, he spotted the 58 painted on the hull of the *USS Denver* secured starboard side to the west of the pier. He stood still for another moment, taking in the majesty of her. She towered before him, taller and wider than he ever imagined. *So, this is my ship. She's huge. She's a beauty.*

In no hurry now, Walter walked a slow pace toward the *Denver* and sensed his ship beckoning to him. *Welcome to your new home. I'm the best fighting ship there is. We're in this war together. Take good care of me, and I'll take good care of you.*

Weak and chilly, Walter dropped his seabag to drag it along as he walked upward on the metal catwalk to board the ship. The first person he met was the Quarter Deck Officer.

"Your voyage begins, young sailor."

Walter saluted, and the officer pointed ahead.

Then he met the Officer of the Deck, saluted, showed his papers, and stammered, "Sir, I think I have a fever."

"Oh, you'll make it," the officer grumbled, dismissing Walter's complaint. "Make your way down to the third deck. Just ask where activation is and show your papers."

Walter followed the orders, dodging other sailors and busy officers, navigating his way around. Overwhelmed, he finally completed all the steps for in-processing, and someone handed him some fruit and water.

Light gray, dark gray, yellow-gray. Even at night, with all the lights on the ship, his new home boasted gray colors throughout with never-ending spaghetti bowls of wires, tentacles of conduit, pipes, electrical panels, hoses, and ropes as accessories.

As Walter made his way through the many narrow corridors called passageways, he ducked his head when he stepped over a number of oval doorways known as hatches to find his berth on the fifth deck. The closed hatch doors of steel he passed offered no invitation to enter, as they were shut for water tightness with hinges as big as his hands. No doorknobs, only levers.

After pulling necessities out of his seabag, he dropped it off at a designated storage room where he would always have access to it. When he stepped into his assigned berth, he understood why his seabag had to be stored elsewhere. The cramped living area allowed no room for all the seabags.

He looked around. Several sailors were talking. Others were trying to sleep. The green and white checkered linoleum floor appeared shiny and clean, even in the dim light. He glanced at a few posters taped to the gray metal walls. One poster read:

Now Hear This!
Camper's Responsibility
Campers are responsible to keep this living
space and other spaces you use
shipshape at all times.

Groups of three vertical beds, known as coffin racks, connected by chains, suspended from the ceilings. He claimed a bed in the middle and tied his mattress to the wobbly frame, wrapped his mattress cover around it, adjusted his blankets, and threw his pillow on. The bed setup did not convince him of any comfort. No one was on the mattress above him. The fellow below his chosen rack was resting on his side with a sheet over his face.

So I'm a camper?

Next, he placed his toiletries and clothing inside the locker below the three racks, a storage space he would have to share.

Some of the other boys appeared to be sleeping while others were chatting the night away. A few waved a welcome hello. He had no idea when he'd meet up with Eddie.

Walter slept fitfully, if at all.

The next morning, he dressed and glanced around the crowded berth. Surprised, he spotted Eddie on the other side of the room, jumping down from his top rack.

His spirits lifted like a hot air balloon, and he hollered over to his friend.

Eddie made his way over to him, and the two clasped one another's shoulders. "Hey, I've been looking for you, pal. I heard they try to put the gunners in the same berths, but I was beginning to wonder about you. When did you get here? I must have been sound asleep last night."

"Yeah, it was pretty late by the time I got off my train and checked in."

"Wait a minute, you don't look so good. The *Denver* ain't moved an inch. You can't be seasick already," Eddie said.

"I'm miserable with a fever. Yeah, seasick is probably comin' around the corner too. But I can't shake this cold."

"Well, guess what, pal?"

Walter put his hands on his hips and eyed Eddie. "Did ya get hitched?"

Eddie smiled like a kid about to get a lollipop. "Yep, being married is the best thing ever. Boy, I can't tell ya how hard it was to say goodbye to my beautiful new wife. We were only together a few days. But some of these other fellas said they got married too and left for the war the very next day."

"Well, I'm happy for ya, Eddie, real happy."

"So I promised Emma I'd get home from the war safe. I gotta keep my promise."

"I'll help you, Eddie, I'll help you. I'd help you even if you weren't married."

———————— ⋙✻⋘ ————————

Walking to the upper deck, Walter took in the sight of many sailors scurrying about like bees on a beehive. Hundreds of teen sailors like him who had endured the Great Depression and had stood in bread lines with their mothers, hoping for another meal to survive. Many had worn shoes with holes, passed down from a sibling. Some had fainted at school from hunger. They had experienced impoverished days only a few years ago they would never forget. They remembered their parents' anguish and becoming resourceful out of necessity. Yes, these young sailors were steeled and motivated when they answered the call of duty to fight for America.

At muster call, Walter found his assigned group and joined about forty others in the gunner division.

He stood at attention. With shaking legs and a hurting head, he fought the urge to sit down. At the first opportunity, he gathered up his courage to approach his division officer, Commander Peter Wells.

"Sir, I feel sick."

"What do you think is wrong with you?"

"I think I have a fever."

"Well, head down to the sick bay if you must. Find deck two and look for the signs."

As soon as Walter entered the medical exam room, he caught a whiff of antiseptic. The room was small but contained all sizes of white metal drawers and cabinets. Jars filled with tongue depressors, cotton swabs, gauze pads, and vials of all sizes filled one corner. A cloth-covered tray with various surgical instruments on the countertop sat next to a white helmet with a red cross on it. A number of folded coarse blankets remained on a chair next to the examination bed.

Climbing up on the bed for his exam, Dr. Horak checked his vitals and confirmed Walter had a fever.

"Take these two aspirins now and the other two at bedtime. I'm going to write out a slip for light-duty and some rest until the fever is gone and you get your strength back," the doctor explained. "Come back if you feel worse."

Walter reviewed the slip he'd been handed. All of a sudden, he felt a surge of strength and a puncture of pride. "Sir, I think I can pull regular duty. I don't want any partiality. I will take the aspirin."

"Hang on to the note anyway, but if you're up to it, we can use your help. We gotta get this cruiser into shape, organized, and ready. The Japs aren't waiting for us."

Walter stepped down from the bed onto the gray and white flecked linoleum floor and thanked the good doctor. As he was exiting the room, he momentarily stopped. Next to the door, he saw a large clear container labeled "Swear Jar." In smaller letters beneath the label, Walter read: *If you slip from the lip, empty your pocket to the jar. Doc.*

Grinning, he made his way back to the gunner division.

The *Denver* consisted of a mixture of naval shipmates— the newly recruited sailors and seasoned sailors from the Pearl Harbor attack who had been reassigned. Tours and orientation meetings began right away.

Petty Officer First Class Peter Gulas explained the bell system to Walter's group. "Some of you may have watches, but if you don't, you'll always know what time it is. The bells ring every four hours around the clock, starting at twelve midnight."

Midnight, 4:00 a.m.? Walter frowned.

He learned the ship had a specific system for laundry, and he supposed it was necessary in light of twelve hundred sailors on board. Not only that, but specific sailors were assigned to the laundry department, and that was their sole job for the war effort.

"All of you will receive two ditty bags, one for whites, one for blues. Make sure you know your colors. They'll be washed and dried as such." Officer Gulas reached into his pocket and held out his pen. "Get out those black pens you have and get your names on all your clothing and on the ditty bags if you want to get your clothes back."

Besides his own understanding of gunners, Walter had no previous comprehension of the vast size of this ship and the inner workings of all the other positions.

Starting with the deck below the main deck, Walter met some of the shell handlers. One of the officers turned on the conveyor belt for a demonstration and said, "For all you gunners, we will keep your guns ready and active. My handlers lunge and squat and slam the shells like clockwork on the conveyor like nobody's business. In a real battle, you can count on us."

When he and the others in his group arrived at the mess hall on one of the lower decks and saw the cooks, he said, "Eddie, look at those mounds of potatoes they're peeling. That's gonna take them hours."

"Well, there's a bunch of us to feed ... like over a thousand of us, I heard."

One of the cooks looked over at the group and asked, "Hey, did you know it takes two and a half tons of food each and every day to feed you fellows? We do our best. Don't complain."

Walter and Eddie looked at each other and shook their heads.

Entering the bottom deck, Walter's group passed by the bridge, and he caught a glimpse of a table full of charts and the steering crew. Edging a little closer, the long panel of buttons, lights, valves, switches, gauges, and levers dazzled him.

"Eddie, which one do you think is our captain?"

"Your guess is as good as mine. But I reckon we'll find out soon enough."

When his group climbed back up to the deck above, Walter saw the chaplain's office. After passing by sick bay, he found himself at the ship's post office with Eddie close behind. He looked through each of the two windows, open enough for hands to give and receive mail yet closed off with vertical bars, similar to prison windows.

When he thought he'd seen it all, he saw the word "Brig" above a closed hatch further down the passageway.

"Well, this is a new discovery for sure. I had no idea our ship had a brig."

"You better mind your manners, Walter, or I'll have to come visit you in the brig." Eddie slapped Walter across the back and laughed.

"You know what? After seeing all these other jobs, I think our ship is like a city. I mean, we have everything we need right here without ever stepping off the ship. We even have our own commissary. I had no idea we had floatplanes and catapults on this cruiser. I'm gonna write home about all this stuff."

"Well, hey, me too. Speaking of new discoveries, did you see the Marine detachment? I just wanted to scream at them and say, "Get off our ship. We're the Navy, not the Marines, you rascals. Are they one of us?"

"Well, they're on our ship. We all want to win the war. There must be some reason for it."

With mail delivery and pick up working fairly easily while the ship was docked, a few days later, Walter decided it was time to write a letter.

Dear Mom and Pop and Arthur,
I hope all is well on the home front. It's cold here at the Philadelphia Navy Yard. We're docked of course. I've heard we won't depart south to the canal until sometime in January. In the meantime, I've been all over this ship, and we always have practice drills. I think I know this cruiser like the back of my hand. Eddie and I linked up right away, and I'm making more friends.

I found out our ship is almost two football fields long. I stared at her for a long time when I first got to the shipyard. Pop, the Denver has four geared turbines, and she can get going to almost forty miles an hour. That's pretty impressive if you ask me. And you won't believe all the other positions besides gunners on this ship. It's like a city. We even have bankers and photographers. We have our own barber shop, and there are sailors on board who just do all the laundry. I'm glad I'm a gunner. I will get to see the action. I've heard that we'll have a shakedown cruise, although I'm not sure what all is involved with that. I guess I'll find out.

Well, write me when you can, especially before we leave the dock. When do you leave, Arthur?
Your loving son,
Walter

CHAPTER TWELVE

Walter worked like a miner in a landslide to prepare the *Denver* for the war effort. He humbly obliged when he got orders to scrape paint, load supplies, work mess duty (kitchen duty), and clean heads (bathrooms). Always busy, he examined and cleaned the guns and reviewed operations in his Bluejacket's Manual.

One day when he ran his hands over some of the guns, feeling the dips and ridges, Eddie asked, "Whatcha doin'?"

"I'm memorizing these beauties. We'll be using them at night, and I want a picture in my mind."

"Well, like Chief Beebe said at Gunner's Mate School, these guns are our new best friends. We need to take good care of 'em."

The cranes from the shipyard continued to load supplies on the *Denver* and other ships, including food supplies. Walter stood wide-eyed one morning as food crate after food crate was lowered on deck. And soon enough, he was ordered to unload them.

"Get a load of all that butter," Eddie said.

"Nope, that's called axle grease," a more seasoned sailor replied. "And see that canned milk? We call that armored cow."

"Well, look, now we're gettin' our dog food. Can't wait for that," another sailor piped up.

"What's that?" Walter asked.

"Corn beef hash. Yum."

Making a face, another sailor slurped his lips and rubbed his belly, mocking the hash.

With no differentiation for seamen first-class jobs, Walter and hundreds of others lifted and moved and counted the crates systematically. It didn't matter that he was a gunner, trained specifically for handling guns and target shooting.

"Men, stop the smoking," barked one of the officers, "You're supposed to save that for the smoking areas and don't look as if you're at a party. More crates are coming. We have to feed 1,200 of you three times a day. If you wanna eat, get these crates moved."

Another officer handed Walter a clipboard with a pen and checklist. "This is your area. Check these crates off from here to here. Turn in your tab sheet to Chief Burgess."

Walter began the monotonous inventory with Alvin Thames, another gunner, counting boxes and looking for the weight and type of food. Alvin called out the food items and the weight, and Walter marked everything off the list.

"White American Kraft cheese, 400 pounds; apples, 2,500 pounds; cabbage, 1,000 pounds; celery, 1,125 pounds; spinach, 750 pounds; dried sliced beef, 1,512 pounds; potatoes, 7,000 pounds."

"Holy mackerel!" Walter whistled when he checked off the pounds of the potatoes. Check, check, check. The vast amount of food dazed his brain.

"Okay, more crates are getting dumped." He stared at the tall crane, edging to the deck again.

Watching other sailors unload the crates from the net, he handed his clipboard and tab sheets to Alvin for more inventory checks, and he took his place at counting the items.

Walter called out canned prunes, franks and beans, spam, sausages, pancake mix, juice, dry milk, coffee, cream, sugar, and potatoes.

"What did you say? More potatoes? Did I hear wrong?" Alvin asked.

"Nope, you heard me right, 3,000 more pounds. Better check the list. This crate is in addition to the other bunch of potatoes. Something tells me we'll be seeing a lot of mashed potatoes on our plates. By the way, where're you from?"

"Denver. I figured that's why they put me on this ship. How about you?"

"Santa Rosa, California. Well, lookee here. I scream, you scream, we all scream for ice cream." Walter slurped his lips when he saw the 140 quarts of ice cream carted away to the freezers.

Later that day, Walter began to climb upward on a ladder to go topside. In his orientation tour, he had learned the stairways, called ladders in the Navy, on the starboard side were for climbing up. And ladders on the port side were for going down. "That's the Navy way," one of the officers had explained.

As he began a rapid climb up the ladder on the starboard side with supplies, he quickly grabbed a bar to keep from falling when someone coming down crashed into him.

Angered and frustrated, Walter yelled, "Hey, why don't you watch where you're going. You're a goofus on the wrong ladder." His supplies scattered below as he and the other man toppled down to the deck.

"I'm sorry, young man. I'm just the captain of this ship, and I haven't learned which sides are starboard and port," Captain Robert B. Carney winked and adjusted his glasses. "Don't tell anyone."

"Uh, oh, uh … okay, thank you, sir, your honor, sir," Walter stammered as his face flushed red and the two men saluted. Walter hoped in that embarrassing moment the captain of the *Denver* would never recognize him again!

For the next few weeks, Walter completed a variety of trainings and performed many kinds of duties, including mess duty, with the hundreds of other new recruits. All this time, the *Denver* never moved an inch.

Muster calls took place every morning at 0815. All sailors stood at attention in their various divisions to be accounted for by the Master of Arms and to receive their daily assignments.

When Walter pulled two weeks of mess duties, he decided to make the best of it, although, in truth, he was anxious to start more training with the guns. He found out he was required to work a certain number of days in the way of TAD—Temporary Assignment Duties—working in the galley as a mess cook. *Chester does this all the time. I guess I can do it too.*

He learned to operate and clean the griddles and became familiar with all the safety precautions for the large ovens and other hot equipment in the galley. His right arm muscles ached from turning the black crank on the three-foot mixer, nothing like the small one in his mother's kitchen.

Shuffling large bags of black pepper, salt, sugar, and flour worked his muscles over quite well. He stared at the large containers of dry yeast, lard, raw oats, cream powder, and vegetable oil, standing next to each other on high shelves like soldiers, hoping he wouldn't have to move any.

Preparing three square meals a day for 1,200 hungry men on board, not to mention the cleanup, was no easy feat, he discovered. Along with the other cooks, he was busy planning and preparing the next meal, hardly before the last meal was consumed. His running legs took him from preparing meals in the galley, to the mess hall for serving, and then on to the scullery for disposing of scraps and washing dishes after every meal. He grabbed his thirty-minute allotment to eat his own meals whenever he could.

He certainly didn't mind boasting to Eddie and others at the end of the day about bread and pastries he'd helped prepare from scratch, teasing them for the next day's meals.

After about three weeks, it was time for Walter to get a haircut to maintain Navy regulations. He headed aft of the Marine Corps Detachment Compartment on the starboard side, third deck, for the barbershop. On his way, he read a posted sign that said:

The Navy Way
Doing so much with so little for so long, proving
that anything can be
accomplished with nothing.

Well, that's probably half true, he thought to himself. Maybe totally true.

When he arrived at the barbershop, there was a short line. But watching the barber whiz over the sailors' heads as fast as greased lightning, Walter moved to the front soon enough. He noticed several bottles of Aqua Velva hair tonic in the background, as well as several pairs of scissors on a tray. Navy magazines as well as *Life*, *National Geographic*, and *Time* filled the rack on the wall behind the chair. Oh, to have a little time to read some of those, he thought.

"Next!"

He walked over, and while standing, the barber threw a

cape around his neck. He scooted onto the barber's chair, but before he'd even settled his behind into a comfortable position, the electric razor buzzed over the top of his head, and he jerked.

"Oh, sorry about that, sailor. I do a bunch of haircuts every day. I'm always maintaining good order, hygiene, and discipline for the Navy with my haircuts. Where're ya from?"

"Santa Rosa."

"What's your position?"

"I'm a Gunner's Mate, and I'm on the—"

Before Walter could finish his sentence, the barber pulled his cape off and said, "See, you're all done. Good luck, sailor."

Walter waded through the piles of hair on the floor, questioning if the barber owned a broom and wondered what his haircut even looked like.

———————⟋⟍———————

When Commander Wells, the Gunnery Department, FC (Fire Control) Division Officer, conducted the first training for the specific *Denver* armament, he explained that each of the gunners would be trained for all the guns but would be assigned primarily to one gun station. He called out names and divided the sailors into groups with assigned supervisors.

Walter heard his name called for the quad forty-millimeter guns. He joined others as they formed a smaller group. Chief Petty Officer Grace's solid frame and majestic bearing did not go unnoticed.

"I am Chief Grace. Pay attention. Most of you are unsophisticated pollywogs, and you will be operating this sophisticated gunnery system. You need to know what you're doing because everyone is counting on you to win the war for us. Am I making myself clear?"

"Yes, sir," rang out in unison.

"Okay, let's talk about the hoists and how everything works." Officer Grace adjusted his cap and placed both hands on his hips. "The powder storage magazines are located on both the port and starboard sides of the lower handling area, right? The powder cartridges are stacked from the deck to the overhead in relatively small compartments. Now, the projectile storage compartment is located in the aft end of the lower handling area. I think you've all seen this, right?"

"Yes, sir" rang out in unison again.

"All ordnance will be moved, stowed, and loaded by you gunners. The hoist mechanisms feed everything up. It's teamwork and clockwork at its best."

The gunners watched and listened as Chief Grace pointed to the 40-millimeter anti-aircraft gun.

"Okay, one of you will be the pointer. You'll sit in one seat and fire the gun. Another of you will be the trainer. You'll sit in the other seat and find the targets and help the pointer aim at them. First loader, you'll keep the ammo in the gun, and second loader, you'll keep your head down and keep the ammo coming from the handlers. You'll work as a team. We want to win this war. I can't do my job if you can't do your job."

Pointing to the shell casings, Chief Grace explained that each ship was assigned a color for the explosives. "Boys, there are dyes in the shells. The *Denver's* color is red. After you fire, look for your splash, look for the red dye in the water, and you'll know if you hit your target. These guns have the capacity to fire 1,000 yards. Your goal is to hit the target within ten feet."

Before Chief Grace finished the specific gun training,

he reminded his group that no smoking would ever be permitted on deck. He smiled, but it was menacing.

"Do you realize that the lighted butts of cigarettes might be seen by the enemy at night? And remember to only wear your blue hats topside. Your white hats could potentially become a beacon of light for the enemy."

Walter paid attention to every detail Chief Grace explained, some of which he recalled from Gunner's Mate School. The big difference, he thought, now is no simulation. He envisioned real action out on the waters with the enemy, which brought not a few flutters to his heart.

One morning after muster call, a siren blared over the loudspeaker, coming from the command deck. Walter jumped like the dickens and looked around. Most of the sailors stood at attention, and he followed suit.

Captain Carney announced over the ship's 1MC, "Men, the less you hear that, the better. But get used to it. That's our General Quarters, GQ alarm, for an impending battle. You will man your stations immediately and prepare for action with the enemy. I will be timing you for future practices."

Walter made many new friends in other division groups, and he especially enjoyed socializing with his gunner mates. He looked forward to some downtime when he could play cards, cut up with the other sailors, and play his harmonica. He and Eddie became fast friends with Buster Tarkington, Jim Thompson, and Claude Fanning, fellow gunners. Alvin Thames, the gunner Walter had worked with for the food deliveries, found his way into the middle of the group.

Buster, from Florida, a wild sort of kid and reckless in

nature, demonstrated strength like a bull. When he worked, he acted like a beast, nostrils flaring. His brawny physique and ruddy complexion demanded respect from the other sailors, and he acted like he knew it.

While Walter ate his breakfast one morning, Buster brought in a bit of drama, cleared his throat, lifted his chin, and said, "Well, we're the best gunners the Navy has, and the Japs aren't going to mess with us. And nobody on this here ship is either." He pounded his fist on the table like a gavel on a court bench, jarring the glasses of milk.

Walter rolled his eyes and grinned. He reckoned this was a true statement as long as Buster stuck around.

The sailors grew accustomed to Captain Carney's demanding ways. Walter figured out right away that his spry captain was a competitor who liked to win, and he expected perfection. During routine inspections, the captain noticed everything, and Walter kept his guard up for the relentless training.

Captain Carney started his daily announcements after muster call one morning with a surprising statement. "Starting this week, I will no longer require Saturday inspections. But the other inspections had better be top-notch. See to it, men."

This caught Walter off guard. When they dismissed, he caught up with several in his group to discuss the matter.

Buster asked, "Well, holy smoke, what's up with no Saturday inspections? That ain't like a captain."

"Maybe we don't have to make our beds on Saturdays?" Alvin asked.

"Guess we'll find out," Walter said. "Maybe he's lightning up because he knows we're already good."

After a few Saturdays with no ship inspections, the *Denver* got her first nickname—The Dirty Dee—with the sailors composing a couple of songs in her honor.

Even with this notice, Walter didn't doubt his ship

would always be in tiptop shape. Everyone wanted to please Captain Carney. Nevertheless, this change reminded him of Saturdays at home when he and Arthur sometimes didn't get their bedroom tidied.

———————⟡———————

"Hey, we're finally moving!" Walter exclaimed. "I feel it."

"Don't get too excited. We're only going to another drydock," Eddie said.

"Well, we know that, but hey, we're still moving." Alvin ran his fingers over his cropped red hair. "I've been waiting to feel this thing move." His tall height and steely blue eyes dominated his features

Claude, a handsome sailor from Kentucky, crossed his lanky legs and leaned against the rail. "Yeah, I like it too. It breaks the monotony. Even if it's just changing piers. We're only going about ten knots, ya know. No seasickness for me." His southern drawl could not be missed.

"Heck, I'll never be seasick." Buster belched and strutted about. "No wimps allowed on this ship. Only sissies get seasick."

"Just you wait, Buster, just you wait," Jim cackled.

Four tugboats pulled the *Denver* until she became waterborne and then cast their lines off.

Claude, standing next to Walter, said, "Those little tugs must have some kind of power to do what they do. I can't believe they can pull this thing."

Walter rested his elbows on the railing. "Yeah, from a distance, I bet it looks like four ants pulling an elephant."

As the ship skimmed the waters for the first time, Walter enjoyed the movement and anticipated what was still to come. He listened. He watched. The gentle lapping of the waters against the side of the ship signaled unknown adventures to him.

When Walter got ready for sleep one evening, he remembered the *Denver* was scheduled to head to open waters for maneuvers at 0300 during his sleep time.

Waking up fairly rested, he staggered out of bed the next morning and ate breakfast. As soon as he reported for muster call on the main deck, the cold wind hit him head on, and he shielded his face with both hands until he started working.

The *Denver*, cruising on the Delaware River on various courses and speeds, conformed with the channel and gradually worked up to twenty-five knots.

More than once, Walter saw a number of sailors running to the side railing, upchucking their breakfast when seasickness attacked. He observed one shipmate running to the side, but before he could make it, he puked right in his cap.

He gripped his own stomach every few minutes while he worked and kept his mind busy so he wouldn't have to join them.

Claude's face turned green, and Jim staggered when he walked.

"Eddie, look over there, Walter said. "Isn't that Buster? He's puking too."

"Serves him right for all his boasting."

"Well, my mother always says humbleness follows cockiness."

No sooner were these words out of his mouth, Eddie ran to the side of the ship. Walter massaged his abdominal area, took some deep breaths, and kept working. Not one for boasting, he never told his friends that the seasickness foe never got a hold of him.

———— ✺ ————

A few days before Thanksgiving, while Walter was busy working on data reports and out of earshot range, Eddie confided in Buster. "Hey, I just read the posted scuttlebutt dispatch. The *San Francisco* got hit really bad. And the *Juneau* blew up right in front of the *San Francisco*. Should I tell Walter?"

"I dunno, why?" Buster shrugged his shoulders.

"I'm pretty sure his brother is on the *San Francisco*."

Buster let out some expletives and shouted, "You gotta tell him, Eddie, or he'll find out anyway! If you don't, I'm gonna."

"Okay, okay."

As soon as Eddie encountered Walter, he scratched his head and asked, "Uh, don't you have a brother on the *San Francisco*?"

"Yeah, why?" Walter stopped writing his report and looked up.

"I just read the latest dispatch post. It says the *San Francisco* got some hits with fatalities. I think forty-five hits total. Must be pretty bad; the captain and admiral were among the dead."

Walter froze and turned pale.

He finally spoke. "I've got to find out more; I've just got to find out more." He squeezed his stomach as if someone had punched him in the gut and stole his breath.

At lunch break, Walter immediately hustled down the ladders and pushed through sailors to get to the posted dispatch. He read seventy-seven men lost their lives with one hundred five wounded and seven more missing on the *San Francisco*. And probably no survivors from the blown-up *Juneau*.

Chester worked as a cook on the heavy cruiser. *Maybe*

he's okay. But suddenly, he felt light-headed.

Finding some privacy, he found a place to sit to collect his thoughts and pray. *Dear God, please no, not my brother, please no. We already went through this with Pearl Harbor.*

With no time to sit around, he stood and walked back up the ladders, camouflaging his worry.

CHAPTER THIRTEEN

On Thanksgiving Day, Walter tried to put his worry aside for a little bit to enjoy time with his buddies. As he entered the chow line for supper, the aroma of cooked turkeys filled the entire area. Walter stood in line behind Eddie.

"Do we get seconds?" Eddie asked one of the cooks when he progressed through the line with his tray.

"Nope, but I'll fill your plates now. And if you don't eat all your veggies, I'm tellin' the skipper. We have twelve hundred to feed, and everyone comes through the line just once as on all other days."

"Well, shucks. My mama gave me seconds, thirds, and fourths on holidays if I wanted it."

"Well, you're not at home, sailor. You're on a cast-iron bathtub."

"Come on, Eddie, keep moving." Walter nudged him with his elbow.

When he watched the server dump a large helping of dressing on his plate with steam rising above it, Walter's stomach growled in anticipation of the festive meal. His appetite had dwindled considerably over worry about Chester. Maybe he would eat better today.

He and Eddie sat on the end of the first table they could grab, along with six other fellows, including Buster and Jim. Thanksgiving dinner consisted of turkey, dressing, mashed potatoes, a slice of bread, green beans, an orange, a stalk of celery, pumpkin pie, and all the coffee they wanted. Walter grabbed his knife and fork and moved his turkey around to keep it out of his green beans and chowed down.

"Ah, this is pretty scrumptious if you ask me," he said, then burped—loudly. "Thank goodness for that. My belly just got more room for my food."

"I can beat you, Walter!" Jim let out a whopper of a belch. A quiet teenager from West Virginia, a steady-at-the-helm sailor, Jim surprised everyone. And soon, the others entered the belching contest.

"Well, later tonight, I'll win the farting contest. Just wait and see," Buster said around a bite of dressing.

"I can tell you right now I'm going to be ready for a blanket drill. Give me some more of that joe." Eddie reached for the coffee pot.

As soon as he took his last bite and deposited his tray in the scullery, Walter got up to walk around by himself, frowning and holding his jaw stiff as he worried about the outcome of the *San Francisco* and Chester. He had no new information.

When someone tapped him on the shoulder, he jerked around.

"Hey, are you okay? You look down in the mouth."

"I didn't see you following me out here, Jim. Yeah, I'm okay, I guess. Well, no, I'm not. I'm still worried about my brother."

"I know whatcha mean. I've got a brother on the *USS Alabama*. I worry about him all the time. I'll leave you alone, but we can talk any time ya want."

"Thanks," he said, and Jim turned and walked away.

Walter watched his friend disappear down the hallway. He admired his easygoing temperament, sparkling laugh, and especially his compassion for everyone around him.

He finally climbed a ladder to his berthing compartment, found a stool, and sat down, staring into space.

A few days after Thanksgiving, Chief Burgess called Walter aside. "Seaman Troyan, step away from duties. I have a telegram for you."

With shaking hands, he thanked the chief and opened the telegram. He blinked and scanned the words quickly.

Msg Walter Troyan ... San Fran got it bad ... I'm okay ... Chester ... 30 November 1942

Walter found a place to sit. With legs apart, head bent, shoulders slumped, he let go of his sobs privately. *Oh, God, thank you.*

That night, with a relieved heart, he pulled his harmonica out and played "Boogie Woogie Bugle Boy."

When he yawned and set the harmonica aside, Buster spoke up, "Aww, don't quit now. I was just starting to relax."

"Maybe I should start charging then. But it's free tonight," Walter said as he put the harmonica to his lips again.

For some reason, Walter sensed a rush when he ate supper the next day. And noting some jitters the other seamen exhibited, maybe they had the same feeling. It had been business as usual since the ship arrived in Chesapeake Bay, yet ...

Before his last swallow, the GQ alarm blared, and he jumped like a cat in a thunderstorm.

"All hands, on deck! Man your battle stations! I repeat, man your battle stations!" Captain Carney's voice rang loud and fierce over the ship's communication system.

Walter shimmied up the ladders to his gunner station. He readied himself and looked around at his shipmates, many still scrambling around. The sailors had switched immediately from supper shifts, routine chores, and some from sleep to fighting readiness when the GQ alarm sounded.

Within a few minutes, another announcement blared. "This is your captain. You took seventeen minutes to man your stations. You know we would all be in the deep six by this time in a battle. In wartime, there are only the quick and the dead. Before I'm through with you boys, you will take only seventeen seconds to man your stations, or I'll be tying all of you over the cannon barrels for whippings until you do. That is all. Carry on."

"I think we just got eggs thrown in our faces." Eddie clenched his jaw.

Walter rubbed the back of his neck. "Yeah, this is just the beginning."

Everyone knew Captain Carney liked rivalry. So when the *Denver* had competitions with other ships during the first shakedown, everyone worked for a win, not just for the *Denver* but for Captain Carney.

After one anti-aircraft competition, Walter anticipated an excellent score, assuming the ship's performance was nearly perfect. However, his jubilance faded when Captain Carney, with his glasses slightly crooked over his nose and a grim expression on his face, stomped up the steps to the podium on the hangar deck.

"Boys, what happened out there—we didn't come in first." His shouting was so loud Walter feared the other ships could hear his reprimands. "If we don't come in first next time, everyone will be swabbing the decks, and I will personally drape you with tar and feathers. Mark my words." He marched down the podium steps with a red, angry face.

Practice makes perfect was now the order of the day.

The *Denver* docked and left for the open waters several times during the shakedown cruise. Right before one docking, Captain Carney demanded the gunners tie empty orange crates to throw over the side in certain areas. Walter followed the order, regardless of how ridiculous it sounded.

"What in tarnation is going on now?" Buster groused.

Walter placed his hands on his waist. "Heck if I know, Buster. Just following orders. No questions asked."

With all the crates bobbing, the *Denver* slowly maneuvered toward the pier. Stupefied, Walter and most of the other gunners watched from the main deck railing as Captain Carney used the crates as markers to begin docking into the pier with no help from the tugboats.

"What's Carney trying to prove now?" Walter asked.

"I don't know, but he needs the tugs," Claude frowned. "He better not split our ship."

"Can we even trust Carney?" Alvin grimaced. Here's what the headline would say: 'Crazy Captain Splits Cruiser Before Japs Can Sink Her.'"

Walter shook his head. "He must be taking his frustrations out from that last competition."

Within a couple of hours after the ship docked perfectly, every sailor heard about their captain getting in trouble. The tattletales traveled from one end of the ship to the other, from the bridge to the engine room. The seasoned sailors had heard the Navy saying you can judge a ship's size by seeing how long it takes for rumors to get from the bow to the stern.

"Serves him right. He got in trouble this time, not us," Eddie said.

"I heard the Yardmaster cussed him out good and threatened to strip him of his eagle and stripes if he tried the stupid stunt again." Alvin laughed.

"Well, I heard the Yardmaster had to say that, you know, but right before Carney got back on the ship, he told him that was the best bit of docking he'd seen in his life," Walter said.

"Yeah, maybe we'll have the need to blackmail him someday," Buster added.

"Oh, come on." Walter looked at the others. "He's a good man. This story will be a feather in the *Denver's* cap."

As the shakedown cruise continued for all of December, watches alternated for days and nights, every four hours, and Walter got his share of night responsibilities. He always familiarized himself with the handling of the ship in darkness.

The cruiser saw cloudy, rainy, and sunny days, but all days were cold on the top open deck. More sailors visited sick bay than usual, fighting colds. The boys donned heavy Navy jackets, and warm beanies took the place of sailor caps. Bitter coldness ruled the nights. Nevertheless, Walter chummed around from time to time, never slacking his duties.

One afternoon while the gunners were inspecting gun magazines, Walter threw up his hands and stretched. "You know, our breaks are so short, I don't think they count."

"My arms and legs hurt like crazy," Alvin said, rubbing them. "I think I'd rather stay home and read about sailors and sea battles than be in one."

Walter tried to rub his back. "Don't they know a skinny 125-pound kid like me needs more rest? I can't even feel my muscles."

Jim arched his back. "I hope I'm reincarnated when we dock."

"Well, I guess we will be when we eat, shower, and shave," Walter answered.

Later that night, when he plopped into his bed, he yawned and said, "You're welcome."

Howard, the seaman across the narrow aisle from him, said, "You're welcome? Who ya talkin' to, Troyan?"

"My body. It just told me thank you when I got into my rack."

The semi-monthly pay disbursed by Lieutenant Hodges, along with mail call, raised the crew's spirits. But truth be told, letters meant more to the sailors than paychecks.

When Walter received a letter from home, he noticed the envelope had been opened. And then he saw a place where a small portion of the letter had been cut out.

"Look at my letter. What's up with somebody reading it ahead of me, and this part has been cut out?"

Buster grabbed it out of his hands. "Heck, it's been censored, is my guess."

"Yeah, one of my letters had three places cut out," Alvin added. "I guess this is the Navy way. When our folks get our own letters, they probably see cutouts too."

Eddie took off his cap and twirled it around on one of his fingers. "Yeah, it's wartime. I guess we have reconnaissance even with our letters."

Walter headed to his berth and plopped onto his bed to read and savor the connection to his family, never mind the cutout. He read the two-page letter from his mother over and over. Pop's bakery was going well despite the sugar ration. Arthur would be leaving soon for boot camp at Farragut. Jacky missed him. Mom and Betty Adams enjoyed visiting while crocheting together. The pastor offered special prayers for all the American enlistees every Sunday. Mom and Pop thanked the good Lord that Chester survived his ship's attack, another miracle, according to his mother.

He held the letter for a long time, thinking about his family and what he'd given up. Then, the picture he stored in his brain of his parents standing at the bus stop back home popped up in his memory. He finally placed the letter under his pillow to save for his seabag, relieved his family was doing well, but missing them more than ever.

CHAPTER FOURTEEN

DECEMBER 1942, SANTA ROSA, CALIFORNIA

Taras coughed as the flour dust flew about his face. The oven was already hot enough for the pumpernickel dough he was kneading when a customer walked in the door.

Mr. Graywitz approached the counter. "Hello, Mr. Troyan, my friend. I will take two loaves of the pumpernickel. Oh, wait a minute, how long for the fresh?"

"About an hour by the time it's cooled and packaged. These other loaves just came out about four hours ago. So I would say that's still pretty fresh."

"Okay, I'll take two. Say, what do you hear from those boys of yours?"

Taras stopped kneading momentarily and rubbed his elbow. "Walter's okay on the *Denver*. He's still on the Atlantic side. His ship is going through a shakedown to enter the war. But the *San Francisco* took a huge hit last month. Really bad. The admiral and captain were killed. Got a telegram from Chester saying he's okay but no details. I know his ship has to go through repairs.

"Oh, that's bad. I know you must worry. Will either of the boys be furloughed for Christmas?" Mr. Graywitz pulled out his wallet.

"Not a chance for Walter, and I don't know about Chester. His telegram only said he was okay."

After Mr. Graywitz left the bakery with his loaves of bread tucked under his left arm, a few more people walked in for purchases. When the last customer left, Taras took off his apron, grabbed the broom, and cleaned up. Even with the war rations, he was grateful that he could keep his bakery going and still get most of the supplies he needed.

His daily routine kept his mind busy and less on the war. Finally, at the end of the day, he locked the door and headed for home, his mind adrift.

As he stepped on the local bus, his shoulders sagged underneath the weight of worrying about his sons fighting in a world war.

Elizabeth feared her neighbor, Betty Adams, would break all her fingers as she wrung them out in a nervous fit. The two neighbors sat against soft cushions on the older couch in Elizabeth's living room. A splash of afternoon sun made its way onto the faded floral rug.

"We haven't heard from Dick for several weeks, and my nerves are just gone, Elizabeth. They're just gone. Why is the postal system so slow? Don't they know all the mothers are sick with worry?" Betty brushed an errant lock of hair from her face and continued twisting her hands.

"Well, I tell you, Betty, I don't even remember what life was like before the Pearl Harbor bombing. I listen to the radio constantly, I read the newspaper, and I pray. What else can we do?" Elizabeth reached for her crochet hook and unfinished Afghan. "I didn't even want to sign for Walter to enlist. But I didn't want to crush his spirit of patriotism or diminish his passion for America. Most of my nights are sleepless now as I think about my boys out on the water. I'm for sure wondering about what's going on with the *San Francisco*. The newspaper report said the attack was horrific. Did you know even the captain and admiral were killed? We heard Chester was okay, but ..."

She sniffled and set her yarn and hook down and reached for her white handkerchief. "We heard on the radio that the *Juneau* took a torpedo hit and blew up right in front of Chester's ship. How many mothers will dread to hear the bicycle bell of the telegram messenger?"

She picked up her yarn and hook again and busied her fingers with her chain stitch. "In fact, Betty, I'm dreading Christmas. Chester and Walter will both be gone. Arthur is only home for a few days before he reports for duty on the East Coast."

"I'm dreading it too," Betty replied with a catch in her throat. "Laverne worries about Dick all the time. She's always asking about Walter and Chester too. I don't even like her listening to the radio, but I can't keep her from it."

Her voice softened, and Elizabeth noticed the weakened tone in her neighbor's voice. "And when we go to church, we hear more about who's been killed, missing, or injured than the sermon."

Elizabeth stood and walked over to the walnut bookcase. She picked up a small oval framed picture.

"Look, Betty. Here are my boys in Navy outfits in 1928. We lived in Hamtramck, Michigan at the time."

Betty fingered the frame. "Oh, Elizabeth, how nice. Did you have any idea your boys would all be in the Navy?"

"Well, no. Not really. And I for sure never imagined they would all be in the Navy fighting in a world war."

Putting the picture back in its place, Elizabeth sat down and decided to change the subject as she unwound more yarn. "How are you managing with your food stamps?"

"I'm getting used to it. So far, we haven't run out of our supplies before the month is over. But half the time I can't even find what I want to buy at the store. I suppose you see all the empty shelves too. Well, at least we know the Navy is feeding our boys well."

Betty stood, moving her hands down the pleats in her shirtwaist dress. "Elizabeth, it's your turn to come over to my house next visit."

When Betty left, Elizabeth continued crocheting, repeating the black, turquoise, and red zig-zag pattern. In between her single yarn stitches, she glanced at another framed picture of her boys on the bookcase. A photograph taken before the war. Chester so tall and handsome in his Navy attire in the middle, Arthur and Walter smiling in their western shirts with cowboy hats on either side of him. She momentarily stopped crocheting and prayed. *God, thank you for my boys. Now, please don't take them away from me.*

The next day, the telephone rang loud and shrill. Elizabeth grabbed it quickly, as was her custom in these days of war.

"Mom, I'll be home for Christmas! We just arrived at Mare Island for repairs. I'm in San Francisco. Oh, and I guess, well, I guess you know I'm okay."

"What ... what ... Ch-Ch-Chester, is this really you?"

Chester's happy laughter dislodged a huge weight from Elizabeth's heart. She skipped around the kitchen after hanging up the telephone.

DECEMBER 25, 1942, SANTA ROSA

On Friday, Elizabeth sat next to Taras in the living room and read the paper while the radio commentator gave updates on the war. She tried to tune it out, being Christmas and all. Chester and Arthur were not back yet from visiting their neighbors.

Outside, Jacky barked, signaling that her sons had finally returned home. Elizabeth turned on the oven and called Chester into the kitchen.

When he wrapped his long arms around her waist in a big hug, lifting her off the floor, she blew out a breath and laughed.

"Son, you're a cook on the ship. You feed thousands. Let me see what you can do in our little kitchen."

Elizabeth busied herself preparing bigos, her favorite Polish dish, and okroshka, Taras's favorite Ukrainian dish. When she chopped the onion, she grabbed her apron corner to rub her eyes. While she wasn't as good with bread as Taras, their native soups and salads were her specialty.

Chester was rolling out the dough for pierogies when Arthur walked in. Elizabeth smiled when he pinched off a corner of dough and offered his own help. The three cooked up a festive Christmas dinner, even with limited rations. The aroma of onions and salt pork frying together filled the kitchen and traveled to the rest of the house.

After she washed her hands at the sink, Elizabeth looked out the small kitchen window. *Walter, I miss you. I hope you're eating well.*

When Chester arranged some dishes on the small, round table, the radio blared news about a British P48 sinking and the bombing of Rabaul.

"*Aye yi yi yi yi. Nie moge w to uwierzyc,*" Elizabeth cried out in her native Polish tongue, saying she couldn't believe this.

"Alzbeta, Alzbeta, вы приглушить радио," Taras yelled back in Ukrainian to tell her to turn off the radio.

"For crying out loud, Taras," she said, "it's Christmas Day. Why can't this fighting stop?"

Chester dashed into the living room to turn off the radio. But when his fingers touched the round knob, Bing Crosby's intimate baritone voice began singing "White Christmas." He let the song spill into the room, hoping his mother's nerves would soothe.

Elizabeth removed the pans from the stove and called her sons and Taras to the table, ordering Chester to turn off the radio when the song ended.

———— ⁓⁓ ————

DECEMBER 25, 1942. USS DENVER, EAST COAST

The ship stayed anchored at Annapolis Roads. The snow from the day before had stopped, leaving a light mist over the area.

After morning muster, Captain Carney announced, "Merry Christmas to my fine *Denver* crew. Boys, we will do necessities today for daily operations, but no training or calisthenics will take place. However, the kitchen crew will be busy as normal. Be sure to thank them. I've heard a rumor about apple pies."

Following orders, Walter shoveled snow off the main deck. "When we head south, I guess we won't be doing this anymore."

Alvin shoveled into his collected pile of snow and scooped it overboard. "Yeah, when we get into the South Pacific, we'll probably be wishing for some of this white stuff."

The more Walter shoveled, the more vapor circles he saw from his own breath in the cold air. After an hour of shoveling, he rubbed his gloved hands together, thankful the sun was trying to make an appearance.

When he arrived on the mess deck for supper, he didn't really expect to see a Christmas tree, but his eyes glanced upward at the homemade red and green paper ornaments the galley crew had hung from the ceiling conduit. Stomach growling, the aroma and sight of hot cooked food filled his senses.

He pushed his tray along as the cooks loaded his plate with chicken, mashed potatoes, squash, green beans, a biscuit, coleslaw, and finally, the apple pie. Separated from his usual friends, he found a table and sat down next to some sailors he didn't know.

"Hey, I'm Davis. Nelson Davis. What division are you in?" The young sailor reached for the coffee pitcher.

"Walter Troyan. I'm a gunner on one of the forty-millimeter guns." Walter cut his biscuit in half. "What about you?"

"I work in M Division in the boiler room, Fireman 1C and these other fellas do too."

"What's that like? I mean, what all do you do in that area?"

"Well, first, we're usually covered with soot from the boilers. It's about a hundred and twenty degrees down there, and I'm not foolin' ya. We pass the day by dreaming about the showers we'll take. We're always recording data and checking the pressure gauges—and looking out for leaks. One little leak, even the size of a fingernail, can make the whole ship, well, never mind that. You don't wanna know." Nelson sipped a little coffee. "What about the guns? What do you boys do up on the main deck?"

"Well, we're all still in training and practicing. I attended Gunner's Mate School in San Diego for sixteen weeks, so I learned a lot of things there. I feel a lot of pressure with the guns, get it? Like the pressure in the boiler room!" Walter cackled at his pun. "Anyway, we always hear that everyone depends on us to win the war. That's pressure, isn't it?"

The conversation continued. Walter cut into his apple pie with his fork, raising the first bite to his lips, smelling it first before chewing the sweetness.

After Christmas supper, he joined his friends in some card games. First, Gin Rummy and then, Slap Jack.

"I'm up for poker," Buster said. "Who wants to join me? I've got me some *do-re-mi* saved. A onesie and a twosie and a, never mind, I ain't tellin' what I got."

"I'm in," Eddie said.

"Count me in, too," Claude added, watching Buster shuffle the cards.

Even with jokes and laughter, Walter remained distracted by thoughts about his whole family and wrestled with homesickness.

Are they thinking about me too? He looked around, then fingered the corner of his eye when no one was looking.

CHAPTER FIFTEEN

When the calendar turned to the new year, the *Denver* crew didn't think much about it. The remainder of the shakedown cruise continued into January as the ship prepped for entering the South Pacific waters for impending war duties. Walter stayed busy with daily inspections and tactical practices. Long duties, short breaks, coveted sleep.

For the next couple of weeks, more drills took place, and the training increased in intensity. The floatplanes launched and performed their own tests while Walter and the rest of the crew participated in shore bombardment practice and dive-bombing runs. Fire drills, drone practices, and air alerts drilled into every sailor his role and action steps until they could do them in their sleep.

Walter plumped his pillow and positioned his blanket in preparation for sleep one evening. "I heard the man overboard drill is coming next and then the abandon ship drill. Am I crazy or what? I don't think any of us will fall overboard. And I sure don't want to abandon our ship."

"All of this is scary if I really think too hard on it," Claude answered.

Alvin grabbed the chain to hoist himself up to his rack at the top of the three suspended mattresses. "Well, I worry about accidents from all the guns and heavy machinery, and I've heard those heavy mooring lines can snap."

"And what about the exposure to the hazardous stuff?" Walter yawned from exhaustion. "I think our lives are on the line every day, and I'm tellin' ya, we haven't even gone into battle lines."

The General Quarters alarm sounded almost daily, and Captain Carney timed the process repeatedly, always yelling over the 1MC. With much practice and hard work, the sailors actually decreased their first time of seventeen minutes to man their stations to seventeen seconds. They finally got it. They recalled the captain's threat if they didn't.

On January twenty-third, Captain Carney announced the first abandon ship drill would take place shortly.

"Men, we conduct this drill to save your lives. It's rarely used, but we must know what to do in the event we have to use this directive. Listen to your division leads when you practice and put the details to memory. A couple more final drills will follow today before we head south for Panama Canal Zone this evening per our schedule."

Before the drills even started, Walter understood that no wartime scenario would be overlooked. He prepared himself mentally to remember the details.

On the early dawn of January twenty-fourth, the GQ alarm sounded yet again. Walter scrambled from his sleep, wondering if an enemy attack might be suspected on the Atlantic coast or if Captain Carney was timing GQ from an awakened sleep since most gunners currently had day watches.

No enemy. Only early morning practice for the timing of GQ, even before breakfast for the first day watch. All the while, the ship traveled at twenty-three knots heading south to the canal.

Breakfast shifts began. Floatplane #4804 launched at 0837, and floatplane #4861 launched eight minutes later from the starboard catapult.

Per orders, Walter assisted in firing test shots from forty-millimeter mounts, firing at a burst from their destroyer escort. He kept a constant watch at his station, ready for simulated enemy action. He looked off in the distance where the endless waters met the sky, creating a faint horizon.

At 1016, an earsplitting crash sounded in the lull of no guns firing. Walter remained at his station, but a few others ran to the stern area.

"Holy Schmoly." Buster returned to the gun mounts and rubbed both hands, lowering his head when he heard what happened.

"What was it? What was it?" Walter stood erect, yet nervous, squinting in the sunlight next to his gun station.

"One of the floatplanes crashed while attempting to land."

Walter left his station, walked over to the railing, and looked out at the waters, swallowing hard. He spotted the crashed plane and could feel the ship repositioning itself to assist with the rescue. Goose bumps traveled across his arms.

An hour later, Alvin walked over to him.

"It was plane #4804. Observer Haley was successfully rescued, but Pilot Post was not found."

When Jim was given the order to sink the capsized plane, he fired on it with his forty-millimeter gun, sinking it immediately while the other gunners watched.

Walter stared in shock. *Why God? We haven't even arrived at the canal, and we've already lost one of our own.*

Later that day, the fading sun, still a crisp circle in the pink sky, illuminated a quivering path across the water. The sailors stood in rows, caps in crossed hands over their hearts, listening to the chaplain's eulogy to commemorate Lieutenant E. M. Post. Captain Carney finished the service, and taps followed.

After the service, most of the crew dispersed and returned to necessary duties. But Walter remained topside. With slumped shoulders, he ambled to the side railing and looked at the waters. An imagined scene of Lieutenant Post fighting for his life and drowning played in his mind, over and over. It was almost more than he could bear.

With a subdued crew, the *Denver* steamed ahead the next day, leaving the East Coast for good to enter the war. Walter sensed how small his ship was compared to the blue waters of the Atlantic Ocean, which stretched forever ahead of him.

When the eastern coastline had almost disappeared, he leaned against the railing on deck five and stretched out his hand as if to touch it. *How long will I be gone? Will I make it back to the United States alive?* When the distant line of barren oak trees disappeared from his view, he lost sight of the shoreline altogether, and a vast emptiness stretched out as far as he could see. He turned around and climbed the ladder to the upper deck to resume his duties.

A destroyer, the *USS Aulick,* affectionately known in the Navy as a "Tin Can" for its thin hull, escorted the *Denver* to the Panama Canal. The *Denver* slowed to five knots and repositioned herself to make her inaugural entrance. The long line of ships waiting to enter the canal sat idle in the ocean, indicating the significance of this water shortcut.

All sizes and all kinds of non-military ships waited their turn, sometimes for days, to pass through.

Humidity draped over the ship like a damp cloak. When much warmer temperatures greeted the sailors, and some tossed their shirts aside, Captain Carney communicated strict guidelines for potential sun burning.

"Gentlemen, expect to be in these warmer temperatures as long as we're in the South Pacific. Shirts may come off during inactive battle times except for topside. If you're topside, you must wear long sleeves and lather up with sun protection lotion. For everyone, no matter your position, no matter what deck you're on, don't make me invoke the Navy's policy for court marshaling you for sunburns."

Eddie swiped at a pesky mosquito. "Court marshaling for sunburns? Who's he kidding?"

"That's just a Mickey Mouse Rule if you ask me," Jim said.

Walter wiped his sweaty brow and flipped his cap inside out, then repositioned it on his head. "Well, I'm not taking any chances. I don't think our captain would joke about a court-martial."

"Or would he?" Alvin asked.

"Like I said, I'm not taking any chances." Walter grabbed a tube of sun protection from a small crate, noticing several other crates had been set out in various places for convenience.

The *Denver* and the *Aulick* navigated to the front of the canal line, passing hundreds of non-military ships, per orders from Navy headquarters. One of the quartermasters reset the clocks in the Control Tower to accommodate the change of time zone.

As the ship neared the entrance, Walter and other sailors scrambled to vantage points on the upper decks to nab their spot for the best view to enjoy the canal journey.

With Jim following right behind him, Walter said, "Come on. Let's head to portside. We gotta see the scenery."

He and Jim gazed at the new landscape as the ship got closer to the entrance, taking in the green foliage and flitting birds, surprised this part of the world displayed summer-like features in January.

Jim glanced back and forth. "I wish we could just stay here."

"Why?"

"This canal is the most guarded place on the planet. We'd always be safe here."

"Yeah, you're probably right about that. Hey, we've practically stopped. It looks like we're about to enter the first lock." Walter stretched his neck to see what was ahead. While they watched, a small boat came alongside, and a man was brought onboard. He was greeted by the Exec and was immediately escorted to the bridge. Walter heard scuttlebutt that the man was someone called a pilot, and he would guide them through the canal.

The ship barely moved to enter gate one to begin the ten-hour transit from the Atlantic side to the Pacific side through the canal's twelve lock gates.

With light duties for the duration of the transit, almost all the sailors moved around from deck to deck, stern to bow, bow to stern, to watch the locks open and close to accommodate the difference in levels of the two oceans as water filled the chambers. Captain Carney grabbed a chair, binoculars in hand, and found a spot on the bridge to observe the pilot. The ship's photography team began clicking away on their cameras, fascinated with the wonder before their eyes.

A few minutes later, Walter's other buddies found spots next to him and Jim. They marveled together as they watched the ship enter the first chamber, which quickly filled with water, raising their ship to a much higher level as water poured in. When the gate opened to the next chamber, the sailors were quiet, watching the well-engineered gates slowly open, creaking like a haunted house in their efforts.

Walter pointed ahead. "Look how mighty thick those gates are."

Eddie studied the precise movements of the gates from side to side. "Yeah, must be at least two yards."

The ship moved into the chamber to face the second gate while the back gate closed. More water filled the chamber after only a few minutes, and the second gate opened for entrance.

Claude trailed his fingers across the railing. "How did that water move us up? I didn't feel anything. And I take it the Pacific is higher than the Atlantic?"

Alvin edged his way to the side railing for a closer look. "Didn't you see the valves open up with the water—"

"Yep," Buster interrupted, "the Pacific Ocean is higher than the Atlantic. Don't ask me by how much. I just know it is. So, we're being raised as we pass through. If our ship had to go all the way around South America, it would take twenty-two days instead of one day."

"Well, how do you know all this, smartie pants?" Walter asked.

"I didn't play hooky in my history classes. I bet you fellows did." Buster waggled his eyebrows, tugged on his sailor pants, and rested his hands on his hips, taunting all of them.

From the side, Walter looked down, pointed, and whistled. "Wow, look at that. Looks like only about three feet clearance on this side. There's hardly any room for this ship of ours. This is a busy place. There's a ship in front of us, and the *Aulick* is behind us."

Eddie looked down too. "It's a good thing the *Denver's*

minding her manners, staying right in the middle. If the captain can steer us through this canal, he can do anything." Walter laughed and said, "I think that pilot might have helped—a little bit."

After crossing Gatun Lake and a second set of locks on the Pacific side, the Denver completed the ten-hour transit of the canal. Captain Carney announced over the 1MC. "My fellow sailors, you have been awarded the Order of the Ditch in the fraternity of sailors for passing through the Panama Canal. You'll each receive a certificate indicative of this status of travel."

"Well, what about that!" Jim said. "I didn't even know we were in a fraternity."

"I guess we're in one now," Walter laughed.

CHAPTER SIXTEEN

The *Denver* moored at Pier 16 in Balboa near Panama City. The Exec escorted the pilot to the gangplank, shook his hand, and thanked him for his service. Before leaving the pier the next day, the ship refueled and received crates of pork loin, chicken, turkey, bananas, potatoes, butter, and boneless beef. The young sailors quickly pulled together for the unloading and the inventory that followed. They already knew what to do.

Balboa civilians and canal workers waved at the friendly sailors as the ship remained moored.

"Look at those kids playing over there in the distance," Walter said and pointed. "Do they even know we have a war going on?"

Jim waved both hands. "Who knows? Ah, I almost feel human again just seeing them."

After refueling and food deliveries were complete, the *Denver* welcomed Hollywood film director John Ford and his Navy Combat Film Team aboard. Their next assignment from the Naval Photographic Division was battle footage in the South Pacific waters. As word got around, the sailors looked for opportunities to spot him, excited about someone famous on their ship.

The *Denver* steamed ahead for her destined South Pacific engagements, sailing quietly through the night.

Before Walter went to his berth, he looked out at the calm waters, wishing with all his heart that the world could be as calm.

"King Neptune's coming to visit—he's coming!" Eddie shouted on January thirty-first.

"Whadaya talking about Eddie?" Walter asked.

"We just crossed the equator. Don't you remember we were told we're polliwogs? Now we're shellbacks since we crossed the equator. And we'll get another certificate for our shellback status. I saw some of the men getting dressed up. Haven't you heard about King Neptune?"

Walter shook his head. He never knew when Eddie was joking or if he really knew what he was talking about. But within a few minutes, he discovered Eddie was right. The Exec bellowed on the 1MC for all who had never crossed the equator to report to the stern for instructions regarding the equator ritual. With a ship full of new recruits like the *Denver,* the polliwogs vastly outnumbered the shellbacks.

When shifts for dinnertime began, the polliwogs humbly ate beans, bread, and water while the shellbacks chowed down on beef and other rich foods. The minions received orders to march to the ship's fantail. They stripped down to their shorts and readied themselves for their prosecution. The polliwogs scurried about nervously like flies on a hot summer day, anticipating what was to come.

King Neptune, played by a shellback sailor, and his party crew triumphantly waited, court bench and all. A sight to behold, the king's white, shoulder-length wig and scepter commanded humility from the polliwogs. Walter shuddered when he saw the ship's forty-foot-long target sleeve, normally used for practice with anti-aircraft guns, had been stretched out on the topside and filled with grease and oil, laced with coffee grinds, potato peels, and eggshells from the garbage. He popped a hand over his mouth. Dread filled him. In minutes, he would be covered with this garbage to become a shellback.

To start the equator ritual, a shellback sailor grabbed a fire hose and sprayed deliberately at the waiting polliwogs to force them into a ramshackle line. Some of the new recruits tried to back away, causing Walter to nearly fall backward.

When he got closer to the front of the waiting polliwogs, he could see the reigning court consisted of several pirates, one acting as an associate judge. Their snarls and smug expressions reigned over the ritual to hold judgment on each participating sailor, determining whether they passed.

Walter scrambled around to find Eddie. Soon Buster, Alvin, Jim, and Claude joined them. They all watched in horror and amusement as each new contestant sat in a chair with arms crossed, waiting to be prepped with diesel oil, vinegar, and paprika. The attending shellback sailor poured the concoction down their hair, covering their faces and bare chests.

King Neptune's exposed belly had been rubbed with some of the garbage. Some of his pirates stayed at his side, ready to fight for his cause. Upon finishing the course on the greasy sleeve, on hands and knees no less, kissing the king's belly was the final requirement for judgment from the court. If King Neptune laughed after the required kiss, the sailor became a shellback. If the king cried, one had to crawl the garbage-filled sleeve again.

Buster pointed to King Neptune and fidgeted. "By golly, the king looks like George Kasper from supply division. If he thinks I'm gonna kiss his belly, he's got another think coming."

"What's wrong, Buster? Ya got ants in your pants?" Alvin cracked up laughing.

Hundreds of sailors nervously stayed in their places for the oil concoction seat prep, the belly crawl through the muck on the target sleeve to reach King Neptune, and the required kiss on his belly.

"Hey, is that the Exec back there in line?" Walter asked.

Eddie grinned. "Heck, yes, Brantly has to do this too. He's never crossed the equator. Serves him right. No one likes him, especially me."

"Well, I'm gonna watch him," Claude added. "Can't wait to see him kiss King Neptune's greasy belly. Yeah, that'll be a treat for all of us. Better than going to the movies."

When Walter neared the sleeve of garbage and grime behind Eddie, the nasty smell engulfed his nostrils like nothing ever had. He watched Eddie gag at the prep chair before he stepped down. He pinched his own nose and heard, "Next!"

He jumped onto the chair, crossed his arms, and endured the oil spray and hair treatment, spitting and coughing when he got down. On hands and knees, he crawled on top of the smelly sleeve, panting his way to the king. He slid and hoisted himself back up several times, enduring the hooting and hollering of the mocking shellbacks. He believed their shouting to be louder than any of the firing guns.

"Keep going!"

"Are you a turtle or what?"

"Look up at his belly. Look up. You're almost there!"

Shellbacks flung towels at Walter's back, and the yelling spurred him on.

"Come here, little sailor, and kiss my sweet belly!" King Neptune shouted while the pirates clapped and cheered.

The king roared a great laugh as soon as Walter planted a kiss on his belly. The pirates at the court of judgment shouted, "You're a shellback, you're a shellback. Grr ... off with you now. Good fightin' matey."

Walter gripped his face as he stumbled away to join the others, trying to keep the junk out of his mouth and eyes.

"Hey matey, you did it, you did it!" Eddie slapped Walter on the back, ignoring his own garbage-filled frame.

Behind Walter, Buster remained stoic in line, holding on to his no sissies allowed attitude. However, when his turn came to step into the chair before crawling on the target sleeve, he turned to Walter and the others who had already completed the ritual and said, "I can't do this, no kidding, I just can't. I think I'm gonna get sick."

Eddie pushed him up to the prep chair. "Well, you have to, Buster. No choice. You're going like the rest of us. You can't stay a polliwog on this ship. You'll contaminate her. And you can't play hooky either."

Soon, Buster's pale face got a lathering of grease. He got down on hands and knees and began his trek across the sleeve.

Walter and others cheered him on.

"Go, Buster, go. Go, Buster, go!"

When he finally kissed King Neptune's belly and walked back to the group, Eddie chanted, "A sissy kissed his belly, a sissy kissed his belly." Everyone laughed, much to Buster's dismay.

As an onlooker who could now relax, Walter laughed every time King Neptune cried when someone he didn't like kissed his belly. And then, in an overly dramatic fashion, he'd shout, "You gotta go again!"

"Whoa, here we go, lookee, here comes the Exec!" Walter maintained his place in the finished line to watch.

The deafening cheers and roars flooded the stern.

"Was that enough for you, my little friend?" King Neptune asked the Executive Officer when he kissed his belly.

Officer Brantly snarled, "Nope."

"Oh, say now, you just get right back in that line for a second try, matey," King Neptune stamped his scepter and roared a cry.

When Officer Brantly started to discreetly walk away from the equator ceremony, pleased that he could get away with his sarcastic answer, several sailors pushed him back in line for a second grease dive.

When he resisted, Captain Carney shouted, "Sorry, Brantly, don't look at me. You gotta go again. King Neptune cried. There's no distinction of ranks."

"Boy, the Exec will never live that one down," Eddie cackled. "Serves him right!"

As the ceremony winded down, the new shellbacks raced to get showers while the veteran shellbacks disposed of the greasy sleeve and tackled the messy deck.

After the cleanup, and satisfied the polliwogs had paid their due respects, the shellbacks called the ship's band so the music could start the closing party. The peppy music pumped up the sailors, and their raucous singing raised the decibels of the noise. The entrance of "girls" strutting around in stuffed bikini tops, hula skirts, wigs, and makeup created a hullabaloo. They danced around, throwing out kisses while catcalls abounded.

Claude shouted, "This is just a bad tease. I only wish the girls were real. This is just a bad tease."

Walter laughed so hard he thought his sides would split when one of the "girls" asked him for a dance.

Although the sailors knew battles loomed ahead, the friendly and healthy camaraderie resulting from the equator ritual gave each one new courage. With pent-up anxiety expended, more friendships developed, and bonds between officers and crew cemented.

Walter developed a sense of belonging to the *Denver* crew like he never had before.

CHAPTER SEVENTEEN

With the *Aulick* at her side, the *Denver* cruised ahead for the Solomon Islands, changing time zones again.

Gunners labored through daily firing drills and maneuvers, with every sailor participating in more fire, collision, and abandon ship drills. The floatplanes went out regularly on routine flights, and the weekly inspections of the magazines, shell storage, and hangar space sprinklers continued.

Never to be taken lightly, the captain repeated orders and inspections to keep his ship combat ready.

The *Denver* steamed ahead most days at twenty to twenty-five knots, zigzagging according to daily plans Captain Carney received from Admiral William Halsey, better known as "The Bull." The admiral's nickname suited him with his bullish look and his imposing leadership.

The ship remained in Condition III through many rainy days and both temperatures and humidity in the eighties, a very different climate than Walter was accustomed to in Northern California.

When the cruiser rendezvoused with hundreds of other Navy ships in the South Pacific waters, Walter whistled in astonishment at the sight.

"Well, get a load of that!" he hollered. "Huge ships, huge guns, huge everything."

"Yeah, it's a huge war," Eddie said. "Like all-over-the-world huge."

Walter stared at the other ships for a long time. The enormity of the war seized his thoughts. How many combats would his ship endure? How long would the war last? Would he make it home alive?

Heavy rain squalls came frequently and without warning in the tropical seas. But the sailors continued tactical and radar tracking exercises even while the ship smacked against the stormy waters.

On February fifth, the Denver arrived at Noumea, New Caledonia, and joined up with *USS Montpelier, USS Columbia,* and *USS Cleveland,* her sister cruiser ships, along with several destroyers and escort carriers to complete their Division Twelve Fleet. Their primary mission was to disrupt the enemy's runs back and forth to airstrips at Munda and Kolombangara, coined the "Tokyo Express."

"Why are you eating breakfast so fast?" Eddie asked Walter one Sunday morning.

"I don't want to be late for Divine Service. You wanna come too?"

"Sure, I'll head there. I need all the prayers I can get."

Jim spoke up. "I'm coming too."

Making their way into the nondenominational chapel temporarily set up in the hangar, the boys squeezed onto a bench toward the back. Walter stared at the steam pipes and air ducts around him, such a contrast from his church back home. The chaplain, wearing a black robe, stood next to a table set up for communion.

After a hymn, the chaplain's still, even voice had a calming effect on Walter. He remembered there was more to life than this war.

"'Be strong and of a good courage, fear not, nor be afraid of them: for the Lord thy God, he it is that doth go with thee; he will not fail thee, nor forsake thee.'" The chaplain read from his large black leather-bound Bible. "Gentlemen, I am reading from Deuteronomy chapter thirty-one, verse six. I have heard our good captain speaking about tension and a possible battle with the Japanese at Blackett Strait. Our Lord does not like war. We serve a God of peace. I believe our Lord will be well pleased if you seek Him and honor Him, even amidst these trying times. Check yourselves for proper motives for fighting. Do not quarrel among yourselves. If you keep your peace of mind and confidence in God, you will better fulfill your war duties."

Walter soaked in the message as the sermon continued. He looked over at Eddie and Jim, watching the chaplain and the other sailors in his line of vision.

When the shipmates finished singing "It Is Well with My Soul," most jumped up to depart, including Eddie and Jim. But Walter remained seated, bowed his head, and prayed privately.

God, it's me, Walter. You know I'm just a humble sailor. We have our first battle coming up, and I know I will have to fire the guns. I might even kill others. I don't like war, but here I am. Keep us safe. Help me to do what's right with the guns. You already know what I'm thinking. I'm scared to die. Would you watch over Chester and Arthur too? This stuff is hard. And please watch over the Denver. She's my ship. Amen.

A sense of peace and wonder washed through his heart like a refreshing shower.

———————— ⤎⤏ ————————

MARCH 5, 1943

Captain Carney relayed his dispatches from Fleet Command on the TBS system, prepping the entire *Denver* crew for bombardment with Japan. All should be prepared to man battle stations in a few more hours, according to plan. The captain explained the positions of the *Denver's* sister ships and their three destroyers in relationship to their own.

"Two Japanese destroyers, *Murasame* and *Minegumo*, have been conveniently undertaking resupply runs to Vila. We have orders from Admiral Merrill to take them out. Their ships will arrive right on time for our fiery reception."

Walter's sleep shift changed to day hours after lunch along with most of the other gunners, anticipating a nighttime battle.

When he awakened in his berth that evening, he stretched and breathed deeply, trying to alleviate anxiety. "Did anybody get any sleep around here?"

Buster rubbed his eyes and let loose with some words no one should hear. "Tell me, how do you sleep when you know you're going to fire the big guns for your first real battle, but the enemy might take you out first?"

Claude pulled up his pants. "Well, you don't sleep. Plain and simple. My body's messed up with this watch change."

As the fleet approached the Solomon Islands that evening, the *Denver* prepared to enter the Espiritu Island harbor. She passed Santa Catalina Island about the time the gunners reached the main deck, waiting for more information.

Even after twilight, Walter could spot the seven Navy Corsair fighter planes overhead and the reconnaissance planes that Captain Carney had described in their briefing. Then, sighting three destroyers from their fleet, he watched them sortie around. They were assigned to protect the cruisers at all costs with hit-and-runs against the enemy ships.

He took in the visible signs that something would be happening soon and tightened his helmet strap. As the imminent battle loomed ahead, there didn't seem to be much to say. This was it. He knew one thing for sure. War meant death and losses. He hoped it was not his own.

The GQ alarm abruptly sounded. Captain Carney ordered Condition 1 for the ship, and the gunners sprinted to their stations. The *Denver* approached the Kolombangara Harbor, her guns loaded with high-capacity projectiles for shore bombardment.

Walter took his position as first loader on one of the four forty-millimeter guns. He looked out into the wind-blown night waters. His choppy heartbeat competed with the choppy waters in his wide-awake state. The southwest Pacific seas were wide-awake, too, with their swells increasing. *What am I made of? Am I going to die? Will this ship sink?* An image of his mother flicked through his mind.

Standing ready at his station, he could see the moonlight glinting down in front of him. His heartbeat thundered in his ears.

When Captain Carney's sharp command came over the 1MC to commence firing at thirty minutes after midnight upon the two Japanese ships, the Battle of Blackett Strait advanced.

Walter jumped into action. His chest heaved, and his body vibrated as the deck shook beneath his feet. His eardrums throbbed, even with ear protection, and the nighttime heavens flashed into daylight from the ferocious firing from both sides. The roar and slap of the salvos commanded the sea.

When the shells came up from the handlers, Walter placed them onto loading trays, slid the trays into breech blocks while the pointers fired at the enemy, and then ejected the empty casings through the bottoms of the turrets to the deck below. The men repeated the clockwork-like cycle again and again as the gun crews worked in tandem with the shell handlers.

After forty-five minutes of intense firing, the *Denver's* blasts straddled one of the targeted enemy ships, the *Murasame,* and she exploded into a ball of fire with large debris, shattering her beyond recognition.

Walter jumped at the explosion. "We got one!" he shouted, his face flushed with exertion and sweat dripping under his helmet as he watched the *Murasame* capsize. "I bet even the sharks are trembling!"

About this time, *Denver's* radar picked up another enemy ship, the *Minegumo,* a Japanese destroyer. The *Denver* boys were ready, already fired up with their successful sinking of the other enemy ship. She fired her guns from a range of 9,100 yards, and the *Minegumo* stopped dead in the water.

"These guns ain't peashooters. The *Minegumo* is going down too," Eddie shouted back, looking to the left.

The vigorous waves sucked the *Minegumo* under in less than ten minutes.

"May their souls rest in peace." Walter stared at the dark waters, his heart still beating wildly.

"What did you say?" Eddie asked.

"I said, may their souls rest in peace. Most of the sailors on the enemy ships are just like us, Eddie—teenage boys who would've had their whole lives ahead of them."

When Captain Carney ordered the cease-fire, Walter's racing adrenaline gradually slowed. He stepped over to the twenty-millimeter mount to ask Jim a question.

"Jim, have you got ... Jim? Jim?" Walter lost all words when he saw his friend collapsed on the deck in a pool of blood, groaning, his breathing shallow.

"Get help for Thompson. And I mean now!" Walter yelled above the clamor.

As the medics rushed across the deck, he scrambled aside. They quickly examined gunner Jim Thompson, whipping out gauze and bandages as they attended him, blood gushing from his head.

"Oh, God, no, not Jim, not Jim." Walter slumped over from the odor of blood and Jim's look of death. Suddenly, his leg muscles were unable to support him.

Although the entire fleet boasted of the successful bombardment against Japan at the Blackett Strait waterway—mission complete—the tactical victory came at a cost. The entire *Denver* crew mourned the death of James William Thompson, who was pronounced dead at 0125 from their own ship's turret blasts from one of the six-inch guns.

Cleanup crews arrived at the main deck to tackle the residual battle messes as Jim's body was covered and removed. Within a short amount of time, muster calls commenced within all the divisions. Even in the dark hours of the night, the solemn gunners' grim and anxious faces couldn't be mistaken. The death of one of their own created intense sorrows, and the dark sky mimicked the sailors' grief.

"I hate this, I tell you, I hate this." Walter walked with drooped shoulders and could barely maintain his duties after the muster call.

Eddie swung his arm around his friend's shoulder. "We all do, pal. Believe me, we all do."

Walter bent over to rub his shaking knees. "Well, it could have been any of us gunners. How's Jim's family going to feel about this when they're notified? I just sat next to him at Divine Service. I saw him pray. He checked on me after our Thanksgiving supper. He worried about me. I just talked with him a couple of hours ago. And now he's gone?"

Eddie shook his head. Like Walter, he had no words.

The sobering reality of war hit Walter head on. The gravity of the death of one of his friends, and not even from direct enemy fire, battled his emotions like an overpowering internal war.

Before dawn, the *Denver* resumed her position within the task force while the gunners sorted and stowed shell casings for metal salvage later on. Walter watched Alvin kiss several cases as if he was demonstrating gratitude for the ammunition doing its job. Or maybe he was thinking about Jim.

Within an hour, with the sun close to rising, a number of Japanese barges came into sight, traveling from island to island.

Captain Carney issued M-1 Garand rifles to the gunners and commanded, "Boys, take potshots and get rid of these barges. Any time you see one, take shots. I don't even care if you want to throw rocks or potatoes. Just aim well."

Walter held fast to his rifle, recalling his weaponry training at Gunner's Mate School. He looked at Eddie. "It's one thing to fire these big guns at ships. It's another thing to fire a rifle at people—enemy or not—at close range. I don't know that I'm cut out to do this."

"This is a war to the death. We gotta do this. It's us or them. And we have to follow Carney's commands." Eddie positioned his gun and stayed close to the rail on the main deck, looking around.

Claude looked through his rifle's scope. "Get ready, get over here. I see a couple of barges within range."

Buster ran over and positioned his gun with great fierceness. "I'm ready to go hunting with my gun."

Multiple men lifted their guns and fired shots with ferocity.

Walter didn't want to close his eyes, but he did and then fired his own rifle several times toward the water, not paying attention to his aim. As other gunners continued firing, he maintained his firing position but didn't pull the trigger again. He swallowed hard, his throat parched and dry. His head pounded with tension like hailstones on a tin roof.

When no live bodies could be seen on the barges, Walter said to no one, "I don't know if I got anybody or not, but I followed orders." *This is hard. What am I made of? Maybe I shouldn't even be here.*

———————⟨∞⟩———————

With cleanup behind them and the barges out of sight, Walter saw John McLloyd walking around before the first breakfast shift. Mac, as he was called, a Boatswain's Mate with twenty-five years of Navy experience, commanded the deck well but also talked freely with all the seamen. Walter admired him a great deal and decided to speak with him.

"Mac, how do you feel about the bombardment and Jim dying and the rifles firing off at the barges and everything?"

"Well, let me ask you." Mac paused, stroked his chin, and turned to Walter. "How do you feel about it?"

"I was scared. Really scared. It was hard to watch those two ships sink, and I had a hard time pulling my rifle trigger at the barges. I aimed in the general direction, but then I closed my eyes. And Jim dying, well, I'm only seventeen, and I've just witnessed my first bloodshed."

Walter coughed to relieve a lump in his throat. His breaths came fast and jagged. "I've never seen death up close. No one in my family has died, and I've never had any friends die. I don't know what to think. I'm wondering if I should even be in this war."

Mac wiped his forehead. "To be honest, I was scared too. Who wouldn't be? This is hard stuff."

"Really? That surprises me. I thought you'd be rough and tough. You've been in the Navy for a long time."

"When I enlisted, WW1 was over. So, just like you, this was my first real battle."

"Well, I don't have a point of reference. I mean, this was my first battle. I didn't know what kind of terrors to expect. And I for sure don't know what the next battles will bring."

The two talked a few more minutes as the night sky changed to morning. It did Walter's heart good to learn from Mac that struggling with scared feelings and hating killing is normal. He believed the Boatswain Mate spoke wise words.

He's right. War involves my emotions but still requires my guts to perform the duties. The two go hand in hand.

An assigned sailor, lowered on a latticed rope, applied two Japanese flag stencils for the score of battle on the bridge of the ship. Proof of victory of taking out the two Japanese destroyers could now be seen by other ships with the stenciled tallies.

The other ships in the *Denver's* fleet received orders to half-mast their colors at 1600 in honor of James William Thompson. All the ships in the area stopped in the waters to show respect.

The *Denver* crew participated in a brief burial service under cloudy skies that afternoon. Following Navy protocol for burial at sea, six crew members walked the deceased's box to a special platform by the side of the ship. The grief-stricken sailors stood at attention with hands over their hearts when the chaplain read a Scripture and prayed. Captain Carney ran his hand down his ashen face, shifted his weight from one foot to the other, and took over the Committal and Benediction. Three cannon shots were fired, followed by taps.

At 1608, the body of James William Thompson was committed to the deep. A flag covered his box as it sunk quickly in the waters, weighted with two projectiles.

The sun appeared for the first time that day, illuminating the clouds with silver linings. Walter swiped the corner of his eye and swallowed hard. *I can't believe you're gone, Jim. I will never forget you.*

In this moment, he strengthened his will and determined not to lose any more shipmates if it was within his power.

Following the service, Captain Carney addressed his crew.

"Gentlemen, on March fifth, the *Denver* was an unproven ship, even with our shakedown and intensive drilling these last four months. But only by going through action with the enemy at the Blackett Strait on March sixth could we demonstrate credibility. I have no misgivings regarding my crew. You can be trusted to do your jobs. You take initiative when necessary, and you carry out the ship's general plan and the general plan of the Force. I have confidence in you. You are determined, cool, and disciplined seamen. You all deserve recognition. This is what we have lived and trained for up to this point. And I will be putting this in my official report."

Captain Carney stepped down from the podium, shaking hands with as many of the officers and sailors as he could get to.

Walter bowed his head, consumed with grief.

CHAPTER EIGHTEEN

With the Blackett Strait battle behind her, the *Denver* maintained her normal routine with readiness drills alongside the Division Twelve Fleet in the Solomon Islands for the next few weeks. Gunnery drills, torpedo evasion drills, aerial missions, and communications and tracking tests filled the sailor's time. The ship idled at Havannah Harbor or ran exercises and patrols nearby. Although not involved in any active engagements, the crew worked diligently to keep their ship ready for battles, both expected and unexpected.

Walter stared at the waves with intense grief one morning, reflecting upon Jim's death and the havoc of a war that no one wanted. However, his attention was diverted when he thought he spotted the *USS San Francisco* in the distance. Could his imagination be playing tricks on him? He squinted and grabbed some binoculars. His brother's ship!

"Hey Eddie. Get over here." He handed the binoculars to him. "Look over there and tell me the name of that ship."

Eddie held the binoculars steady and focused them. "Looks like the *San Francisco*. Hey, wait a minute. That's your brother's ship, right?"

"Yep, it is. Can you believe that? How can his ship be so close to us, yet we can't see each other?"

"Hey, man, you gotta at least send him a telegraph. See if he can come over here or find out if you can go to his ship. Go talk to one of the officers. Maybe Mac can help you out. If you ask me, you gotta at least try."

Spurred on by Eddie's prodding and with the necessary permissions, Walter sent Chester a telegraph:

> Msg Chester Troyan F Div ... I am on Denver ... If possible come see me tonight ... Walter ... March 30 1943

When he received notification a couple of hours later that Chester got permission and would be arriving at 1800, Walter paced the deck like a leopard with no place to go.

Surrounded by his friends, he ate his supper at 1700 like nobody's business and chattered about Chester's visit between bites he hadn't fully chewed nor swallowed. Hiccups consumed him.

Alvin slapped him on the back and said, "Walter, slow down. Hey, we're all excited to meet your brother."

Claude grabbed his napkin and wiped his mouth. "Well, it's not every day two brothers' ships are this close and arrangements are made for a visit. What time will he get here?"

"He's supposed to get here at 1800," Walter answered.

Eddie piped up, "Well, you know he's not gonna be late. That ain't the Navy way."

An hour later, Walter made his way up to the main open deck and spotted Chester with an escort officer walking toward him. Moisture gathered in the corners of his eyes. *What's this? Tears?*

When he and Chester finally embraced, he cleared his throat a couple times. He pulled away and placed both hands on his brother's shoulders.

"Hey, look at you. You made it! Welcome to the *Denver.* You gotta check out my ship." He swiped a finger across his eye. "Sorry, I think I've got something in my eye."

"That's funny. My eye's got something too, little brother."

Walter gave Chester an abbreviated tour, and the two exchanged small talk as they made their way down to his berth for the two-hour visit.

Eddie, Buster, Claude, Alvin, and other gunner friends gathered around Walter to meet his brother.

"Walter, you never told us your brother was so tall!" Alvin reached out to shake Chester's hand.

"Yep, I bet you can imagine how I bump my head all the time on the ship. My hair dusts the ceiling conduits every day," Chester said.

"Well, hey, we hear you're a hashburner over there on the SF." Eddie patted Chester on the shoulder. "Can you get a transfer to the *Denver*?"

"Yeah, I'm butchering and firing up the food right along with the guns firing away. Heck, sometimes I pretend I'm butchering the enemy. Be sure to thank your hashburners, boys. They're cooking and baking their butts off to get all of you 4,000 calories per day. We get it."

"Get what?" Walter asked.

"Well, the health and morale of everyone else depends on us to a great extent. We wanna get great food into your bellies. We all need that many calories a day to keep up with our duties. Like I said, thank your hashburners."

Walter stared at his older brother in admiration. The group discussed the Japanese, the Nazis, Admiral "Bull" Halsey, and girls, of course, for nearly an hour. When Walter's friends slipped away for their jobs, he was thankful he had Chester to himself for the last hour of the liberty visit. The brothers talked nonstop, understanding they might not see each other again for a long time.

"Have you heard from Arthur? How are Mom and Pop?" Walter asked.

"Yeah, I wrote Art and got a letter from him about a month ago. He talked more about wanting to marry Marcia than his training or anything else."

Walter chuckled. "That sounds like him. What have you heard from Mom and Pop?"

"Pop's bakery is good, but he only uses recipes with less sugar, and he's had to lower prices. Mom's fine. She said they bought some war bonds. What have you heard?"

"Just about the same thing. I got several letters from Mom while we were at the Navy Yard. Now, the letters are fewer and farther between, I guess because of delivery delays on the waters."

"Hey, your birthday is coming up—the big one. I can't believe my baby brother will be eighteen."

Walter grinned. "Yeah, I don't know what they do on ships for birthdays, probably nothing, I guess." He playfully punched Chester's arm. "And don't call me your baby brother. I'm a sailor on a ship too." He checked his posture and sat up straighter.

Chester cleared his throat at Walter's comment. "Do you like your captain?"

"Yeah, Captain Carney's a good man. Strict, but he's got our backs. I hope he doesn't remember the day I yelled at him."

"What?" Chester folded his arms and stared at Walter in disbelief. "How can you yell at your captain? I don't think you're my brother!"

"Well, here's what happened. I was only on the ship a few days." Walter proceeded to tell the story of Captain Carney's mix-up with the ladders. Chester laughed.

"I want to hear firsthand about the *San Fran* getting hit at Guadalcanal," Walter continued. "I was so scared for you. I couldn't sleep, and I could barely eat. Your captain and admiral were killed? And what about when the *Juneau* exploded? I heard there were five brothers on that ship."

Chester placed both elbows on his knees, resting his chin upon his interlocked fingers, and said nothing for a moment. Walter took this signal that his brother would struggle to recount anything. He shifted, got comfortable on the bench they were sitting on, and waited for Chester's story.

"Well, first, I gotta tell you our gunners mistakenly took aim at the light cruiser *USS Atlanta*. We caused damage and casualties. It was dark, the battle was urgent, and I heard there was confusion with an intermingling of friend and foe. Their admiral was killed, and some of his staff, too. So, the morale on our ship was not good. But what do you do? You just keep going."

Chester rotated his neck and rubbed it and then massaged his temples, clearly distressed in the retelling.

"I was in my normal place in the galley at about 1400 when a Jap torpedo bomber plane tried to hit us. The torpedo only passed alongside our ship, but the plane itself crashed into our control aft and killed fifteen of our men. Wounded a bunch more. The control aft was demolished for sure. I gotta tell ya, the impact of that no-good idiotic kamikaze bomber plane crashing into us was felt on every inch of our ship. I thought we were done in. It was sheer havoc."

Chester flicked a fly and continued. "Most of us hashburners sleep the night shift, or at least we try to. But all of us found ourselves in a fierce battle at Guadalcanal. You can't sleep while firing is going on unless you put in earplugs, and you don't give a darn about the war. You know that. Well, anyway, at 0200, three Jap ships hit on us at once; a battleship, a cruiser, and a destroyer. What I found out was the starboard five-inch battery got hit, and then we took another direct hit on the navigation bridge. That's when our captain and admiral and sixty others were killed. It was awful."

Walter stared at Chester. "And what about the *Juneau*? What do you know about the five brothers?"

"When the *Juneau* saw how badly we were hit, they immediately sent their medical team over to our ship to help our wounded. And believe me, there were a bunch of 'em. Those medics had barely stepped on board when the *Juneau* totally exploded and sank like a stone. Those five Sullivan brothers wanted to fight the war together. And look what happened to them. All gone, just like that." He looked Walter in the eye and snapped his fingers. "I heard one of the officers saying the Navy had a policy that brothers could not be assigned to the same ship, but that they didn't enforce it."

"Well, that makes sense. I guess it's a good thing we're separated." Walter bit his upper lip and shook his head. "I saw my first bloodshed just three weeks ago. I'm not the same. I still haven't recovered from my gunner friend, Jim, dying."

"What happened?"

Walter sighed, recalling the nightmarish event. "We were fighting it out at Blackett Strait. The battle didn't even last that long, but the fighting was fierce. We took out two Jap destroyers. When the firing ceased, I turned around to ask Jim something, but he was collapsed on the deck in a pool of blood. I called for help right away, but he didn't make it. The thing of it is, he wasn't killed by a hit from the enemy. He died from turret blasts from one of the big guns."

Chester stared at Walter's slumped frame. Not sure what to say, he patted him on the back.

Walter blew out a breath and continued. "After that, I questioned why I ever dropped out of school to fight in a war. I hate this war. I asked myself, should I even be in the Navy? Why did I put those weights in my pockets anyway?"

"Huh? What do ya mean by that?"

Walter's lips formed a slight curl. "Well, I was afraid I wouldn't pass the weight requirement, so I put weights in my pockets at the Navy Recruiting Office when I had my first exam. I clutched them in my hands when I stepped on the scales."

Chester sniggered. "My little brother did that? I can't believe you came up with that idea."

"Well, I didn't want to take any chances. Look at you. You're tall, and Arthur is muscular. And look at skinny me. I'm still the baby brother, just like you said. You and Arthur always have confidence. I wonder what I'm made of and if should I even be here." Walter's voice trailed off as he stared ahead.

"Well, this war is tough. I hate it too." Chester decided to distract Walter.

"Hey, I brought you something." He reached into his pocket and pulled out a piece of folded paper.

Walter relaxed his shoulders and opened it. He chuckled at the cartoon picture of Chester with knobby elbows, butt sticking out, and exaggerated flared sailor pants, playing the violin.

"Who drew this?"

"My friend, JR Mac. We call him our ship's artist. You can keep this to remember me."

Chester looked at his watch and rubbed the back of his neck. "Well, my liberty time has run out. I guess I gotta go."

The brothers stood and embraced each other, and Walter walked with Chester as far as he could until the escort officer met them. Swallowing a lump in his throat, he watched each step his brother took when he departed the ship. Out of habit, he wanted to shout out to him to take care, but he couldn't get the words out of his mouth.

———————— ❧ ————————

Walter's eighteenth birthday occurred a couple of weeks later, on April fifteenth, with a subdued celebration. A few well wishes and pats on the back came from his friends. In times of war, birthdays faded into oblivion on a fighting ship. No birthday cake, no presents.

That evening he looked over the railing, trying to get his mind off his birthday. The sunset cast its colors over the seascape while the frothy waters splashed against all sides of the ship. He could still see Chester's ship in the distance. *That's the best present of all.*

———————— ❧ ————————

A few days later, Eddie, whistling and hands in his pockets, approached Walter. "I'm heading to the post office. Do you wanna come with me?"

"Sure. I'm due a letter or two." Walter followed Eddie up the ladder to deck five.

"Same here, but I try not to get my hopes up."

When they arrived at the post office, a few other sailors were ahead of them, hopeful for a word from home.

When Walter approached the barred window, the mail clerk asked, "Name?"

"Troyan."

"Okay, let's see." The clerk turned around to locate the correct box. "Yeah, you got one."

Walter thanked him, grabbed his letter, and grinned. "I got a letter from my mother."

Eddie waved two envelopes in the air. "It's our lucky day. I got two. One from Emma and one from my mother, too."

Walter followed Eddie, who was dashing, to get over to the port side of the ship to go back down to his berth. As soon as he walked in, he grabbed one of the suspended chains that held his middle rack and climbed up to open his letter.

Dear Walter,
I'm writing this before your birthday with hopes you'll receive our letter in time. But I know you have to wait for a ship to deliver the mail. When I'm finished, I'll write Chester and Arthur too.
I miss my boys. All three of you are gone. Arthur called after he got to the East Coast. Two boys on ships, one boy on a plane. He's a radioman, flying up and down the coast with surveillance pilots.

Life is not the same since Pearl Harbor. I listen to the radio every day. We purchased a couple of war bonds for what we could afford. Betty comes over to visit, and we talk about our boys—how proud we are, all of you fighting for America. She says LaVerne is always asking about you. Marcia walks over to visit sometimes and talks about nothing but Arthur. I'm wondering if they will marry.

I've been working in the garden, and it's getting off to a good start. We've always had a garden, but Betty says I need to call it a Victory Garden for the war effort. Our plum trees are filled with white blossoms, and I smell them when the wind blows. I hope we have a good harvest for prunes come August. Are you eating well?

I pray for you boys all the time, and I worry. We shouldn't be having this war at all. And I hear horrible things going on in Europe. I'm wondering how my Poland is faring with the Germans taking over. It's been a long time since I've heard from my brother, Wincent. I hope he's not been forced to fight for Hitler's regime. Pop is always worrying about what's going on in Ukraine with your Aunt Olga and Aunt Anna and their families still over there.

Jacky mopes around outside, but he's still a good dog. I know he misses you. Please write when you can. You are fixed in my memory. Keep your faith, and always do what's right.
Love,
Mom

Walter re-read his letter several times. He stared at the gray bulkheads inside his berth and looked around at the posters and pictures on the walls, drumming his fingers on his one-inch mattress. Nothing like his bedroom back home. Even below decks, he could smell the salt water. His rack vibrated gently with the constant movement of the ship. He longed to step foot on dry land again.

He finally jumped down from his rack and walked to the storage room to place the letter inside his seabag. Thoughts of home lingered in his mind and were never far from him.

On Sunday afternoon, June twentieth, the sailors were abuzz in anticipation of a boxing match, often called "smokers," their ship would host in conjunction with the *USS Cleveland*, one of their sister cruiser ships. With a lull in active battles, the sailors thrived, and morale was boosted with fun diversions. Programs circulated titled "The Denver Showboat" with the front cartoon picture in red featuring two sailors boxing it out.

Everyone was excited that Fred Apostoli, former middleweight champion of the world, serving on another sister ship, the *USS Columbia*, would be officiating.

The "Amateur Hour" preceded the matches with entertainment beyond what the sailors could have imagined. The *Denver* band opened with the peppy song "Here Comes the Show Boat," followed by six sailors competing in a jitterbug contest.

When Seaman First Class Cornea jumped onto the platform to perform the "Hula Hula Gal," the shrieks and shrill whistles probably could have alerted the enemy.

Sailors Gould and Ferri nearly brought the ship down with laughter when they performed their duo Fat Lady Act.

"Oh boy, there they are. This will be good." Walter pointed to the six *Denver* sailors lined up, with their boxing gloves on, facing their opponents from the *Cleveland*.

"Well, at least Apostoli should be fair with his refereeing since he's from the *Columbia*," Alvin added.

"Look at crazy Avalos. I didn't think he had a boxing bone in his body," Claude said, watching the sailors casually duking it out in line with one another before the first match.

The boxing matches ignited everyone with more whistles and cheers in the makeshift ring. Captain Carney shouted his own cheers for his *Denver* boys and tossed his hat in the air when they won four of the six matches.

When Fred Apostoli rang the bell to conclude the last match and the last two boxers held their fighting gloves up together, the drummer in the band hit his symbols and got the music going again. Silly dancing and laughter filled the area, and pop and candy bars were served.

That night before sleeping, Walter stuck his fists out at Howard in the bunk across from him. "Oomph, pah, foup, gotcha Howard!" And soon, the two were going at it, with Walter claiming victory before he climbed up to his rack to settle down.

CHAPTER NINETEEN

JUNE 1943 SOLOMON ISLANDS

"Men, I have received orders from Admiral Merrill for a shore bombardment of Japanese positions in the Shortland area, south of Bougainville Island, on twenty-nine June midnight." Captain Carney's voice traveled through the ship over the communication system.

"We'll join up with our sister cruisers *Montpelier*, *Cleveland*, and *Columbia* in column—in that order—with our ship positioned last in the lineup. Our destroyers will conduct mine-laying at the enemy's base at Buin, placing them strategically in the waters, sequestering the Japanese ships, and preventing them from getting out at all. We're heading to Visu Visu Point, New Georgia, as I speak."

Captain Carney cleared his throat and continued with the announcement.

"Because this is a planned bombardment, we'll have drills during dawn and dusk alerts starting this evening. On June twenty-eighth and twenty-ninth, all divisions involved in this planned bombardment will sleep during day hours. When practicable, operating personnel will be relieved from time to time. For the next two days, gunners are allowed to stand easy at battle stations unless new orders are given."

Prior to the first drill, Walter and the gun crew listened to the specific firing instructions from their division officer, Commander Peter Wells. They studied the targets on transparent tracing cloth placed over a grid. The surprise shore bombardment would be aimed at taking out the Japanese military installments on Ballale Island.

Walter's confidence, his patriotism for his country, and his personal desire to be the best sailor on the sea played war with the eddy of fear that swirled around him. The thought of Jim's death never left him. Instead, his heart pumped harder, and a flush of fear crawled up his throat at the thought of going into the next battle.

He looked out over the gray waters and sky, hinting of a storm, and his imagination anticipated all kinds of battle events. The change in weather heightened Walter's sense of vulnerability and fear for what might come next.

After lunch, he walked to his rack for his afternoon sleep shift in preparation for the first dusk alert rehearsal. The stifling heat hung over him like a hot dust vapor. But he finally drifted off, sweating in his clothes.

On the evening of June twenty-ninth, hours away from the surprise shore bombardment against Japan, Walter ate his supper at 1730. The ventilation systems opened and operated to full capacity to alleviate the muggy heat but didn't accomplish much in lessening his wet shirt from perspiration sticking to him and beaded sweat dripping from his forehead.

At midnight, right before the gunners assumed their assigned positions at their stations, Walter adjusted his earplugs and tightened his helmet. He squinted at the dark waters, nearly invisible with the hovering fog that welled up from the sea, creating an opaque view.

In position with other gunners on one of the forty-millimeter weapons, he said, "I can't see a thing. Radar, we're counting on you!"

"Yeah, the radar's our eyes for sure." Eddie ducked his head and threw up his hands as torrents of rain streamed through the darkness like a deluge from heaven with no warning. "Well, here it comes. I knew it."

The gunners scrambled to grab their jackets. The rainstorm was so thick Walter couldn't see his hand in front of his face. He swiped the rain from his neck and jacket as it continued to fall stubbornly and insensibly without a care for the sailors. He waited for the order to fire while enduring a pelting madness.

"Well, this is fun." Walter clutched his rain jacket even tighter.

"Somebody, hand me an axe. I'm gonna make a trench right here on the deck." Buster swung his arm upward in a hitting motion.

Within minutes of the pouring rain, the *USS Montpelier* fired the first shot, and Captain Carney gave the order at 0155 for the *Denver* to fire away. The gunners weathered the worst of nature and the enemy at the same time.

Caught off guard by the surprise attack, the Japanese shore batteries fired lightly and fell short of their targets while the rapid fire from the Navy fleet replied fiercely.

"Looks like somebody's mad at us," Eddie yelled.

"Surprise makes a good ally," Walter yelled back.

The gunners, never ready to quit, fired away, seventeen-to-twenty rounds per minute coming from each gun mount.

Walter gritted his teeth in his position as first loader, keeping the ammunition coming from the magazines like clockwork.

"Keep it coming; keep it coming," Claude shouted, rapid firing his words.

"We are, we are. The shell handlers below us are almost ahead of us." Walter's hands jerked with each shell he moved as if they were on fire. Sweat dripped down from his helmet, mixing with the rain.

The *Denver* danced with the storm, decreasing speed and changing courses multiple times due to extremely poor visibility, relying totally on radar to maintain her station.

The rain abated for ten minutes, allowing the steerage crew and topside sailors to observe the *wake* of the *Columbia* ahead of them. Despite the rain squall, the ships moved in precise formation, always working together. The remorseless rain paid another visit when Captain Carney gave the order to cease firing.

Before the beleaguered gunners could dry out, the GQ alarm sounded again, this time for an enemy air raid.

They manned their stations immediately, prepared for sky action, hands ready at the guns with radar control.

In a dark place of his mind, Walter's chest tightened like a leather strap wrapped around him when he imagined a bomb dropping from above. *What am I made of? Can I keep doing this?* Images of Jim in a pool of blood played havoc with his emotions. He prayed. *Oh, Lord, keep the Denver safe. Keep all of us safe.*

At the command, the gunners fired at the enemy planes, totally relying on radar triggers, creating billows of smoke that neatly blended with the fog.

Captain Carney secured the ship from GQ and changed its course, which allowed a breather for the frazzled gunners.

But thirty minutes later, the GQ alarm blared for yet another air raid. Walter seized the shells from the loaders as Claude and other pointers fired the 40-millimeter guns at the Japanese. Vibrations from the rapid firing of all the guns traveled throughout the entire ship.

When the cease-fire order came, Walter's adrenaline finally slowed. He breathed deeply, relieved that no casualties had occurred on his ship. And so far, no news about other casualties within the fleet. The runway and dispersal and supply areas of the enemy had been wiped out.

Through the 1MC, Captain Carney addressed his crew.

"All hands were enthusiastic but cool and collected and went through the operation after the customary manner of any other well-rehearsed exercise. To date, this raid represents the greatest penetration by surface craft into enemy territory. It's impossible to single out individuals for praise in such an operation as this, which adhered to a planned schedule and offered no opportunities for heroism since the enemy was too surprised to offer much opposition. So, I say to all of you, well done, men, well done."

Commander Wells dismissed the gunners in the middle of the night after their division muster call.

Changing into dry clothes in his berth, hunger pangs stirred Walter's insides like a small animal.

"I don't care if it's only beans and water. I'll take anything. I'll even eat Spam 'cause I'm as hungry as a bear." Walter headed to the galley, one deck above his berth, with the rest of the gun crew close behind.

The aroma of meat pervaded the mess hall as soon as Walter arrived, and he soaked in the savory smell as he quickly grabbed his tray. The cooks loaded his plate as they always did after a battle—no matter the time, regular meal shift or not—as the galley remained open twenty-four hours a day. The gunners ate the ham and biscuits and green beans like ravenous gulls over a fishing boat.

"I thought that zigzagging would never stop. I wasn't sure if we were going up or down or sideways." Eddie shoved one bite of ham after another into his mouth.

"Yeah, kind of like how you're eating." Alvin swiped his chin with the back of his hand and slurped his milk.

"I've seen rainstorms back home, but nothing compares to these awful rain squalls. They're blinding." Walter reached for the coffee pot. "I don't feel dry, even though I changed my clothes."

Relieved of day watch, Walter fell into his bed, accepting the sleep invitation, and snored like a snare drum for several hours.

———————⚬⚬⚬———————

Shortly after midnight, on July first, Captain Carney darkened the ship as the sister ships filed in formation for more anticipated night engagements with Japan at Visu Visu Point. The *Montpelier, Cleveland, Columbia,* and the *Denver* joined up with the same destroyers who had previously laid the mines but were now providing an anti-submarine screen.

A quarter moon shone a luminescent path across the sea, but the waters still frowned after yesterday's rain squalls.

Walter manned his station and prepared for more action with the Japanese at the shore and bombers in the sky.

The next eight hours proved tense, with all four cruisers meeting up with the tanker for refueling right along with the destroyers. Their speeds decreased considerably during the refueling procedures, creating a vulnerable situation with the enemy. Battle or no battle, the ships needed fuel.

The *Denver* launched floatplane number seven to scout for enemy submarines in the very choppy waters.

Zigzagging and changing course repetitively to allow for refueling of all the cruisers and destroyers, the *Denver* subsequently launched floatplane number eight for more surveillance.

With no more apparent threats from enemy fire, Captain Carney secured his ship from GQ and announced Condition III shortly before dawn.

The morning sky appeared with scarves of color, releasing soft gray and white clouds.

An unexplained explosion startled Walter, and he searched the waters within his sight. "Holy cow, what was that?"

"Look over there." Eddie peered through binoculars before handing them to Walter.

"That's one of our floatplanes." Walter spotted the capsized plane, unsure of the status of both men inside, the pilot and his partner observer.

As it turned out, when floatplane number seven approached for landing on the water, the depth charge became disengaged and detonated, damaging the plane beyond functioning ability. After rescuing the two men bobbing at sea, *Denver* gunfire sank the plane completely.

Walter watched floatplane number eight approaching the *Denver*. Aware the floatplane's surveillance missions were crucial for their safety, he watched the successful landing and heard the ship's crane hoist the floatplane back onto the ship.

Muster call on July twenty-fourth included a ceremony of transfer of command when Captain R. P. Brisco replaced Captain Carney, who had received a promotion to Chief of Staff for Admiral Halsey.

Captain Brisco's thick eyebrows, sea-weathered face, and straight lips that barely smiled projected a straightforward captain, but his demeanor softened with his southern Mississippi accent when he addressed the *Denver* crew for the first time.

"Oh, please don't tell me we'll start having inspections on Saturday with this new fella," Eddie complained to Walter, Buster, Claude, and Alvin.

"We can't. We're the Dirty Dee," Walter said. "No one's gonna strip our ship of that title if I have any say-so in the matter. We'll just have to sing our Dirty Dee songs for this new captain of ours. He'll love it."

"Well, I'll miss Carney," Claude added. "Remember when he had us throw out those orange crates for docking this thing? Ya know, he was pretty good. Demanding, yeah, but I got used to that. I wish I could shake his hand."

Walter chuckled. "Not me. I've been avoiding eye contact with him since I first set foot on this ship."

"Why?" Alvin asked.

"I yelled at him. I called him a goofus. That's why."

"You what?"

The other four exchanged dubious glances and stared at Walter.

On the hot seat, he explained the incident he'd already shared with Chester about the time when he was going upward on the starboard side and Captain Carney was coming down, in error, at the same time.

"Well, I think we just might work out a plan for you to personally say your goodbye to our captain." Buster raised his eyebrows and tapped a finger to his chin. "You know, there's more of us, and there's just one of you. Whaddya say, boys?"

Walter stood and made for a dash. But not soon enough. In spontaneous fashion, Buster, Alvin, Claude, and Eddie grabbed him by the arms and legs and began to swing him, chanting, "Let's go see the captain, let's go see the captain."

On July twenty-eighth, one of the *Denver's* radiomen, Paul Vrolijk, broadcast President Roosevelt's Fireside Chat for the whole crew to hear.

While performing light duties, Walter listened, as did other gunners. He paid close attention to the president's references to Pacific warfare.

> For several months we have been losing fewer ships by sinkings, and we have been destroying more and more U-boats. We hope this will continue. But we cannot be sure. We must not lower our guard for one single instant.
>
> In the Pacific, we are pushing the Japs around from the Aleutians to New Guinea. There too, we have taken the initiative—and we are not going to let go of it.
>
> Our naval, land, and air strength in the Pacific is constantly growing. If the Japanese are basing their future plans for the Pacific on a long period in which they will be permitted to consolidate and exploit their conquered resources, they had better start revising their plans now. I give that to them merely as a helpful suggestion.

At this, Walter grinned. He heard some of the other gunners shout some cheers. He watched Buster beat his chest like Tarzan and continued listening to the speech for the next few minutes. President Roosevelt ended his Fireside Chat with uplifting words for all Americans.

> We shall not settle for less than total victory. That is the determination of every American on the fighting fronts. That must be, and will be, the determination of every American here at home.

It was time for Walter's supper shift. He stopped his work in gun maintenance and headed for the ladder to get to the mess hall. He thought more about the president's chat and the weariness of the war. Would a victory for the Americans come soon?

The end of the summer transitioned into autumn with hardly a notice. The *Denver* and her division ran "the slot" nightly, as the channels surrounding the Solomon Islands were referred to. The Pacific Fleet commandeered the Solomon Islands for weeks on end for the bitter struggle to drive the Japanese away. The ships were ready to defend and protect the islands as well as dispose of enemy threats.

For the next several months, the *Denver* zigzagged according to delivered plans and changed courses constantly. Her crew remained at battle stations on the lookout for the enemy, almost always staying in Condition III.

The Navy destroyers, also known as "Small Boys," guzzled their fuel as they maintained their anti-submarine screen for protection around the *Denver* and her sister ships for many days.

Winter was almost upon them in the Solomon Islands, situated south of the equator, but the warm temperatures seemed to be fibbing.

The *Denver* steamed ahead day and night with store ships, escorts, aircraft carriers, auxiliary and ammo ships, along with the destroyers and attack cargo vessels. The aircraft carriers, known as "The Queens," got prime positions in the waters. The *USS Relief*, a hospital ship, remained stationary in the waters to serve the American Navy in this part of the world.

Walter resolved to never let his guard down during the summer and autumn of 1943. The *Denver*, his home, remained the same, but he did not. He prayed more. He trusted his officers and captain and worked hard to please them, never expecting praises. His faith and the magnificent fleet encircled his spirit with a new maturity with each passing day.

CHAPTER TWENTY

OCTOBER 1943

Before the next battle engagement, radioman Paul played the fifth game of the World Series over the 1MC. In the days prior, he had announced the wins. The New York Yankees were ahead of the St. Louis Cardinals, three to one. On October eleventh, game five, the sailors went about their duties while listening to the game, played at Sportsman's Park in St. Louis.

Although both teams were depleted of some of their best players who had enlisted in the war, this did not affect the enthusiasm of the American sports fans nor the sailors on the *Denver*. When the question arose if the national pastime should be suspended during the war, President Roosevelt defended the sport. Of course, he declared, baseball should continue. He called baseball a wartime morale booster.

Cheers erupted for both teams on the ship. In the end, Bill Dickey scored two runs for the Yankees, and Spud Chandler, the Yankee's pitcher, shut out the Cardinals with a two to zero win. The liveliness of the last game produced banter and friendly competition among the sailors, a coveted distraction and connection to home.

"Well, the Yankees won, even if Joe DiMaggio couldn't play center field," Walter said. "I heard he joined the army air force. Where is he anyway?"

"I think I heard he's stationed at Santa Ana," Eddie answered.

"I bet the Cardinals could have pulled this off if they'd had Johnny Beazley as their pitcher," Alvin added. "He shut games down with his strikeouts. But the war called him, too."

By the end of October, the outcome of the Pacific War hung in the balance. The Bougainville Island Campaign opened, and the ships were put on high alert. Captain Brisco received orders to bombard Japanese military installations at Buka Airfield, the largest Japanese outfit in the Pacific.

On the night of October thirty-first, the *Denver* and her running mates, the *Montpelier, Cleveland,* and *Columbia*—each 1,500 yards apart and escorted by eight destroyers—prepared for battle as they steamed ahead toward Buka. The code breakers at the US Office of Naval Intelligence based in Pearl Harbor had determined that the Japanese task force intended to intercept and destroy the Navy's ships and bombard the Marines who were already ashore.

Admiral Merrill's orders were clear. He communicated to all the captains. "Prevent any such occurrence," he stated.

The firing began at 0022. The *Denver* let loose her six-inch batteries toward the shore, securing direct hits on the Buka Airfield landing strip and burning Japanese planes on the western end. Relentless shelling from the *Denver* softened up the shore for the Marines to take over.

That night Walter methodically pounded the enemy with his firing, as did the others. But when he watched the Japanese fire their own guns skyward, he yelled, "What in the world are they doing?"

Commander Wells announced, "Keep firing, boys. They're confused by our surprise attack. The Japs think they are under air attack. Keep it going."

The shockwaves from his firing gun rattled through Walter's entire body. He watched the fire from the explosions leaping toward the sky like dancers. Graceful, yet deadly. When he fired his gun, he could see his star shells dazzling like fireworks.

Seven minutes later, the *Denver* sailors received a new order to cease fire at Buka. Two enemy vessels had snuck up on their port side, only three-thousand yards away, and the *Denver's* orders were redirected. Star shells and flares from Walter's ship lit up the sky with a constant glow. Dark brown clouds of gun smoke billowed up everywhere, merging into the low-lying rain clouds. Great geysers of water shooting up from enemy fire nearly engulfed the *Denver*.

The cease-fire order came only thirteen minutes after the penetrating engagement began.

"By golly, look at those explosions! Have you ever seen anything like this?" Alvin shouted as the gunners watched the distant fires grow. "We got 'em good!"

Walter pushed his helmet slightly back to wipe his brow. "Well, yeah. You have a short memory, Al, if you don't remember the explosions at Ballale. But I tell ya, there's probably not a fish around for miles. They probably all swam away, cussing about the war."

When the last firings subsided, Walter watched gunner Lawrence Jurovich head to sick bay. Even in the darkness of night, he could see that his hand was wrapped in a bloody cloth.

"What happened?" Claude asked.

"I don't know." Walter rubbed his nose with his fingers. "If he got his hand caught between a heavy shell and the breech mechanism, then it's crushed for sure. I'm gonna check up on him as soon as I have a break. I'll let you know."

Executive Officer Brantly's debriefing for the sailors came over the 1MC.

"Good job, men. That was a baptism of fire. There won't be any Japanese planes flying out of Buka anymore. Clear the decks of interferences and missile hazards. Prepare for early breakfast. We're heading for another shore bombardment and possible air attacks at Shortland Area at Bouganville. The Japanese intend to intercept and destroy our transports and supply ships unloading there, and I'll betcha they plan to bombard the Marines ashore."

The officer's angst could be detected in his rough voice.

Walter heaved his lean frame in the middle of the night as he began moving empty cartridge cases from the vicinity of the turrets and mounts to the hangar. The night's darkness was that of a coal hole—no moon in sight with the dense clouds.

When Captain Brisco set the *Denver* for Condition II, he ate his breakfast ration at his gun station at 0420.

Fast approaching northern Bougainville, the *Denver* crew could see the shore batteries open fire. At 0623, the gunners received word through the sound-powered phones to "go ahead with scheduled bombardment missions" and began their own firing in the morning darkness.

Several enemy single salvo shots began falling in the *Denver's* wake, about two hundred yards short of hitting the stern, forcing her to change course. The ship began maneuvering to maintain the usual order with her sister ships. The spectacular Battle of Empress Augusta Bay took off in full force.

With American ships strategically blocking the entrance to Augusta Bay, the Japanese approached from the northwest, aiming to fire on the ships along the shore.

Admiral Merrill subsequently ordered his entire task force into three columns, sending the destroyers to attack the Japanese and ordering the cruisers to turn about and remain out of torpedo range. The Japanese fleet separated in their confusion of the admiral's three groups.

In a heavy rain squall, the American ships twisted and turned, constantly maneuvering in their own scene of utter confusion. Yet they never lost sight of their respective targets.

Smoke billows spread themselves out like infernal clouds, and the firing guns burst like thunderbolts from both sides. Walter recalled Officer Beebe's words from gunnery school: *You'll fire, or you will be fired upon. You'll kill, or you will be killed.*

Because the incessant illumination from the firing guns appeared to be helping the Japanese's accuracy of their own gunfire, Admiral Merrill ordered all the ships to make chemical and funnel smoke by counter-illumination of star shells just short of the enemy line. As a result, great, thick black rolls of smoke slid out of the funnels, adding to the eeriness of the picture.

While the battle continued throughout Monday, November first, the gun crews welcomed alternating sleep shifts. Although the four-hour reprieve was needed when his time came, sleep evaded Walter's weary mind and body as the nerves of his body frayed.

"Hey, Buster, I feel messed up. My ears are pounding." Walter rubbed his eyes. "I'm still hearing the guns. In fact, I think my body is still vibrating. Is it Tuesday yet? I've lost track. I can't sleep if I think this ship might blow up."

"No kidding. It's not Tuesday yet. Probably will be when we go back on the guns. Having fun, aren't we?" Buster pounded his pillow.

"Sure, we are." Walter couldn't get comfortable on his thin mattress as he thought about Eddie, Alvin, Claude, and the others still at the guns. Out of nervousness, he poked a couple of fingers into one of the hanging chains that held the three-tiered racks together. He wondered what was going on with Lawrence's hand injury. He remembered Eddie's promise to his wife to return safely from the war. Despite his twists and turns, sleep finally overtook him.

⁂

Hardly feeling rested at all, Walter returned to his gun station for night duty, his forty-millimeter gun primed and ready in the early hours of Tuesday, November second. By 0245, the Navy destroyers launched a number of torpedoes. The *Denver* commenced firing all her guns on enemy ships and planes with all batteries in a ferocious attack.

The ship made a sudden change of course to the left with a full rudder to avoid hitting another ship. Nearly falling, Walter staggered and grabbed the bottom railing of the turret mount. His stomach roiled with every turn as the cruiser continued with extreme maneuvering throughout the battle.

With no submarine screen available, the fleet's destroyers worked over two Japanese groups of ships. Finally, the backbone of the enemy battle line broke. The Japanese ships that were able to do so fled. A destroyer salvo fired after the last crippled enemy ship.

Venus, now a morning star, illuminated bright and clear in the early dawn as the clouds gradually disappeared. Walter and the *Denver* gun crew staggered below for coffee.

The muffled morning sunlight peeked through the remaining clouds before making its grand entrance. At 0607, the *Denver* passed through a heavy, wide oil slick of undeterminable length, adding to the already stale air.

The coffee break respite didn't last for long. Doing their best to ignore the odor when they returned topside, the gunners worked as a team, efficient and alert, watching for all potential danger. At 0745, the harsh blare of GQ sounded again.

A large group of enemy planes consisting of *Vals*, *Bettys*, and *Zeros* descended upon the American ships at about ten-thousand feet, bombarding as they swooped past. The whole Navy fleet communicated with one another for coordinated firing through the sound-powered telephone system.

The destroyers let loose with more torpedoes.

When the *Denver's* Gunner Division officer received orders from the CIC (Combat Information Center), the gun crew activated rapid and calculated salvo firing along with the other cruisers.

Walter watched a downed enemy plane fall off the port bow of his ship, the dead pilot in his parachute. He shuddered. *Oh, Lord, help us all.* Instinctively, he closed his eyes and hit his helmet with both hands, trying to rid his mind of the horrible image so close in his range of sight.

At 1804, nearly seventy enemy planes began attacking the whole Division Twelve Fleet. Walter's ear protection did little to diminish the deafening noise.

The billows of smoke grew larger every minute. He couldn't determine which was brighter—the morning sun or the firing blasts. *Is this what the attack on Pearl Harbor looked like?*

He worked hard to determine the difference between the glare of the sun on the water and the target hits. With each successive wave, the bow of his ship appeared to be dipping underwater. Amidst the firing, the *Denver* endured the fiercest saltwater shower she'd ever had.

"Something's not right with my gun. I need help!" Walter's heart rammed against his ribcage as a blast of saltwater spray hit him head on.

"Back away," Lieutenant Commander John Wiley ordered.

Upon quick examination, the gunnery supervisor determined Walter's right gun of mount three had been damaged by a forty-millimeter shell fired from one of their own guns during the strafing attack.

The commander called for damage control to effect repairs, and he and two others began immediate action for the minor repairs and adjustments. Walter got right back on his gun within minutes.

Unfortunately, the *Denver* became an easy target for the enemy as she was now illuminated by flying eight-inch star shells. Usually behind her sister cruiser ships in the lineup, she was now the leading cruiser due to all of the formation's evasive course changes. Japan's cruisers concentrated on the *Denver* with shots straddling her repeatedly.

Without warning, the *Denver* lurched severely three times. Every rattle and vibration from the striking enemy shells made Walter wince and worry about his fate. The wild waters sloshed across the main deck.

"We've been hit. I can feel it!" Walter yelled at the top of his lungs. Terror rolled over him in waves. "Oh, please God, not us, not us." Blood rushed through his ears and pounded in his head. Torrid breaths filled his lungs. The magnitude of the horror of the war came sharply into focus, no longer an incomprehensible blur.

"Oh, Lord, save our ship!" Buster screamed when another water bath hit the sailors head on.

The fighting crew that they were, Walter and the gunners continued firing at the enemy, although shuddering and wary with fear, their senses strained from their own apparent hits.

"Keep going, boys. We'll assess the damage later," Commander Wells ordered. "Get those Japs, and I mean get 'em now! It's us or them!"

The effect of the enemy's fire subsequently fell off when the Pacific Fleet's fire on them intensified. The Japanese's tactics had been aggressive hits at first, but their consequent efforts were directed toward escape. The enemy was taking severe punishment.

Each ship made strategic moves on the sea-like water chessboard, with the Americans achieving checkmate.

As the Japanese force eventually retreated from the engagement, the *Denver* gunners refused to let their guard down until the radar was clear except for friendly planes.

When lunch shifts came, the sailors digested their food as they digested the news that three compartments in the Dirty Dee had flooded. Water had gushed in from three large holes where the enemy shells had struck on the third deck, resulting in two and a half feet of water.

"Attention, my fellow seamen," Captain Brisco announced shipwide. "We sustained three holes from two shell hits that apparently played tag with each other. The first eight-inch shell entered the second deck, stateroom 205, and took a journey like I've never heard of before to other places as it traveled through our ship. This shell proceeded to pass through the second deck, stateroom 203, then entered third deck stateroom 309, passed through the Warrant Officer's Mess door, and then into the Warrant Officer's Stores. It then passed through the hull in the Small Stores Issuing Room on the first platform level, and there it still quietly lies. Another eight-inch shell entered the starboard side of the Paravane Stowage and passed out the port side about eighteen inches above the waterline."

The captain cleared his throat. "We have three holes necessitating repairs. But it will remain a mystery to me as long as I live as to why the first shell incredibly never detonated. No explanation whatsoever. Someone from above was obviously watching over us. We could have all been goners."

After a brief pause, the captain continued. "No personnel were hurt, gentlemen, and for that, we can be grateful. In fact, that first crazy shell ricocheted and twirled in unbelievable ways, sizzling six inches over one of our men's heads. Just a little lower, and it would have taken his life. When I take off my cap, I expect my hair will be white from thinking about this. Our repairs will be quick, and we will carry on. I commend you. Your conduct and performance were most credible, and your firing was like razors."

And soon thereafter, the Dirty Dee acquired her second nickname—Razorbacks—and word spread to the other ships.

With repairs underway for the three holes, the cruiser proudly traveled at ten knots toward the south, catching up with her sister ships as if to say, "No checkmate for me. I'm still in the game."

Walter finished his lunch, headed back to his station, and waited for the next directive, all the while wondering about the flooding below him and thanking God the *Denver* lost no lives that day.

———— ✦ ————

"Get a load of that!" Walter's jaw dropped, and he stopped dead in his tracks, hands on his hips, at the sight of the shell.

Eddie stood as still as a statue. "That's just downright scary. If I was asked to transport that dead shell, I wouldn't. I just wouldn't. I'd quit the Navy before I'd carry it."

Walter and Eddie watched Commander Wells walk methodically with the shell that hadn't detonated and carry it to the side of the ship to dispose of it.

"Maybe he won spin the bottle," Buster said as he watched the officer walk calmly back to his station. "I mean, holy cow, I bet no volunteers lined up to take it. Who would?"

With deck log entries and reports written, the *Denver* crew could talk of nothing else regarding the Battle of Empress Augusta Bay for several days. The Division Twelve Fleet had been attacked by almost seventy enemy planes. During this action, the *Denver* crew took credit for destroying six enemy aircraft, adding more stenciled victory tallies to her bridge.

No sooner was the ration lunch in the sailors' bellies when a new directive was given for the entire fleet to return to the vicinity of Empress Augusta Bay, Bougainville Island, yet again. The destroyers formed their anti-submarine screen as the ships steamed ahead.

At his first chance, Walter made his way to sick bay to check on Lawrence. In the dim light, he saw him resting on the framed metal bed under a white sheet, eyes closed, his wounded hand wrapped in layers of medical gauze. He smelled antiseptic as the doctor wrung out a cloth in a large steel bowl of water on a small table next to the bed. A wall fan above oscillated in circles to move the air.

"How is he?" Walter asked, biting his upper lip.

Doctor Horak sighed. "I had to amputate his left thumb. As you know, his injury occurred during the line of duty through no fault of his own. He's still groggy from the anesthesia, and I'm monitoring him for signs of infection. He knows his thumb's gone, but I don't think he's fully comprehended how it will affect the rest of his life. Out of necessity, he'll be taken off the guns."

Walter looked at Lawrence for a moment with a thousand-yard stare. He had no words. He shuffled away, shaking his head. He'd let the other gunners know Lawrence would not be returning to the team. *This could have happened to me.* When he walked back to his station, he wiggled his fingers, thankful to have them all.

After the most exhilarating seventy-two hours of her existence, the *Denver* retired to Port Purvis in the Solomons.

But most of the gunners remained at their stations with little sleep while Japanese planes heckled their cruiser by dropping flares.

Walter looked out at the night sky and caught sight of a shooting star. As a youngster, his mother had told him to make a wish when this occurred. He closed his eyes and made the wish that any sailor would make in a time of war.

CHAPTER TWENTY-ONE

NOVEMBER 1943

The *Denver* was still licking her wounds when she was called upon with new orders to cover the third Echelon of the Empress of Augusta Bay occupation. By November tenth, the entire fleet began to monitor unidentified planes in the area.

"Here we go again—what's that awful smell?" Alvin asked.

Walter stifled a sneeze. "Guess we're passing through another heavy oil slick, I reckon."

Claude coughed. "Smells worse than my dirty socks."

While the gunners were eating a ration of ham sandwiches, apples, and coffee at their battle stations, they watched five Americans parachute from a Liberator B24, and four of them were recovered by other ships.

"That thing is huge," Walter said, watching the plane disappear to the west.

"Yeah, we sure don't see those very often," Eddie replied. "I hope the fifth guy made it okay."

"I wonder what parachuting down from the sky feels like," Walter said. "I guess I won't find out being a sailor on a ship. But it kinda looks fun."

Eddie stuffed the last bite of his sandwich into his mouth and garbled, "Yeah, it probably is if it's not in wartime."

The *USS Claxton* reported a torpedo plane might be heading toward the *Montpelier*, one of the *Denver's* sister ships, but the destroyers opened fire on the Japanese planes and headed them off without loss.

The *Denver* crew remained vigilant for the next three days. The enemy loomed close, keeping Walter on his toes. The ship remained at Condition I, and sleep shifts were short—if any were offered at all.

Throughout the watch, the full moon and cumulus clouds illuminated the entire fleet, even when scattered rain squalls drenched the *Denver's* deck from time to time. The Japanese bombers appeared to break off their attacks, even in good positions, as if they didn't have the courage to press onward.

"What in tarnation are the Japs doing? Inviting us to come over?" Walter asked.

"Look at my hands," Eddie fumed. "They're staying glued to these guns. I'm ready to blast again. They're just cowards."

However, on the night of November thirteenth, everything changed. The Japanese opened fire with a ferocity the *Denver* crew had never seen before. The PT boats went crazy trying to protect the big ships, firing into invasion lines determined to harass and track the enemy.

The waters received their own attack as the entire Navy fleet began twisting and turning in choreographed evasive patterns.

Walter watched in horror as the flashes of Japan's big guns with their smoke billowing out seemed to stare him down. Frazzled, he found himself in another fierce battle, not fully recovered from Empress Augusta Bay. The conveyor hoist moved nonstop as he fired his forty-millimeter gun constantly. Walter knew the shell handlers below deck were probably going crazy dealing with the constantly moving empty casings.

Suddenly, the *USS Stanley,* a destroyer screening enemy ships, reported over the TBS, "Razorback, three torpedoes coming at you. Two at thirty degrees port, one at two hundred forty-five degrees starboard."

Captain Brisco yelled to everyone over the 1MC, "Well, we're between the devil and the deep blue sea!"

Panicky thoughts consumed Walter in an instant. He knew, as did all the men on board, that if the two torpedoes hit the *Denver* at the front, all their ammunition would blow up, resulting in countless deaths, certainly his own. He also knew if the ship took a side hit, the engine room would explode and put them dead in the water, but they would have fewer fatalities.

Counting the seconds to the torpedoes' time of impact, he waited for Captain Brisco's orders, ready to act upon command. His heart beat wildly with fear.

The captain's voice boomed over the ship's communication system, "Hard to port! Prepare for impact!"

And just like that, the enemy escort plane came into view out of nowhere. The *Denver* took an aerial torpedo hit at 0455, amidships, starboard side, by the light of a full moon. When the torpedo detonated, a massive geyser exploded hundreds of feet into the air and created a shock as if the ship had been picked up and thrown into the air. The earsplitting explosion blasted oil, molten metal, splintered decking, and even rained down debris on other ships in the area.

Walter doubled over and screamed, "Help! Help!"

"She took it from the side, Walt," Eddie screamed back as he pulled Walter's shoulder to stand him back up.

Walter stood. He opened his eyes in shock, clearly disoriented.

The Nip pilot who landed the hit on the *Denver's* engine room never knew he'd been successful. *Denver* gunners on a four-inch turret struck him immediately, and his plane rolled into a blinding orange ball of fire. The other two torpedoes intended for Walter's ship sailed away.

The hit to the *Denver* brought the cruiser to a sudden halt due to a loss of engine power, steering control, and gyrocompass function. Out on the waters, the PT boats twisted like angry eels, fending off the enemy.

Panic, confusion, and chaos engulfed Walter and the other sailors. The decks and ladders vibrated with the stampede of hundreds of quick footsteps, and pipes rattled with the shock of the hit. Other ships blasted at the Japanese to get rid of them.

An emergency TBS message was sent to Admiral Bull Halsey: *Denver out of commission.*

Admiral Halsey received this notification, and he immediately ordered the *USS Eaton* and *USS Stanly*, destroyers, to stand by the *Denver* for protection. She lay vulnerably dead in the water, too close to Rabaul, a major Japanese base with two hundred planes, for comfort.

In their panic and over-reaction, many sailors from all divisions went into abandon ship mode, even though no order from the captain had been given. Life rafts and nets lowered down the sides. Walter could see many sailors scrambling down to the dark and murky waters.

"Come on, leave the guns! We need to get off," Buster shouted and started running. He was never inclined to run, so most other gunners took their cue from him.

"We're dead in the water now," Claude shouted back. "This is worse than a death sentence. Come on, Walter, move it."

"I ain't gonna be a sitting duck," Alvin yelled, running behind Claude.

Walter's chest heaved with a surge of panic. No longer disoriented, he shouted as he ran with the gunners, "What the Sam Hill do you guys think you're doing? I'm not leaving the Dirty Dee until I hear the abandon ship order! We still have our captain, and he'll give the order." His mother's face flashed before him. *Do what's right, son.* "I mean it, I'm not leaving!"

Alvin scowled at him and shouted, "Our ship is on her way to the graveyard, Troyan! You're crazy. Come on. We need to get off. It's only a matter of time until she sinks or the Japs blow all of us up."

"Well, this ship might be dead in the water, but she ain't dead!" Walter yelled back. "I'm staying at my station to see what I can do to help."

"Well, if those Japs surround us, we'll be heading toward a meatgrinder. Now's the chance to save our lives. We gotta get off." Alvin ran to the nearest ladder.

"Where's Eddie? Where's Eddie?" Walter shouted. Tempestuous wails, shrill and loud, assaulted Walter.

With no power, Captain Brisco looked down at the waters at a number of his crew already on lifeboats and did the only thing he could do to communicate. He grabbed his megaphone and shouted, "Hey, down there, get back on this ship. And I mean now! I never gave the abandon ship order. We're taking her home, boys, if we have to swim and push her in."

With not a second to waste, the sailors already in lifeboats steered back. They helped one another climb back up the ropes. Shellshocked and exhausted, the determination of the *Denver* sailors to save their ship was incredible from that point forward.

Flooding in the aft compartments did not deter repair parties from snapping into action. Six men were trapped in the engine room when the torpedo tore open that side of the ship to the sea, their means of escape from death a mystery even to them.

Although shaken up like he'd never been in his entire young life, Walter stayed at his station and listened for the next orders. Dead in the water. He looked around. He rubbed his face, exhausted, scared. *What does that mean for all twelve hundred of us? Where's Eddie?* His stomach churned like the ship's rudder.

"You know, Buka Airfield is just ten miles away," Claude panted when he got back to the main deck. "Those leftover Japs might grab rowboats and attack us with hand grenades. We have no way of defending ourselves."

Alvin, who'd just come back, very wet from jumping into a lifeboat, bent over, hands on knees. "I'm feeling jittery. Who knows what's lurking around out there?" And then he keeled over with fright and lightheadedness.

Walter bent over him to make sure he was okay. He shook his shoulders. "Alvin, Alvin."

His gunner friend stared back at him in fright.

"We need to pray." Walter held Alvin's arms and looked skyward. Then, with open eyes, he shouted a desperate prayer.

With no time for sleep, most of the crew was on the verge of collapse from fatigue. Nevertheless, they all worked together for damage-control assessment and cleanup, like the great team they were.

Walter worked and listened for the next orders from his division officer while still looking around for Eddie.

As water filled the gaping hole left by the torpedo hit, Captain Brisco and the steerage crew monitored the list angle of the *Denver* as she was tilting to starboard.

Rumors circulated that some of the engine room crew had lost their lives.

The ship's listing to starboard worsened by the minute.

After a quick trip to a lower deck, Claude returned to his station, frantic and out of breath. "They are reporting that we're listing fifteen degrees. What's the degree for capsizing?"

"It has to be forty-five degrees. I remember that from boot camp," Walter said. "We'll be okay. We'll be okay, as long as it doesn't get worse. We have a good captain. We have a good damage-control team." He released the pent-up breath he hadn't realized he was holding until then.

"Yeah, even The Bull knows what's going on with us," Buster added.

"What about fatalities?" Claude asked. "I heard we've had some deaths. And where's Eddie?"

"I don't want to think about death." Walter's raspy voice and blank stare revealed his shaken state of mind. He decided to leave his station to search for Eddie.

The mechanics had rushed to the mangled side of the ship to assess the damage and possible repairs. But the flooding, dead bodies, and floating equipment parts hindered their efforts. The hole in their hull was roomy enough for a large truck to drive through and turn around. Although the engine room flooded, two men from the repair crew stayed with the one trapped man until he could be removed.

The *Eaton* and *Stanly* circled steadily around the *Denver* to protect her.

At one point, Walter stopped his search for Eddie for a moment and watched both destroyers, only a little more than half the size of the *Denver,* hoping their defense would be enough to safeguard his ship.

His paralyzed thoughts seized him. *Dead in the water. Dead in the water. What will happen next?*

Two hours later, the *Denver* was back on even keel. A tugboat, the *USS Sioux,* came alongside her to begin the mammoth effort of pulling the enormous vessel to the closest shore. Lines, the diameter of human arms, were thrown out, reeled in by the *Sioux,* and tied off. Although the engineers soon had one shaft operating, the tugboat exerted tremendous effort to get the *Denver* to move an inch.

But she finally moved at six knots, shuddering and groaning as if defying her own death. She rumbled louder and louder, not willing to give up the fight to survive in the enemy waters with no engine. Her two destroyer escorts faithfully flanked her sides as she got underway for the nearest safe shore.

Captain Brisco informed his division officers, "With the angel on our ship, two destroyers, our capable tugboat, and a plane umbrella, we'll get her in. We'll get her in."

The captain's remarks spread to everyone else.

Walter looked to the sky in vain to see the air support. He shrugged his shoulders and continued his assigned duties.

No one said a word as the *Denver* crawled—slow mile by slow mile. The magnificent ship spoke for herself. The crippled cruiser remained in full fighting condition and would have taken up another fight had it presented itself. The *Denver* was seaworthy except for speed. She had her spirit, thanks to her indomitable crew.

Walter understood that a vessel draws life from the essence of the men aboard her. He watched the difficult labors required for his ship to move at all. Pride and relief stirred his heart.

A few hours later, Captain Brisco passed the word to all his division officers that twenty lives were lost and twenty wounded. One man was paralyzed from the waist down with four broken vertebrae. Word traveled to everyone.

Walter swallowed a wail and moaned when he heard about the fatalities. He sat on the deck with his head between his knees. Word of the deaths of his own comrades hit him like a sucker punch in the gut. *Oh, God, no more deaths. Please, God, get the rest of us to safety, wherever that may be. And where's Eddie? God, where's Eddie? He made a promise to Emma.*

The news finally reached Walter and the other gunners that Eddie was among the wounded. He'd scrambled down the ropes and jumped into a lifeboat as many others had. But when he'd seen two other sailors clinging to ship debris, close to drowning, he jumped out of the lifeboat to rescue them, injuring himself when a chunk of wreckage slammed into his side.

A few hours later, the arduous task of placing the dead bodies into boxes wrapped with flags was indescribable. Walter placed his hand over his heart as his ship's flags were lowered to half-mast in respect of their deceased. He discreetly swiped his cheek with the back of his hand, getting rid of a forbidden tear, staring into a sorrowful space.

Normally, other ships would have stopped in the water and lowered their own flags to honor the *Denver's* deceased. But an active battle continued to encircle the whole area of Augusta Bay.

Walter stared at the numerous ships, both allies and enemies. They looked like flies caught in a huge spider's web of the sea to battle it out until some of them went down.

With no power through the communication system, everyone waited for messages and announcements from their division officers.

The gunner crew finally heard that Captain Brisco said that General MacArthur had ordered an umbrella of P38s to fly over their ship for protection.

But the terrified sailors looked skyward and saw nothing.

"Awe, that's just MacArthur flappin' his jaws to the captain," Buster sneered. "There's no protection up there."

"Don't see a thing. Don't hear a thing," Claude added, looking upward. "The Skipper doesn't know what he's talking about."

But no sooner had those words come out of their mouths when an eerie sound came from the sky. Then faint shots could be heard. Two enemy planes were shot down and spiraled from the sky.

"See, we do have the umbrella!" Walter placed his hands on his waist. "Haven't you figured out what the P38s sound like?"

"Well, I doubt I'll sleep any better." Alvin sighed and walked away.

The rest of that day and night, the cruiser traveled at six knots toward Tulagi, remaining in GQ in constant fear of an air attack with less than half of the main battery operative. The sea battle still raged, but the *Denver's* distance from it kept them from immediate danger.

Some of the gunners welcomed sleep that night in four-hour shifts. However, Walter was back on the forty-millimeter guns for his 0000 to 0800 watch. Even with the ship removed from active battle, he could still hear underwater charges going off miles away. He remained alert and vigil at his station for potential firing commands as he watched the flashing daggers of explosions stabbing the waters in the distance.

Thoughts tumbled in his head. Grief for the lost lives. Worry for his compromised ship. Hatred for the war.

CHAPTER TWENTY-TWO

DECEMBER 1943, NEW HEBRIDES, SOLOMON ISLANDS

Captain Brisco submitted his action report for the *Denver*. "The control of damage and rapid rate of emergency repairs is a fine tribute to training. Every man has a job to do, which he knows to its last detail, and he has no time to do anything else. In my two years of experience in the South Pacific, I have found this to be the case in all types of combat ships. The ability of my men to do their job under most trying conditions is the reason we are still here."

The tugboat got the *Denver* to Florida Island on November fifteenth to the welcoming cheers and blasts from other ships in the harbor. She stayed anchored for a week for temporary repairs to stop the flooding in the mess hall, forcing nearly everyone to eat topside.

Sailors from all departments worked night and day in oil and debris of all sorts as they removed ammunition and aided in the repair of their ship. But, within a few days, word spread that permission would be given, division by division, for sailors to deboard the ship for limited periods.

When Eddie was released from sick bay, Walter lost no time catching up with his friend, asking all kinds of questions about his rescue mission in the dark waters only a few nights ago.

"Boy, everything was going through my mind. Ya know, sharks and everything," Eddie said. "But I was down on the lifeboat, and those two boys were screaming for their lives. I knew I could help. The water was loaded with all kinds of wreckage. Everyone was panicky." He drew in a breath and crossed his arms over his chest. "I'm tellin ya, I've never been so scared. Someone from above must have been watching over me. I'm still here. I'm keeping my promise to Emma, no matter what."

Walter swallowed hard and embraced his friend.

When Walter finally stepped off the cruiser, he teetered for a moment, unsure of solid ground. An odd feeling took hold of him—no vibrations beneath his feet. It had been a year since he'd boarded the *Denver*.

He walked around the docking area to see the hole in the ship for himself. His stomach churned at the image. The death. The damage. Yet, here he was, still alive.

His eyes widened in shock as he stared at the massive hole. He turned around to Eddie, who had just walked up behind him, hobbling, and said, "This is worse than I ever imagined. I don't even see how it can possibly be repaired."

"Same here." Eddie walked closer to the side of the dock. "This is bad to the bone. I don't know how repairs will work, but our ship's a tough ol' girl. If the captain wants to save her, he will."

Claude, Buster, and Alvin walked over to them.

Alvin squatted and fingered some pebbles on the ground. "You know, none of us would be here if the captain had taken the two torpedo hits from the front."

Walter took off his cap and crossed his arms. "I really don't even know how to think about all this. But what I do know is that if Captain Brisco hadn't turned the ship and we'd taken those two torpedoes head on, our ammunition would have exploded right along with the impact. Half the Dirty Dee would be gone, and we'd all be goners. We would have been out so fast that we wouldn't have known what happened."

"You're right about that," Claude said. "Our whole ship faced death in the seconds before those torpedoes came at us."

Buster, unusually quiet, cleared his throat a couple times before speaking. "We have a good captain. He knew what he was doing. But I still hate it that we lost twenty lives. I'm telling you. I hate this."

Walter looked toward him. "We all do, Buster. The United States shouldn't even be in this mess." The magnitude and severity of the war crashed all over his mind.

The group of five remained quiet, staring at the hole. Other sailors also came over to assess the damage.

Walter sauntered back to the main area of the dock, unsure if the other would follow. Finally, he found some shade beneath a clump of tropical trees and sat down. The waving flags at the top of the masts on his ship caught his attention, and he stared at them. To him, they represented life for the *Denver*. Although he grappled with the lost lives and all the damage, his heart stirred with hope for his ship's recovery as the American flag waved gently in the afternoon breeze along with the signal flags.

Ammunition from three turret mounts was removed for transfer to the nearest Naval Ammunition Depot to be utilized by other ships. The immediate temporary work continued for several days so the ship could move yet again to the New Hebrides for more repairs. She rested on keel blocks in the dry dock and received electrical power for the first time since she'd been dead in the water.

A somber air surrounded the sailors on November eighteenth as the deceased, in their flag-wrapped boxes, were carried off the ship for burial at the Tulagi cemetery. The *Denver's* chaplain, Lieutenant Hindman, assisted by a priest from a neighboring ship, led a memorial service as part of the Marine detachment played "Amazing Grace" on their bugles, followed by taps.

Some of the crew remained on the base for reassignments to other ships. But most stayed with the *Denver,* according to orders, and continued on with light duties during the repair time.

The haggard sailors were somewhat disappointed with their liberty time during their brief stay at Tulagi. An advanced American base, it only offered the jungle, coconuts, large natives, and not-too-friendly ones at that.

A few days later, the watertight enclosure repair was complete in the mess hall, and the ship got underway for Espiritu Santo in the New Hebrides with help from the tugboat *USS Pawnee.*

She settled in a floating drydock for more temporary repairs before the long sea journey to Pearl Harbor. The *Denver* would then sail on to Mare Island in California for permanent repairs.

Walter's soul had also taken a hit in the latest combat. Nightmares, headaches, diarrhea, sleepless nights, and a resultant loss of energy plagued him for several days. The loop in his brain ran constantly, always starting and ending in the same place with firing the guns to fight the enemy while protecting his ship.

But he figured if the *Denver* was getting repaired, he would too. Not one to give up, he pushed through his personal turmoil for the sake of his cruiser and his sailor friends. So, he claimed hope for himself and his enemy-struck ship.

Six days later, on Thanksgiving Day, the seagulls soared in circles, chattering in the cloudless sky of penetrating blue, oblivious of a war. Divine Services were held on the upper deck, and more than the usual attended.

Walter's rich tenor voice blended in with hundreds of other sailors when they sang "How Great Thou Art."

In the meantime, taking advantage of their replenished food supplies, the cooks busied themselves making apple pies.

A lighter spirit prevailed within the crew. Despite the troubles, the boys finally enjoyed cutting up and laughing again. They were already anticipating wetting their whistles with their liberty time when the *Denver* would be out of commission for a few weeks at Mare Island in San Francisco.

As Walter sat down to eat, surrounded by his buddies, he smiled and grabbed his fork to dig into the Thanksgiving dinner. Steam rose from his hot green beans and mashed potatoes, and he breathed in the savory scents.

"The first thing I'm gonna do is head to a restaurant for a burger. A big fat juicy one, I hope," Buster said. "I reckon Florida is too far away for me to head for home. I bet there'll be some gals hanging around in San Francisco for dancing, don'tcha think?"

"Probably. Virginia's too far away for me too," Alvin added. "Pass the joe ... and the side arms, too."

"When I get my liberty time," Eddie said, "I'm gonna be a husband again. Emma's gonna get the biggest kiss she's ever had, mark my words. Can't wait to see the folks too. My pop got a new job, and he's working at Mare Island. What do you think of them apples? I guess I better be good while I'm there. What about you, Walter? Heading up to Santa Rosa?"

"Yeah, for sure, I'm going home. I'm lucky I'll only be fifty miles away. I can't wait to eat my pop's bread from the bakery and my mom's pierogies."

"Do you think we'll have the whole time off for liberty leave?" Claude asked. "I mean, can we do whatever we want while the Dirty Dee gets repaired?"

"Guess we'll just have to find out." Walter swiped his mouth with the back of his hand. "But I'll take whatever I can get. I need to get these guns out of my head. We're off the guns now, but I still feel like I need to be at my station. I constantly feel like I need to fire. Once a gunner, always a gunner, I guess. I wish I could shake it, even for a little while."

While waiting for the ship's repairs at New Hebrides, the crew enjoyed some leisure time with movies in the mess hall and card games. Slapjack, war, crazy eights, acey-deucey, and poker offered some mental relief from their war-stricken minds. The scuttlebutt sheet hanging in the galley listed the titles of the movies and what days and times they would play.

Walter twisted Eddie's arm to watch the movie "Life Begins for Andy Hardy." Even though Eddie had seen the movie before, he agreed to go.

The American comedy film had played in Santa Rosa before the war, but Walter never got to see it. When he settled into his seat in the mess hall, he watched the main stars' names scroll down the screen—Lewis Stones, Mickey Rooney, Fay Holden, and Judy Garland.

When the movie was over, Walter chuckled. "You know, Eddie, you kind of remind me of Andy in the movie. He sure got into some fixes."

Eddie playfully stuck out his tongue. "Well, that's funny. My mama said the same thing!"

Three weeks later, with temporary voyage repairs complete, the *Denver* got underway on December twentieth for her journey back to the States. But not before six Japanese Prisoners of War came on board for transfer to Pearl Harbor. After examinations by the senior medical officer, they were placed in the brig. As word got around that the POWs had just boarded, expletives flew.

"Well, now I know what that odor is. They have contaminated our ship forever," Buster snarled and balled up his hands into fighting fists.

"I'd like to get my hands around their scrawny little necks. I'm gonna sneak down to the brig tonight when everyone's asleep," Alvin fumed.

Walter faked a loud cough to get his friends' attention. "Okay, okay, look, they didn't want to be in this war any more than us. And the last place they want to be is on our ship. I wouldn't wanna be a POW on one of their ships. Would you?"

Eddie stared at Walter. "Well, yeah, for sure, but what makes you think they didn't want to be in this war? They seem to enjoy firing their guns to kill us all off if you ask me. They even like diving their planes into our ships."

Walter briefly hesitated, then went on. "The way I figure it is they didn't really have a choice. Yamamoto started this thing. They're teenagers, just like us."

The *Denver* stayed in communication with her sailing buddy, the *USS Boyd*, a destroyer, for the duration of the repairs. The destroyer had sustained battle damage and lost lives, and both had arrived at Espirito Santo Island at the same time for torpedo hit repairs. They were commissioned to sail together to Pearl Harbor and then to Mare Island, San Francisco, keeping company with each other.

While steaming ahead to Pearl Harbor, the gunners resumed their firing drills as soon as they got underway. Both ships crossed the equator and the International Date Line together.

When this occurred, Captain Brisco made an announcement. "My fellow sailors. In the order of our fraternity as sailors, you will now be awarded two more certificates. The Order of the Golden Dragon will be issued to you for crossing the International Date Line. And on top of that, the Golden Shellback will be issued to all of you fine men, as we have just now crossed the equator where it just so happens to cross the International Date Line at the same time."

Cheers and whistles erupted across the ship.

On Christmas Day, the cruiser and destroyer blew their horns for the holiday, offering best wishes for each other through the air.

Three days later, the *Denver* and *Boyd* entered Pearl Harbor, Oahu Island, and refueled. The *Denver* released her Japanese prisoners. In accordance with directives from the Commander of the Third Fleet and with routing instructions from the Commander of Hawaiian Sea Frontier, the two ships left for the United States the next day.

While the gunners did maintenance on the guns, Walter shook his head with worry. "I don't know that I trust that flimsy patch. I mean, really, I looked at it from up here, and I looked at it when I stepped off the ship yesterday. It looks like it was glued on with paste. And we're gonna be in rough waters in the San Francisco Bay Area. I feel like we're still crippled, and the *Boyd* is too."

Alvin looked at Walter. "So what? We've been in rough waters already."

"Yeah, but I used to live in San Francisco when I was a kid, and I know for a fact there are mountains on the floor of the ocean in the San Francisco Bay. The waters are crazy there, I'm tellin' you. Go ask Eddie."

"I'm scared, Walter. You got me real scared," Alvin laughed.

"Yeah, me too." Buster winked and chuckled. "I'm gonna sit in the corner and suck my thumb."

Claude placed both hands over his eyes in a mock gesture. "Well, I'm real scared too. I'm not one for buoyancy, but whatever floats your boat."

Three days later, when they approached San Francisco, twenty-foot swells greeted the *Denver* and *Boyd*. The biting air and cloudy skies produced mad waters in the roiling bay. Most of the *Denver* crew on the upper decks scrambled to sit or hold on to something while standing as the ship rocked. Walter looked out at the waves, slapping in all directions as if they were confused.

Before long, he noticed Buster, Alvin, and Claude holding their stomachs as they raced for the heads. Walter stifled a grin. *Probably to barf.*

CHAPTER TWENTY-THREE

The *Denver* sailors sighted the Golden Gate Bridge as their ship limped into Pier 35 at Mare Island and moored on the second day of the new year. Walter watched more than six thousand gallons of diesel oil as it was transferred off the ship.

Nothing is wasted, just like in the depression days.

A couple days later, the cruiser moved to Pier 22 for dry-docking for her extensive repairs.

Except for security, Seabees, and select officers, the rest of the crew disembarked the *Denver* and were assigned to various barracks in the Navy Yard. Security watches were set throughout the ship, especially around the anti-aircraft batteries.

Before Walter walked over to the gangplank to leave the ship, he stopped and rubbed both hands along the railing.

"What's that for? C'mon." Eddie nearly bumped into him.

"Well, I say the Dirty Dee's going into surgery. I hope her doctors can put her back together."

Eddie shook his head and grinned.

The weary *Denver* crew received a well-deserved liberty time, alternating as assigned, for thirty days off the Navy

Yard for however long the ship needed repairs. The other days required the sailors to stay in the yard for various duties and specialized training, although additional brief liberties could be granted with discretion. Captain Brisco reminded his crew to be a credit to the Navy with no engagement in horseplay of any kind while on leave.

Whooping and laughter could be heard everywhere as the teenage boys went their various ways, some to new barracks, others to leave the Navy Yard for their thirty-day leave.

Walter was thankful his personal leave came on the front end for him. He decided he'd pick up his civilian life as best he could after the horrors of the war and damage to his mind. He'd keep repairing himself and trying to get the guns out of his head.

Walking around the Navy Yard, the numerous propaganda posters caught his attention. He stared at the red and blue poster with a sinking blown-up ship that read, "Loose Lips Sink Ships." A reminder of Navy warnings for gossip and keeping confidentialities during wartime.

Others caught his attention.

A Careless Word ... A Needless Sinking.

Bits of Careless Talk Are Pieced Together by the Enemy.

Sailor Beware! Loose Talk Can Cost Lives.

He'd already called home and was making arrangements for a bus ticket when Robbie White from the ship's maintenance division approached him about a blind date.

"Well, ya see, I met a pretty girl here who's working in the shipyard factory right here at Mare Island, Mildred, and well, she has a friend. And well, I was wonderin' if you'd join us tonight. And then, well, you see, you'll have a date too. And we have our Navy pay from Uncle Sam. So, whaddya think, Walter?" Robbie's Alabama southern drawl could not be missed, nor his nervousness.

"Uh, I'm not sure. I was about to head home, and my mom and pop are waiting for me. Uh, would we go someplace? What do you have in mind? And does Mildred's friend want to meet me?"

"Sure, sure, yeah, sure she does. We'll take the girls to a nice restaurant. Maybe do some dancing. That'll be fun. We have to have some fun after all we've been through, right?"

Walter reluctantly agreed to the blind date. While Robbie worked out the details, he made another call home to delay his family visit. He didn't explain why and hung up the phone before his mother could ask questions.

Later that day, he took a fresh shower at his assigned shipyard barracks and dressed in his formal Navy uniform. He slicked back his short black hair and dabbed on some borrowed men's cologne. Shining his black Navy dress shoes until he could see his face in them, he wished they fit better. His feet had grown in the last year.

Taking a city bus to head into San Francisco, he and Robbie walked a few blocks until they stood in front of the St. Julien Restaurant. He slipped his hand into his pocket to finger several two-dollar bills, some of his pay he'd received.

As soon as they walked in, Robbie spotted Mildred and her girlfriend sitting at a booth with a half-circle burgundy cushioned seat.

He pointed them out and whispered, "The one on the left is my gal, Mildred."

Walter gulped. The young woman sitting next to Mildred was stunning, her face a perfect oval. He rubbed his damp palms on his pants as he followed Robbie over to their booth. His heart thumped a military march as he checked his posture and tried to swallow when the girls stood.

Robbie started the introductions. "Walter, this is Mildred Brown, my girl."

"Nice to meet you, Walter." Mildred cocked her head and smiled. "This is my friend, Alberta Thomas."

Walter reached to shake Alberta's hand. His knees wobbled when she smiled. He cleared his throat and hoped she hadn't noticed his sweaty palms.

He and Robbie scooted into the booth on opposite sides next to the girls. As the two couples looked over the menu to order their food, Walter's nerves moved like a current through his belly. He couldn't take his eyes off his beautiful date. His legs jiggled under the table from nerves.

The four made small talk as they perused the menus and placed their food orders.

When the waitress set their warm dinner plates before them, Walter breathed in the aroma of his broiled spring lamb chops, blocking out all memories of the ship's mess hall meals.

"Well, this fried filet of sole doesn't look half bad," Robbie said. "You girls probably wonder why I even got fish after spending so much time with them on the sea. So, how are your factory jobs going?"

Mildred and Alberta chatted about their experiences on the assembly lines at the shipyard, making parts for the ships, and even learning the art of welding. Listening to them talk, Walter assumed they were both from California. His mouth dropped open in surprise when he learned they both came to the West Coast from Indiana.

Astonished at this news, Walter fired out questions. "How did you get out here? Where are you staying? I know everybody's been pulled into the war, but, well, weren't there any jobs out in the Midwest? What did your parents—"

Robbie cut him off. "Let's let the girls talk. Wait until you hear how they got out here."

Walter placed his elbow on the table and rested his jaw on the back of his hand.

"Well, we had a couple of bus rides, but we mostly hitchhiked." Alberta's large brown eyes sparkled as she talked, her voice melodic. "Just the two of us. And it took several weeks to even get to San Francisco. When we ran low on money, we'd stay in whatever town we found ourselves in, get a local job, save our money, then put our thumbs up on the highway. Each new driver took us further west."

"You hitchhiked out here?" Walter gasped. "Just the two of you?"

"Well, yes. It was okay, Walter. Really, it was. We always felt safe, and the drivers were always kind and wanted to help us." Mildred went on to explain how they heard the call for duty during wartime and figured out their travels to the West Coast, leaving their families behind.

"We took off for factory jobs on the West Coast right after high school graduation, and our friends did too. You know, we have steady work, housing, and the California sunshine. And who knows, maybe we'll find love." Mildred batted her eyelashes at Robbie while Alberta looked down at her lap.

As the evening progressed, Walter and Alberta continued to talk, mostly in their own conversation. As soon as they finished eating, the two couples headed to the dance floor.

Walter placed a tremulous hand on Alberta's shoulder. His feet tripped a few times during the first dance, especially since his shoes were too tight. But he finally relaxed when he and Alberta danced to Tommy Dorsey and Frank Sinatra's song, "There Are Such Things" and Dolley Wilson's, "As Time Goes By."

When the songs ended, the band revved up. Alberta and Mildred linked up together and danced the jitterbug to Harry James's "Two O'Clock Jump." The saxophone player watched the girls, and his lively notes spurred them on. All the other patrons in the restaurant watched them move around the dance floor, their skirts swirling about.

Walter put the hard times on the *Denver* out of his mind and concentrated solely on Alberta. *I feel like I'm human again, really human. In a restaurant. Dancing. Talking with a beautiful girl.*

When the girls said they needed their sleep to be ready for work the next day, the two couples walked toward the front double doors. Walter drew a deep breath and asked Alberta, "May I see you again?"

"I'd like that very much," she demurely replied.

Walter floated out the door on a cloud, holding Alberta's elbow. *This is too good to be true.*

"What in the world did you say, Walter?" Mom shouted over the telephone.

"I said I won't be home right away like I thought I would. I've met this girl, and—"

"You mean to tell me you're not coming home? Aye yi yi yi yi!" Holding the phone in one hand, she rubbed her forehead. "Well, I'll have you know your pop and I have been worried sick. We listen to the radio and read the paper constantly. We've been trying to follow you and Chester and Arthur every day, and it's hard to sleep at night, especially when we hear about the torpedo hits. We have three boys in the war and—"

"I know, Mom, I'm still coming home, but—"

"Aye yi yi yi yi! Nie moge uwierzyc, ze to mowisz," Mom shouted, saying she couldn't believe what her son was telling her.

When his mother ranted in Polish, Walter bristled. He knew this conversation was not going well.

"Can't you just bring that girl here? I may like to meet her."

"Well, that's what I was getting ready to ask, but you didn't give me a chance."

Mom settled down a bit when Walter promised he'd bring Alberta with him. He drew in a deep breath to calm his pounding heart.

For the next three weeks, although he was officially on his thirty-day liberty leave, Walter stayed at the shipyard for meals, leisure time, and sleeping in his barracks. In the evenings, he made his way into the shipyard factory to meet with Alberta. They spent as much time as they could when she got off from her factory job.

Walter fell hard for this new beauty of his. He was a proud sailor wherever they went, Alberta's arm tucked into the crook of his elbow. They strolled around Fisherman's Wharf, window shopped in Chinatown, and rode the trolley cars across the city.

"This is my new favorite place," Alberta said when they walked around the Japanese Tea Garden one Sunday afternoon. Even with the cooler January temperatures, the lush ornamental trees and flowers spoke of beauty and tranquility.

Frowning a bit, Alberta pressed her fingertips against her lips. "You know, it doesn't seem right to me that the Japanese Americans were forced to leave their homes to go to internment camps. I mean, they're Americans like we are, and they did nothing to start this war. My supervisor's Japanese neighbors were snatched away from their homes at the beginning of the war. They were uprooted and lost all their property. I don't get this part of the war at all."

"I don't get it either," Walter answered. "I agree with you. It doesn't seem right. The same thing happened to our neighbors, the Hashimotos. What really gets to me is that a bunch of Japanese Americans have been recruited to fight for America in segregated units in the army. I guess it's the tension of the war."

One evening, they rode a bus to the Golden Gate Bridge and walked across, hand in hand. Walter worked up his courage and asked, "May I take you to Santa Rosa to meet my parents?"

Alberta hesitated briefly. "I'd like that, but don't you think you should go back home by yourself first? I mean, I'd feel a little awkward since your parents haven't seen you for quite a while."

Surprised by her answer, Walter stammered, "Umm, you're, uh, probably right. That's a good idea. But only for a few days, then I'll come back to get you."

As usual, Alberta's eyes sparkled when she smiled. "I think that can work. I need to ask my supervisor for the time off, depending on what day I go. I'll look forward to meeting your parents. How far away is Santa Rosa?"

"My home is less than an hour away from here. I'm lucky."

The couple continued talking and making plans. When they reached the other side of the bridge after a thirty-five-minute walk, they looked out at the bay waters and the hilly city on the other side, birds wheeling and swooping all around.

Walter hugged Alberta and planted a light kiss on her forehead. To his blissful state of mind, it seemed the long walk across the bridge had only taken five minutes. He couldn't deny the love bug had bitten him.

CHAPTER TWENTY-FOUR

SANTA ROSA AND MARE ISLAND, SPRING 1944

"Son, I can't believe you're finally home. Drat on the *Denver's* torpedo hit, but I'm glad you got this leave." Elizabeth hugged and kissed Walter until he nearly stumbled.

Taras cleared his throat a couple of times when Walter also embraced him.

After plopping his seabag in his bedroom, he went outside to play with Jacky and tossed him some balls. Then, smelling the fresh air from his yard, no ocean in sight, he dismissed thoughts of guns, torpedoes, deaths, ships, rain squalls, and everything about the war from his mind.

Instead, the sight of the family's plum trees, the Plymouth sitting outside the shed, and Jacky running around intoxicated him, lifting his spirits to a new level of gratefulness for his home. Birds flitted from the bird feeder to the trees and back to the bird feeder, singing their songs. Walter glanced up at the maple tree where a squirrel looked back at him, flicking his bushy tail. The fresh air held him captive.

When he walked back into the house, he smelled borscht simmering and heard his mother softly humming.

"How much more time until dinner, Mom?"

"A little while yet. Maybe another hour."

Oh, good. Walter headed to his bedroom and took out his violin. Feeling a little rusty with his fingers at first, he made sure it was in tune and then played some scales to warm up before breaking into some of his favorite solo pieces. The solitude of his bedroom and time for playing his violin created a peaceful feeling in his heart that he hadn't sensed for quite some time.

After he finished playing "Flight of the Bumblebee," he set his violin aside and rested on his bed, missing Arthur, who would normally be next to him on the other twin. Staring at the ceiling, his thoughts floated from home to Chester to Alberta and back to the *Denver* drydocked at the shipyard.

"Chodźmy jeść." Mom's usual call for dinner in Polish ended Walter's trance.

As the three sat down for dinner, Walter inhaled the aroma of his favorite soup with every bite. His eyes feasted on the bright red beets.

He looked at his parents and asked, "Any news from the Hashimotos?"

"Not a thing," Mom answered. "Mrs. Adams checks on their house. I keep their weeds pulled. None of us have any idea when they'll be back.

"Well, what's the latest with Chester and Arthur? Did I write you that Chester got to visit me on my ship for a couple of hours? Do you think they've heard about the *Denver's* hit?"

"They probably heard about it before we did." Mom said. "In fact, I think you boys hear the latest in the war faster than we do. And yes, Chester wrote us about your visit. I can't believe your ships lined up together like that."

"Hey, save some bread for me." Pop said. "From what we hear, Arthur still makes runs in the reconnaissance planes, and his letters don't give any details, what with the censoring and his top security missions. You already know Chester's ship is still navigating the Pacific. Your mother and I were mortified when we heard about his ship getting hit, and then a year later, we heard about the *Denver*. Sometimes, I don't know ..." Pop clamped his upper teeth over his bottom lip and lowered his head.

"You better go see Marcia while you're on liberty leave," Mom said. "You can cheer her up. She really misses Arthur. Say, maybe she can meet your new friend, Alberta. You know, Alberta sounds a lot like my Polish name, Alzbeta. What do you say to that?"

Walter grinned.

"Tell us, Son, about the firing of the guns during the battles. Did you have any warning about the torpedo coming your way?" Pop asked.

"Uh ... umm ... I don't think I want to talk about that."

Silence hung in the air.

"I wasn't finished talking about Alberta anyway." Mom glared at Pop. "We can't wait to meet her. Tell me more about her,"

"Well, she has brown hair and big brown eyes, and oh, you'll just have to wait until you meet her. You'll love her." Walter fidgeted with his spoon, heat rising in his cheeks.

"You say I'll love her? I'm wondering if you already do!"

Walter slurped his soup, enjoying the familiarity of his mother's cooking in the kitchen he loved, keeping the bad memories of the war at bay.

Three days later, Walter stepped into the family Plymouth to head back to San Francisco to pick up Alberta. The engine sputtered, and the wheels picked up some traction on the loose gravel, producing clouds of dust. He cranked the handle on the side door to roll the window down a bit to catch some mild breezes, even in January.

All smiles, Alberta scooted into her seat and thanked Walter for holding the door open for her. On the short drive, she asked Walter about the torpedo hit and what it was like to be a gunner. He shifted uneasily in his seat, gave short answers, and took the conversation in a new direction.

"You know, the whole time I've been on my ship, I've witnessed horrible things. But I always thought about the Americans back home, all pulling together to help with the war. When I first got off the ship last month, I was grateful to see all the women working so hard at the shipyard for us. And you're one of them. Well—" Walter cleared his throat. "Thank you. All you gals are working hard for us."

"When Mildred and I first discussed traveling to Mare Island, I wasn't sure what to expect. I just knew I wanted to help. A lot of the boys from my high school didn't even graduate. Their patriotism called them to the war."

"Same for me. I quit high school too. My oldest brother was on the *USS San Francisco* when Pearl Harbor was bombed. I made up my mind right then to enlist in the Navy. And my other brother enlisted too. I know my parents worry about all three of us. It kills me when my mother cries about the war."

Alberta rested her hands in her lap when Walter shifted gears and pulled the car into their gravel driveway. Jacky came dashing out to greet both of them.

When they walked in the front door, Mom came in from the kitchen, all smiles. "Welcome, welcome sweet girl!"

Following introductions and small talk, Walter led Alberta to the sofa to sit. But only minutes later, she stood and made herself at home when she stepped into the kitchen to help Mom with lunch preparations.

The two talked up a storm. Walter remained hopeful he might be in better graces with his parents for his abbreviated visit.

Later that evening, he drove Alberta back to San Francisco.

"Tell me about the rest of your leave time. Do you know when your ship will be fully repaired?"

"I don't know for sure, but we were told it would take several weeks. You know, it's so tempting to not even go back to the war after what we've been through. It was sheer—" Walter paused. "I'm sorry. I don't want to say the word. Anyway, I don't wanna be AWOL. I've been through too much without adding desertion to my record. I need to see this thing through to the end."

The couple made more plans to see one another over the remainder of his thirty-day leave before he stopped the car in front of Alberta's flat. With night approaching, the city lights flickered like a stage set, mimicking the light in Walter's heart being in Alberta's presence.

The immense repair work continued on the *Denver* while the sentries kept their posts for security. A change in command took place as well. Captain A. M. Bledsoe took over from Captain R. P. Briscoe, who was transferred to Washington, DC.

When Walter's thirty-day liberty ended, he received word that he was selected to attend the three-day Anti-Aircraft Training Center at Point Montara starting March twenty-second.

Always ready to be a student, he listened attentively to his instructor, took notes, and practiced new simulations.

About the first of April, the *Denver* received ammunition in preparation for battle duties, scheduled to depart in early May. The entire crew returned to the ship in staggered sections on specific dates.

During this latter part of the Mare Island repair, the time came for new clothes and shoes to be issued to all the sailors as needed. Walter got in line for new pants and shirts first, then he got in line for shoes, relieved his old too-tight shoes would be replaced.

The clerk asked, "Name and rank?"

"Walter Troyan, Seaman Second Class."

"Here you go, size ten. Next."

"Wait a minute, my shoes are getting too small for me. I think I will need a size ten and a half."

"No, I have the inventory record right here. It says you wear a size ten." The clerk showed the tracking sheet to Walter.

"Well, I was seventeen when I enlisted, sir. I'm almost nineteen now. My feet have grown, and I'm taller."

"It says right here, size ten. We always go by the inventory sheets. Take your shoes so I can help the fellow behind you."

Frustrated, Walter argued back. "No, I can't take those. I'm telling you, my feet have grown. We're all teenagers here, you know. We're growing boys."

The equally frustrated clerk left the table to confer with another clerk. Walter waited. The two men looked over at him. The first clerk finally walked back and said, "Here, size eleven. These should last you a while. Two pairs— working and dress shoes. Next."

Walter took both pairs and walked away, shaking his head about Navy protocols.

Whenever he could get liberty, Walter would meet up with Alberta for more dates. It became more difficult to separate from his lovely girlfriend, and he was becoming distracted while performing his naval duties. Nervous, but with his mind made up, he hatched a plan.

Finding a jewelry store, he used a portion of his Navy savings to purchase an engagement ring for his first love.

Should I tell the boys? What if she says no? Maybe I should ask Eddie about this?

Deciding it was best to stay mum, he took Alberta back to the Japanese Tea Garden one Sunday afternoon. Walking hand in hand, he spotted a special tree next to a bench, and they stopped to sit. Clearing his throat, he pulled the simple solitaire diamond ring from his pocket. The diamond flashed like drops of frozen light. He gazed into Alberta's brown eyes for the longest time, heart throbbing.

"Alberta, I know we have a war going on and all, but I, uh, want you to be my wife. I want to make a life with you as soon as the war is over, and ... will you marry me?"

Walter drew in a deep breath when he saw moisture from Alberta's eyes right before she flung her arms around his neck.

"I will," she whispered, "yes, I will."

The two hugged as if the world had only known one love, and it was theirs.

———— ⊸≫∾⊶ ————

Word spread fast in the barracks. Rapid-fire questions assailed Walter.

"You really popped the question?" Buster asked.

"You never even said you bought that gal a ring," Alvin said.

"When will you tie the knot?" Claude wanted to know.

"As soon as I step off this ship when the war's over," Walter beamed.

Eddie flung his arm around Walter's shoulder and grinned. "This is the best news I've heard yet, ol' pal of mine. Nothing beats love and marriage. I know. I can't wait to meet this gal of yours."

When Walter called home to break the exciting news to his parents, his mother gasped and said at once she would plan a quick engagement party. "How much more time do we have?" she asked him.

"The ship's still not ready, but I'm told we'll head out about the first of May."

Walter could hardly contain his excitement. He was on board as his parents made celebratory plans for him. Eddie and his new wife Emma would be invited as well as neighbors and other friends.

One evening, Walter made arrangements for Alberta to meet Eddie and Emma when the two couples met to take a walk. He grinned from head to toe watching Alberta and Emma giggling and talking up a storm.

The next day, he whistled and skipped around the Navy Yard while working, anticipating his engagement party on Saturday, April fifteenth, his nineteenth birthday.

When the big day arrived, Walter and Alberta met up with Eddie and Emma to take a bus ride up to Santa Rosa. The two couples were excited to use the Troyan car to drive to the Russian River for some swimming fun before the engagement party.

Taking a picnic lunch, the four enjoyed frolicking in the water for a couple of hours. Alberta, in all her excitement, kept reminding everyone of the time and cautioned them not to be late.

When the four picked up their belongings and hopped into the car, Walter got behind the wheel and confidently pulled away on the sandy road a little too fast. With an unexpected jerk, the car halted when he edged it too close to a small drop-off, the back wheel falling down into a ditch.

Walter and Eddie got out to assess the situation.

"Piece of cake, girls. No worries," Walter said as he and Eddie confidently used all their muscles in an attempt to push the car out.

But the car would not budge.

Eddie frowned, scratched his head, and said, "Well, okay, looks like the car's dead on the street, kinda like our ship was dead in the water."

Alberta and Emma joined in the rescue effort. The two couples pushed and lunged, creating swirls of dust that landed all over them, but to no avail.

Finally, Walter spotted a pickup truck coming down the road, and he waved his arms to call him over for help. With a big push from the truck and Walter and Eddie's exertions on both sides, the car finally edged back to the road.

Red as a beet from the tug of war with the car, not to mention embarrassment, Walter got behind the wheel again.

"Walter, what will your mother say?" Alberta asked. "I'm sure we're going to be late now."

"We can't walk into an engagement party with all this dirt on us," Emma added.

"Well, the most important worry is the food," Eddie said. "I just hope if the guests arrive before we do, they won't eat everything up."

"They better not," Walter said. "I'm starving now."

Alberta looked at Emma and winked. "Come on, fellows. Forget the food. We just need to get cleaned up and arrive on time."

"Yes, that's food for thought," Emma added.

When Walter finally pulled into the dirt driveway of his home, his mother ran out to greet them in a dither. She stopped abruptly, arms akimbo.

"Where have you been? This is an engagement party. And it's for you, I'll have you know. It's almost time to start. It's almost time to start! Come on." Elizabeth took off her apron and flung it at Walter's behind.

The couples dashed into the house, laughing, all talking at once about their adventure with the car.

Right before Walter's assigned date to officially report aboard the ship, he called home to say a final goodbye to his parents. Then he asked for personal liberty for his last evening. Eddie did the same. When granted, the two couples met at a trolly car station.

After they posed for a photograph to remember their last night together, the trolley car went up and down the hills. They later walked around downtown San Francisco. As they passed another strolling couple, Walter called over to them, pointing to Alberta, and said, "This is my beautiful wife-to-be!" The couple laughed and walked on.

When Eddie and Emma departed, Walter was glad to have some time alone with Alberta. She held out her hand with her cherished diamond several times.

"Promise you'll write me?" Walter's heart flipped and fluttered.

"Of course. Promise you'll come back safe and sound?"

Walter could see the sheen of tears on Alberta's face.

A cloud of sadness hovered over both, knowing they would not see each other again for quite some time. Who knew what was ahead with the interminable war?

With promises to write letters, emotions filled Walter's heart like nothing he'd ever experienced. They shared a kiss he would never forget.

"Has anyone seen Eddie?" Walter asked a few days after he boarded the *Denver*.

"Nope. Maybe he went AWOL." Buster laughed. "Haven't you noticed some haven't returned at all?"

"I'm serious. Today is the last day for boarding," Walter answered.

"He'll be here," Alvin said. "We always hear him before we see him, right? Nothing to worry about when it comes to Eddie."

Each division performed readiness duties for departure on May third. Still no sign of Eddie. Walter worried and constantly looked for him.

The day before departure, Walter approached his division officer to inquire about his friend.

"Walter, he's a no-show. No word from him at all. He knows how to find a telephone. You know that going *AWOL* is a serious offense. Unless he shows up today, Eddie's done with the *Denver* and probably with the US Navy."

Walter thanked his officer, shook his head, and walked away. This just wasn't like Eddie.

With a new camouflage paint job, food provisions, refueling, a full tender of ammunition, and successful testing of all functions of the cruiser, the *Denver* pulled away from Mare Island with cheers and whistles. The ship made good on her escape for repairs—down but not defeated or out. She still had a soul and her fighting spirit. The ship made her second appearance on the open seas as if she was slowly walking out of surgery, saying, "The doctor did great. Here I am. Where's the next battle?"

Moving out of San Francisco Bay, they headed south to North Island, San Diego, where post-repair shakedown exercises started. The *Denver* successfully completed all the exercises in company with other ships.

Upon arrival at the Naval Air Station, all decks and living quarters were inspected as well as the navigational lights, sirens, and communication system. The *Denver* launched her floatplanes and participated in several simulated attacks.

Naval blimps and the usual anti-submarine screen with the destroyers offered high security for the entire bay area. Local United States security had ramped up since the Pearl Harbor attack. The seamen continued daily drilling and exercises and remained on GQ. Even so, Captain Bledsoe played the Dirty Dee song on his accordion at dusk with enthusiasm and encouraged his crew to sing along. The sailors needed no convincing to sing a song of praise for their ship.

Tune: She's a Grand Old Flag

She's a grand old ship, she is really a pip,
And her crew is as true as can be.
They've learned to fight, with all their might,
To protect and preserve Liberty.
And the captain, grand,
when he gives a command,
Knows it's carried out to a "T."
For he has trained us all,
And we're always on the ball,
We're all proud of the Mighty DEE.

Following some fun singing along with the captain's accordion and hooting and hollering, Claude gathered around the gun crew and said, "Let's go play cards."

"No, we can't." Buster stood tall, puffing out his chest.

"Why not?"

"The captain's standing on the deck!" Buster hooted. "Get it? Are ya coming, Walter?"

"Nah, not tonight."

"Okay, you're as jumpy as a grasshopper. Is it Eddie or your new gal you're missing?" Claude asked.

"Both."

Claude motioned with his hand. "Well, come on anyway, you need to get your mind off things."

Declining, Walter excused himself and got situated on his thin mattress with paper and pen to write letters—one to Alberta and one to his parents—even though he'd just seen them. Although still anchored in California, he didn't care. He reasoned maybe his letters would get picked up quickly since he wasn't yet out on the open waters.

When he finished writing his letter to Alberta, he closed with, "Frankly, I don't know what I'm going to do if this war drags out. All I know is that I want to be with you."

He sealed both letters and stared off into space, worried about Eddie.

On May eighteenth, the azure blue sky displayed clouds that resembled cotton balls. Calmness pervaded the ship. But in the blink of an eye, an explosion shattered the peace. Above them, two planes met head on and crashed into the bay and produced an indescribable boom.

The sailors screamed in shock as they witnessed the air crash only a half mile away. The seagulls dispersed quickly, frightened even more than the sailors.

"That's real! What happened? Oh no!" Walter cried out. He tried to pray but could barely string two words together.

"What on earth?" Alvin covered his face with both hands.

Captain Bledsoe immediately communicated with the other ships to get a rescue search underway for any survivors. The simulated air attack of two planes repelling from Fleet Air Detachment based at North Island had gone wrong—very wrong. Two blimps that had been taking part in the exercise, the *USS Rockford* and the *USS Carson City,* all joined the *Denver's* search efforts but failed to recover any survivors.

A somber air filled the *Denver* cruiser yet again. Witnessing the blood bath in the sky and lives lost before they had even traveled to the open seas for battle with the enemy, a wave of sorrow threatened to pull Walter under.

CHAPTER TWENTY-FIVE

JUNE 1944, SOUTH PACIFIC

The ship slowed to five knots as she prepared to enter the channel for berth H4, Pearl Harbor, Oahu. It was now summer, and she'd already received new orders to report to Task Group 58.1 for duty in the Marshall Islands.

As the ship prepared for docking, Walter stood on the main deck and gazed out at the waters. He watched a couple of seagulls glide toward the berth area. And then, totally caught off guard, he watched a young sailor waving his cap like a madman at the ship. He squinted.

Could that be ...

He scaled down to deck three for a closer look, but the sailor was gone. Hoping against hope the sailor could have been Eddie, Walter stopped by the commissary for a few minutes before making his way back up to the main deck.

Within half an hour, Walter heard Eddie laughing.

"Okay, I'm dreaming, right? Somebody, wake me up!" Walter ran to meet his buddy, took off his cap, and slapped him on the back.

Confused and surprised, the other gunners gathered around Eddie and Walter.

"Eddie, no way you're here. What's up with you just appearing when ya want?" Buster reprimanded.

"Yeah, what happened? The Navy doesn't tolerate lateness. You know that." Alvin's steely blue eyes bore into Eddie's.

Other sailors joined in with the group, and everyone peppered Eddie with questions—all at once.

"Okay, okay. This is not what you think. I wasn't thinking about AWOL. I wouldn't do that. I was just late for boarding, plain and simple. I was busy with Emma, and I was also helping my parents. I tried my best to make it back on time, and I almost did. I was at the berth when the ship started pulling out. The authorities were no help to me in stopping it. The *Denver* had pulled out, and there was nothing I could do about it."

He looked back and forth at everyone who was listening. "Arrangements were made for me to board another smaller ship that was also headed to Pearl. And so here I am. I beat the *Denver*. I'm mustered back in and ready to use the guns."

Eddie made a mimicking gun sound. "I explained everything, and the Officer of the Deck just happened to remember how I rescued a couple fellows, and I got wounded and all when the ship got hit. And I did what I could to get over here to Pearl."

"Oh, shut your trap, Eddie. Heck, that's what I'm gonna do next time around, just get busy with other stuff," Buster hissed.

"No one just shows up late for the Navy. What were you thinking?" Alvin cursed and walked away.

"Eddie, can't you spin a tale better than that?" Claude stood with his hands crossed over his chest.

Eddie defiantly crossed his hands over his chest too and said, "Well, it's the capital-T truth."

Walter ignored the cussing and jokes that followed. Some were laughing—some were mad. He didn't care.

He knew Eddie was genuine, through and through. He embraced his friend with a quick, heartfelt hug.

When the others walked away, Walter pulled Eddie's elbow and said, "Eddie, I promised Alberta I'd return to her safely. I told you when we first met up on this ship that I'd help you get back to Emma. Now I want you to help me."

"Oh, for sure. It's you and me and me and you. We'll keep our promises no matter what."

———————

After refueling, replenishing food supplies, and receiving more ammunition, the *Denver* headed out on her new mission and crossed the International Date Line again.

Walter pulled deck-sweeping duties after muster call on June twelfth. The sweeping turned to mopping as he and a couple others frowned at the souvenirs the albatross birds left on the main deck around the turrets recently when they'd visited the ship.

All deck floors throughout the ship were steel, but the main deck had teak wood over the steel for better traction. While sweeping and mopping, Walter's ears perked up when he heard President Roosevelt's Fireside Chat broadcast over the 1MC.

He listened while he worked, as did the other gunners. The president spoke of victory in North Africa and Sicily, but he said the heaviest and most decisive fighting was currently going on in Russia. And that naval, land, and air strength in the Pacific was constantly growing.

The president went on to say that rationing coffee in the American homes would be terminated, and he anticipated that in a short time, sugar allowance would increase.

In the Pacific, by relentless submarine and Naval attacks, and amphibious thrusts, and ever-mounting air attacks, we have deprived the Japs of the power to check the momentum of our ever-growing and ever-advancing military forces. We have reduced the Japs' shipping by more than three million tons. We have overcome their original advantage in the air. We have cut off from a return to the homeland tens of thousands of beleaguered Japanese troops who now face starvation or ultimate surrender. And we have cut down their Naval strength, so that for many months they have avoided all risk of encounter with our Naval forces.

At this part of the speech, the gunners added their own speeches in angst while the broadcast continued.

"Well, if they're that bad off, why don't they just surrender?" Eddie asked.

Following some expletives, the gunners got fired up. Their commentaries grew loud enough to drown out the rest of the Fireside Chat.

"Well, they shouldn't have messed with us, to begin with, when they bombed Pearl Harbor," Alvin said. "Too bad about their shipping losses. I'll fire these guns nonstop and cut off more."

"Well, I'm just gonna say it." Claude twirled his cap on his pointer finger. "Hirohito is their god. They believe he is their living god. So they fight for him at all costs to bring him honor, even if it means they'll die. That's what I think."

"They're too prideful," Buster added. "They don't value life the way we do. Their people are fundamentally different. The Japanese view their warriors as expendable."

More lashing out against Japan continued. Finally, Walter said, "They're too proud to surrender, and they'd prefer to die instead. I just don't get it. I don't think they'll surrender any time soon. And so here we are, having all this fun."

The gunners continued daily drills while out on the open seas. Finally, the cruiser arrived at Eniwetok Atoll, Marshall Islands, at the end of June. The next mission for Task Group 58.1 was to proceed to the vicinity of the Bonin and Volcano Islands and attack Japanese aircraft, shipping, and installations at Haha Jima, Iwo Jima, and Chichi Jima on July fourth.

"Our mission is to bombard the airfields, dispersal areas, and fixed defenses," Captain Bledsoe announced. "We will render their air facilities and shore establishments as unserviceable. Each ship will get their specific assignment. We're going to give them a Fourth of July they'll never forget!"

The *USS Burns* came alongside starboard of the *Denver* to receive and deliver mail. Walter walked quickly to the post office with his two letters in hand, hopeful some mail might be handed back to him.

His lucky day, he received two letters from his brothers. Arthur wrote a couple sentences about his reconnaissance flights on the East Coast and the high security that surrounded him like bees on a honeycomb. Of course, he included no specifics of his missions. The rest of his letter was filled with things about Marcia.

Chester wrote about his cook duties, the *USS San Francisco's* battles at Satawan Atoll, and his homesickness for Santa Rosa.

Walter read the letters more than once. A connection to his family was worth more than any amount of gold.

The task force was on high alert, and preliminary attacks began on July third when a Japanese snooper plane was shot down. Several carriers sent plane strikes against the three Jima Islands.

Early on July fourth, the *Denver* turned on her white truck lights during the predawn aircraft launching operations. The American carriers launched more plane strikes against the installations in the Bonin and Volcano Islands. The calm waters and remarkable visibility assisted the actions. The *Denver* crew knew this battle was primarily going to be air and carrier strikes, but always a fighting ship, she wanted to get in her licks too. At short range, the gunners fired on Iwo Jima airstrips and other installations.

As soon as her portion of the bombardment was completed, the cruiser pulled off a bit, and many of the sailors came topside to watch the heavies bombard for a while.

With binoculars, Captain Bledsoe spotted the enemy airfields as they came into view on top of a long plateau on Iwo Jima. The Japanese planes presented an astonishing sight silhouetted against the sky, parked on the runways, almost nose to tail.

About the time the enemy planes came into view, the captain also sighted a Japanese submarine chaser very close to the beach. Following his quick orders, the gunners let loose as their forty-millimeter and five-inch guns fired in precise syncopation. They shot off a section of the enemy boat's bow. The submarine chaser lamely fired back on the *Denver's* spotting plane but missed.

The attacks by the Navy task force were well executed and precise. The naval planes and ships communicated in tandem with one another, battling it out as a force not to be reckoned with. Their savvy planning and military flamboyance paid off.

Walter turned and elevated his gun by turning the brass-handled wheel on the side of the mount. He cranked the wheel back and forth, and his gun howled in the air as he depressed his foot pedals with precision.

"We're gettin' 'em good, real good," Eddie shouted as they persistently fired away. "See that water tower over there? I want to get it. Let's finish them off."

"Holy cow, this thing is jammed," Walter shouted when his forty-millimeter gun stalled at his station.

"Mine is, too," Buster hollered from a few feet away.

Before panic set in for the brief interruption, two jammed cartridge cases were cleared after a quick assessment. Within a minute, the *Denver* gunners destroyed the water tower. With binoculars, the seamen witnessed the water flooding like small rivers in all directions.

"Well, that's the cat's meow. Look at that, will ya! I wish I had a camera." Walter handed the binoculars to Eddie.

Adjusting the binoculars before passing them to Alvin, Eddie shouted, "Hot diggity dog!" He put two fingers inside his lips for a shrill celebratory whistle.

The "cease firing" command came loud and clear at 1557 for the task force when the entire airfield area and adjacent buildings were in flames.

The *Denver* crew knew the Japanese runways and buildings took a crushing beating when they heard the explosions and witnessed several heavy black-oil fires. Dense, black smoke billowed upward like dark giants walking on water.

Later that day, Captain Bledsoe got on the ship's communication system. "Men, the gunnery was extremely effective, and a shore bombardment could not have been fired under more ideal conditions. We had unlimited visibility and no enemy opposition to speak of. All those Jap planes that were obligingly parked on the runways made this bombardment almost too good to be true. I plan to get out my accordion in a few moments for some good singing. Meet me topside. Happy Fourth of July!"

Within the hour, Walter joined his shipmates on the main deck for some fun singing with Captain Bledsoe. The "Dirty Dee Song" came first, followed by "Stars and Stripes Forever" and other foot-stamping songs, leading into clapping and silly dancing.

Walter dismissed the guns from his mind. American pride flowed through his veins. With unbridled enthusiasm, he grabbed hold of Eddie's and Buster's shoulders as all the sailors linked up together in long lines, kicking their legs to the rhythm of the music.

Although the *Denver* was not in the vicinity of the Saipan battle, which ended on July ninth with an Allied victory, the crew nevertheless heard about the disastrous suicides committed by the Japanese civilians who lived on the island.

The scuttlebutt posts on the ship served as an informant as the sailors learned of other victories and defeats of the Pacific War outside of their specific assignments. Japan's Prime Minister, Hideki Tojo, resigned when he heard of the loss of Saipan. It was the last remaining body of land close to their homeland to control the sea and win the war.

When the Americans secured Saipan, a prisoner encampment was offered to the civilians with the promise of three warm meals a day and no risk of being shot. However, the natives believed the false propaganda they'd been fed when the Japanese soldiers used their voices as weapons. They chose to take what they believed was their privileged afterlife option. Reports of the thousands of Japanese civilians, including mothers and children, who jumped from cliffs on the Saipan Island to end their lives rather than face defeat, brought incredulous shock among the *Denver* sailors.

At this news, Walter battled headaches, fatigue, and sleepless nights. Even with these plagues, however, he never gave up. Rather his determination to work the guns to end the war grew.

CHAPTER TWENTY-SIX

AUGUST 1944

After the Bonin exercise, word came to the *Denver* crew that their ship stuck out like a sore thumb on moon-lit nights with the new camouflage paint she's recently received at Mare Island. The black and white scheme in jagged lines, like a zebra, showed more white than black, and rumor had it that General Douglas MacArthur did not like the look. While anchored, gallons of battleship gray paint, rollers, and brushes suddenly appeared, and the crew took on the colossal task of painting the superstructure in one day, all hands on deck.

"This is for the birds." Claude stroked his brush back and forth.

"No, it's for the ship." Buster moved his bucket of paint to the next section.

Walter painted a large cross. "See, I know where to draw the line."

Experimenting with swirls and joking around when no one was paying attention, the sailors knew every stroke of paint would get the job done. They did not want the Dirty Dee to be conspicuous during battles.

The *Denver* continued to operate with the famous Task Force 58.1 in the Marianas Campaign until early August.

Then the substantial completion of the Saipan Campaign and the start of the Guam and Tinian operations took place. The task force flew their planes for daily strikes against Guam, Tinian, and Rota. They made a two-day raid on Yap, Woleai, and Ulithi.

Walter's ship remained ready on a moment's notice for reinforcement as the seamen pushed themselves to the limit through one dangerous passage after another. Watching. Keeping their guns ready. Remaining on high alert in Condition I. But thanks to the twenty-four-hour vigilance and firings from the carriers, all enemy aircraft were shot down.

Meeting up after nine months of separation, the *Montpelier*, *Cleveland*, and *Columbia* sister ships finally welcomed the repaired *Denver* back into their division. The whole task force was an impressive sight. It looked like most of the American Navy was on the sea together— battleships, light cruisers, heavy cruisers, aircraft carriers, PT boats, and dozens of destroyers.

Toward the end of August, the naval force held a dry run off Guadalcanal in anticipation of bombardment and control of Angaur Island. They simulated air attacks and anti-aircraft machine gun practices for several days. The directors and trainers were drilled using the gridded and intelligence charts so that all of them would be thoroughly familiar with the target areas when the time came.

"I feel as safe as if I was sitting in my living room at home." Walter's gaze roamed the waters filled with the vast number of American ships.

"We're in a battle. You know that, right?" Claude stared at Walter.

"I know, but hey, who's going to mess with us? Who can take us down? Just look at the hundreds of Navy ships. There's no way the Japs can match this."

The Americans assumed there would be counterbattery fire from the enemy's coastal guns. Enemy air, submarines, Japanese PT boats, and mined waters would oppose them.

But this formidable American Naval force, in conjunction with the Marines, was ready! With deliberate firing from plane spotting for almost a week in September, the task force commenced destroying the enemy's coastal defense guns, mobile and mortar batteries, beach defenses, buildings, and communication and transportation facilities. A precise firing schedule was followed for the whole task force, which allowed time for servicing planes, feeding the crews, ship-keeping, and rest.

The *Denver* crew eyed the Angaur lighthouse. Although thick foliage lined the beaches for three-to-four hundred yards inward, the lighthouse stood out as a tempting target for the gunners to take aim at. They'd been informed this particular lighthouse was suspected of being used as an enemy command and observation post. They'd also been told that previous air and ship bombardment, though extensive, had failed to dismantle it.

When Admiral "Bull" Halsey ordered the *Denver* crew to take it down on September fifteenth, the gunners were all too eager to oblige. Their adrenaline ran faster than a herd of cheetahs as they took their shots. And when the concrete lighthouse toppled over from thirteen projectile hits, a cloud of dust and debris scattered across the beach with terrific roars.

"By golly, we got it. We got it!" Walter pushed back his helmet to wipe beads of sweat trickling down.

"We're the *Denver*. We shoot the guns like no one else can!" Eddie cheered. "And just look at the mess we made. Boy, we knocked it to pieces!"

With the collapse of the second lighthouse on their record, the *Denver* acquired her third name, Lighthouse Buster.

Walter and the gunners kept tight to their schedule of firing guns, eating, and sleeping during this battle time. Some slept in the day, some at night. But no matter the watch, sleep was difficult at best.

"I can't sleep at all just feeling the firing vibrations," Eddie lamented, climbing up to his third-tier mattress with fatigue.

"Same here, I can't either, but at least it's a break," Walter answered. "Sometimes I feel like my hands are always shaking when it's this intense, even when it's time to sleep. You know, like I'm a gunner, twenty-four hours a day. Well, I've said that before."

"I just lay here thinking about what if we take a hit in our sleep, and then we wake up and we're just corpses. Okay, that's not a joke. I guess we wouldn't wake up," Alvin said. "The engine room crew never saw that torpedo coming last fall, and they were awake. Twenty of 'em met their deaths before they even knew what happened. And their mothers never got to tell 'em goodbye."

"It's war, Alvin. I didn't lie, but I didn't tell my mom anything about this scary stuff when I was home on leave." Walter clutched his bed chains. "Like Captain Carney said a long time ago, we're either fast or dead."

"I never get a break from the guns. Never. I eat, sleep, dream them." Buster rubbed his temples. "A couple nights ago, I dreamed my hands were dripping blood from squeezing the guns too tight. And I kept tasting my own sweat as it dripped down my lips. All of us were screaming, 'Kill the Japs, kill the Japs!' And then, suddenly, the Exec blows his whistle and tells us to quit firing. We stared at him, and then he laughed, 'Come watch me kiss King Neptune's belly again.'" He chuckled. "Well, that part of the dream wasn't so bad."

Claude sat up from his top mattress, looked down, and said, "Get out your harmonica, Walter. Play us a tune. C'mon, let's relax."

Soon, low humming could be heard from the berth as Walter played "When the Saints Go Marching In."

With the Angaur Island attacks complete, the *Denver* moved ahead for another workout at Ulithi—this time to cover a landing in conjunction with the Marines. She bombarded the islands outside the lagoon while minesweeping was conducted in the shallow waters. The gunners maintained a scheduled firing at the northern end of the island.

Walter spotted a shaggy dog running along the beach when he looked through the scope of his forty-millimeter gun. He hesitated before he could make another move.

Lips curled and gritting his teeth, he shouted, "I see a dog, no kidding."

"No way you do. Not in the middle of these firings are you seeing a dog." Alvin worked the ammunition as the first loader.

"I did too. It was trotting along, wagging its tail, oblivious to this war." Walter looked at Claude, who was the pointer. "Get the Japs, but don't get that dog, whatever you do."

At that moment, the boys on the six-inch gun fired a salvo from the main battery with a roar. When the debris cleared from the explosion on the beach where the dog was spotted, there was nothing to be seen but sand.

All firing ceased when the bombardment mission ended, and Captain Brisco ordered a reconnaissance detachment ashore. A couple days later, they returned with two indigenous natives who informed the *Denver* interpreter that all Japanese had left three weeks before, explaining the lack of return fire.

And with this great news, the *Denver* crew enjoyed a picnic and swimming party on the beach of Ulithi for some brief but much-needed R&R.

Walter took off his shirt and sat down on the sand, scooping up a handful and watching it run through his fingers. His mind took him back to the little dog he'd spotted. Was it shot up? Did it get away? *This war affects everything, even animals.*

CHAPTER TWENTY-SEVEN

OCTOBER 1944

Walter stepped up to the gangplank to board the ship and turned around to look at Eddie. "You know, I feel really small. Do you ever feel that way?"

"Whaddya mean?" Eddie asked

"Well, you know, this war is so big, and I feel small in it. Like I'm caught up in a whirlpool of battles, and I keep spinning. We finish one and go right on to the next, and this war still isn't over. I wonder if I'm accomplishing anything. Sometimes I wish I could talk to my brothers about this."

"Yeah, same here," Eddie replied. "It's been about two years since we stepped foot on the Dirty Dee. We've all been through a lot. But hey, we're doing things right. We're always accomplishing something."

Changing the subject to distract his friend, Eddie added, "Do you think we'll see MacArthur when we head to the Philippines?"

"I guess we'll find out," Walter said. "MacArthur and Bull Halsey will make sure the Navy and Army work together. I just wish we could make some big splashes and get this war over with."

"Well, heck, me too. Hey, the World Series is about to start. I hope Paul plays some games over the 1MC."

Beginning on October fourth, the first five games played over the ship's comm system in certain parts of the ship. On October ninth, while performing their normal duties, the entire *Denver* crew listened to game six, where the St. Louis Cardinals were leading three to two against the St. Louis Browns.

Cheering for both teams erupted whenever runs brought scores to the board. The sailors couldn't see the scoreboard, but they could imagine it. Captain Bledsoe walked around the ship that day, cheering for his own team.

Ted Wilks, pitcher for the Cardinals, brilliantly took out the Browns he faced, clinching the necessary win in the ninth inning for the St. Louis Cardinals to claim victory in the World Series. The camaraderie that filled the ship that day for the final outcome also created a connection to home and a much-needed distraction.

Although gambling wasn't permitted aboard ship, Walter heard conversations as evidence that bets had been placed. He grinned. Maybe he'd bet next time. But for now, his thoughts took him to the win he really wanted—America defeating Japan. There had been too many innings for the war, and he wanted this all-important game to be over.

Cooler tropical air enveloped the ship as she steamed ahead to Leyte Island in the central Philippines by the middle of October. She joined hundreds of other ships, including Australians, in isolating Japan from the countries it had occupied in Southeast Asia—vital sources of her industrial and oil supplies.

General Douglas MacArthur and Vice Admiral Thomas Kinkaid planned four main engagements: the Sibuyan

Sea, Surigao Strait, Cape Engano, and Samar. The *Denver*, assigned to Task Force 77.2, met up with her fighting comrades for the Surigao Strait battle.

The ship's next mission was to destroy enemy personnel, installations, and facilities along the East Coast of Leyte. The *Denver* crew was expecting mines in Leyte Gulf, and they knew the enemy would resist with their PT boats and airstrikes and probably their heavy ships.

Japan proudly occupied the Philippines and had driven General MacArthur and his troops out in 1942. The death toll for the Americans before the retreat was higher than the lost lives from Japan's attack on Pearl Harbor. Even seventy-seven American nurses had been taken prisoner.

In cooperation with the Marines for the battle of Leyte, Walter and hundreds of other topside sailors passed around binoculars in hopes of seeing General MacArthur as they came closer to shore.

"That's got to be him!" Walter shouted, waving and pointing. Sure enough, on October twentieth, Walter watched the general wade ashore onto the island with sunglasses on and wet pants up to his thighs.

"Pass me the binoculars." Buster clambered over to Walter's side.

That day, General MacArthur made a radio broadcast in which he declared, "People of the Philippines, I have returned!"

———————⟨⟩———————

The *USS California, USS Maryland, USS Pennsylvania, USS Tennessee*, and the *USS West Virginia* had rejoined the Pacific Fleet. Only three years earlier, these battleships had all but been destroyed at Pearl Harbor. Now refitted for combat, known as the ghost ships, they proudly joined the war effort at Leyte. Even Japan's Admiral Yamamoto had prophesied these ships would be daunting if resurrected from the dead.

The task force knew the Japanese would be well dug in and camouflaged. The *Denver* sent out her spotter plane only to learn there was little evidence of any activity.

However, on Admiral William Halsey's radar, The Bull knew the Japanese Imperial ships faced fuel shortages. As a result, the US Naval Intelligence had learned to spot the Japanese fleet oilers and track their maneuvers. Following the trails of oil aided the American fleet with hints of the whereabouts of the Imperial ships.

"Where are those crazy Japs?" Buster muttered.

"It's a cat and mouse game. You know that," Walter said.

The gunners were mostly silent and nervous as their ship moved closer to the shore.

"We're definitely unwanted guests," Walter added. "But Captain Bledsoe is tracking everything. We gotta trust our captain."

On October twenty-fourth, the Japanese ships were no longer hiding. Admiral Halsey sent a brief, but terse, order over the Sound-Powered Phone circuit. "Strike! Repeat: Strike! Good luck!"

When the Japanese ships approached the Surigao Strait, they ran into a deadly trap set by Rear Admiral Jesse Oldendorf's force comprised of six battleships, four heavy cruisers, four light cruisers, twenty-eight destroyers, and thirty-nine PT boats. Always a fighting ship with a doctrine, mission, and tactical plans, the *Denver* took her place, and she was ready!

The waters grew rougher, and the large masses of dark clouds looked like they had their own bombs to drop when bombardment commenced between the American and Imperial ships. Captain Bledsoe issued orders to batten down the ship when the weather changed. With only 700 yards between the *Denver,* the *Columbia,* and the *Minneapolis,* the wind kicked up, and the ferocious rain attacked the whole area like a blitz.

As usual for a battle, the *Denver's* photography team had taken various positions to capture images of the ship-to-ship engagements. But with the dangerous storm surge, they disappeared intermittently, protecting their cameras.

The gunners held fast at battle stations, sometimes holding on to one another for stability. Captain Bledsoe had warned of a predicted typhoon. The Pacific was an unforgiving sea when typhoons formed. The high winds commanded the sea, ordering water trenches to form. When the *Denver* dipped into one of the trenches, a wave over a hundred feet high slammed over the ship, creating enormous fear among the sailors of capsizing and drowning.

The seventy-mile-an-hour winds hampered the *Denver's* operations as it did everyone else's. In spite of the weather, the gunners continued bombardment, nearly swimming in the waters collecting on the deck.

The whole fleet took calculated aims toward the shore and the waters, fighting off the enemy ships.

Oh, Lord, protect all of us. Walter prayed with a dizzy head while fighting the enemy and the storm. His body endured fatigue from both fights. Wet to the bone, no complaint came out of his mouth, and he never gave up. But that small feeling haunted his spirit again. Then he remembered Eddie's words that he was always accomplishing something. He tugged his thoughts back to the war mission.

After sinking a Katori class enemy cruiser and a Japanese destroyer, the *Denver* moored alongside the *SS Durham Victory* to receive more ammunition. The sailors watched the burning wreckage of enemy ships disappear beneath the waves.

Sighting a Japanese-class light cruiser, the *Asagumo*, dead in the water with her bow blown off, the order came for the *Denver* boys to take her out altogether. And that they did. The gunners fired at the hapless enemy destroyer and watched her sink ten minutes later. Debris, fires, masts settling, small boats, and wreckage littered the waters, robbing nature of its beauty.

The *Denver* broke off from the local engagement when she received orders to assist an escort carrier unit east of Leyte Gulf, which was under attack by a larger enemy task force. By the time the ship finished this engagement, she was running low on ammunition along with her sister ship, the *Columbia*. Both ships detached from the task force for ammunition replenishment.

The typhoon had settled into a slight rainstorm before disappearing altogether that evening.

The next day an enemy plane appeared with no previous warning from the hills on south Leyte, headed for the *Denver*. The Japanese Mitsubishi twin-engine Ki-46 'DINAH' hurriedly dropped its bombs one thousand yards ahead of the ship before departing. Although the gunners were grateful the *Denver* avoided a hit, all they could do was shake their heads at the poor aim and wonder.

"Don't the Japs offer a pilot training school?" Walter smirked.

"Who knows." Alvin adjusted his helmet.

"They're losing this war," Eddie said. "Why don't they just go ahead and surrender?"

One Japanese plane, in particular, continued to circle overhead while being fired upon by other American ships. But it still flew a steady course when the *Denver* struck her down with five-inch guns, causing the plane to burst into flames as it landed on Leyte Island. Another proof of victory to be stenciled on the side of the ship.

Eddie called over to Walter, "We got it. Others tried, but we got it. Now isn't that something? We're not so small. We're all making things happen."

"I know. You're right." Walter adjusted a loose earplug.

The American ships continued to strike the enemy with hard, fast, and furious blows. Two Japanese heavy cruisers sank while another sustained serious damage. When the enemy's super battleship, *Musashi*, began to sink, the Japanese soon realized the Americans were penetrating their defenses nearly at will.

Groups of Japanese sailors could be seen clinging to wreckage, and many cried out for help as they floated frantically in the oily waters, destined to drown.

Not to be undone with the sinking of their ships, the Japanese pushed forward with unpredicted aviation operations filled with kamikaze bombers—a form of war the Americans certainly didn't want. With total allegiance to Emperor Hirohito, young Japanese pilots willingly gave up their lives for the honor of making their country proud.

The kamikaze warfare raised philosophical questions. The attacks were like a death cult. The *Denver* sailors didn't know if they should respect or pity these young pilots. What went through their minds when they took off from the runways, facing their own deaths in an attempt to kill others?

As one Japanese suicide bomber started a dive toward the *Denver*, the gunners opened fire. Before the enemy plane hit the water in annihilation, the pilot released his bomb about fifty feet starboard. Walter's ship fell victim to the hit. The exploding ordnance jarred the cruiser and sent up a cloud of black smoke.

Although no casualties were sustained, several compartments in the *Denver* began to flood. But the damage-control crew assessed the impairment quickly and began the necessary repairs. Seawater continued to find its way in, and fire hoses were prepared just in case. Divers jumped in the water to ascertain the extent of damage to the hull. The ship slowed to five knots, took a three-degree starboard list, but later righted herself when repairs were complete. Burst seams in the fuel tanks resulted in the loss of about 50,000 gallons of fuel oil.

Walter fired away without stopping, even in the chaos of the hit. While their ship was compromised, he took more aims at an enemy plane, bringing him down with his forty-millimeter gun.

"Another one down!" he shouted.

Fighting continued for several days. The sister cruiser ships, the *Denver* and the *Columbia*, were along for more than a ride with the fleet. The gunners from both ships went to rapid salvo firing, and their targets were on fire in minutes. They observed another Japanese ship dead in the water and burning fiercely from their hits. Fast action produced more fires and sank more enemy ships.

By this time, any remaining enemy ships that could run were sprinting away. The rear admiral ordered the *Denver* and *Columbia* and three destroyers to chase the cripples and finish them off.

"What a sight." Buster shook his head sadly. "These waters are supposed to be beautiful, but they're filled with oil, debris, fires, and litter from all these small boats and stupid wreckage. Just look at this awful mess."

"No kidding," Eddie said. "I don't think the water likes the plane fragments and junk any more than we do. I can't even imagine what's already at the bottom of the ocean."

Walter had cooled down a bit with the breeze, but the air currents couldn't ventilate his mind. "Well, we're not on easy street here. War is ugly. There's no other word for it. Even the waters suffer. And I can't imagine that any fish are around this mess. At least ones that are still alive."

The Japanese Imperial Navy had suffered its greatest loss of ships and crew ever. Its failure to win the Leyte battles meant the loss of the Philippines. They would be all but cut off from its occupied territories in Southeast Asia, which provided vital resources for them, including the oil needed for her ships and aircraft.

Toward the end of the engagement, natives in great numbers could be seen marching up the beaches. As they waved white flags in jubilance, they headed toward the *Denver*. The native boats came out from the beach asking for food and offering enemy information.

Captain Bledsoe was happy to oblige, but the natives presented a nuisance, a distraction, and a hazard for their own deaths with the last of the firing in the area.

Walter observed food donations given to them while the captain and other officers did their best to shoo them back to shore.

A little later, Walter sat down and rubbed his forehead, frowning.

"I just don't know how much more death I can take," Walter sighed. "I mean, I can't even think clearly about these suicide bombers. They're still right in my mind's eyes. I can't shake it."

"I hate it," Claude answered. "I hate the war. I hate the killing. And the good Lord only knows if we kill innocent civilians."

"How do the Japs have the courage for the suicide bombings? Is a strike at us worth their own lives?" Walter asked.

Claude shrugged his shoulders. "They accept their own death to harm us. They're not afraid of death; their admiral has said so. I think they prepare themselves mentally, knowing they're honoring their country."

Walter could only reply with a blank stare, clearly fatigued physically and emotionally.

CHAPTER TWENTY-EIGHT

NOVEMBER 1944

More patching up. The *Denver* was well cared for by the repair ship, *USS Medusa*, at Manus Island in the Admiralty Islands at the Naval Base after the kamikaze hit. The repair experts performed amazing feats when they purposely listed the ship fourteen degrees to port so they could patch the hole to her starboard side.

While being worked on, Captain Bledsoe saw to it that the ammunition hungry *Denver* got stocked up on shells over the next several days with transfers from the *USS Honolulu*.

It was one thing to load shells into the guns and fire them. It was another thing to travel through the water on a Higgins Boat to transport ammunition. So, the task at hand brought no little trepidation among the gunners involved in the process. Of course, Walter took it as a compliment when he was assigned to oversee each trip, and he was compliant, but the edginess never quite escaped him.

On one such run, Claude asked, "How many more runs for the ammo, Walt? I mean, we're used to firing the guns, but transporting all these shells is not my cup of tea."

"Yeah, I feel like we're passing around dynamite," another gunner remarked.

"I don't know when we'll be done, but it comes with the territory. Someone's gotta do it. And it falls to us. I don't like it any more than you do, but do you wanna run out of the shells in the middle of an engagement?"

And so it went for several days. On November eight, Walter led another ammo retrieval on a Higgins Boat, this time to *USS Mount Hood*, hoping it was his last. Climbing the ropes back up to the *Denver*, he expected to be done with the ammunition runs. *Surely, we have enough now.*

Aware that fighting continued in the distance at Seeadler Harbor, where Walter made the ammunition runs, he was not prepared when Chief Thornton approached him for yet another run to the *Mount Hood* on the morning of November tenth. Dread and fear welled up inside him. He thought the ammo runs were done.

"But Chief, with all due respect, bombardments are continuing around us," Walter stated. "And the Japs always go after the ammunition ships." Anxiety snaked its way down his chest, creating a rapid heartbeat.

"Seaman Troyan, it's imperative we get more armor-piercing shells, or we'll all be goners. I'm counting on you, and this next run will complete our stock. This will be the last run, at least for now."

"Yes, sir."

With no more discussion, Walter, Claude, and five other gunners lowered themselves by ropes to the restless Higgins Boat below that rocked up and down with the lapping waves. The morning sun produced bright light, but not enough to dispel the dark fears the gunners contended with. As usual, they strapped their helmets tightly around their chins before getting underway.

Once they began moving, the pilot cussed up a storm, complaining about his own orders for the ammunition retrieval.

"Just so ya know, this ain't my idea. I didn't sign up for this," he yelled.

"Well, heck, we didn't either!" yelled one of the other gunners. "Just get us to *Mount Hood* so we can get our shells quick. Then we can forget about this."

"I hope I keep my biscuits and jam I had for breakfast this morning," one of the gunners bellowed as the small vessel rocked up and down.

The barge finally lined up with the ammunition ship. Walter and the gunners waited impatiently for the shells to be lowered so they could be on their way.

However, the Officer of the Deck of *Mount Hood* signaled to the *Denver* that their men had arrived safely, but they had run out of the specific shells requested.

Chief Thornton signaled back to *Mount Hood* for his men to stand by until further notice.

"What's this about?" Walter yelled.

"Okay, so we put our lives on the line to get to this ammo ship, and they don't have any shells for us? How in the heck did this happen?" Claude was madder than a sack full of rattlesnakes.

"Well, how in the world did this war happen?" Walter yelled when the *Denver* group began cussing and losing patience.

A few minutes later, the gunners received orders to leave and head to the *USS Honolulu* to retrieve the shells. The men accepted the new orders with the motivation to be done and get back to their own ship.

"Let's get going, Skipper," Walter said. "We've got more jobs to do today. I want my men to get the ammo as fast as we can and get home."

"Home?"

"Yeah, you heard right, the *Denver's* our home."

The pilot steered the craft away in total agreement to be done with the ammunition run, even if just for himself.

Ten minutes later. Boom!

Walter and his crew suddenly heard an earsplitting explosion like no other. Before they could even determine the cause, the massive blast temporarily blinded them. The *USS Mount Hood* exploded in a cloud of smoke at 0850 that filled the morning sky. The airbursts of lead and steel crashed high. Explosion fragments rained down on Walter and the others like an avalanche as they all hit the deck.

The emergency sirens from other ships around wailed in distress.

Disoriented and fearing for his very life, Walter raised his head and tried to look around. The close-up view of the deafening explosions was horrific. Assuming the Japanese had just fired on the ammunition ship, Walter prayed that their barge stayed hidden from the enemy while floating vulnerably in the open waters.

Hide us, God, hide us. Fear spun at lightning speed while his beating heart pounded in his ears. *Get us to safety, God.*

"Keep us going, pilot, keep us going! Get us outa here!" Walter shrieked, hugging his helmet. The waves absorbed his prayers. *Am I going to die? Am I going to die?* The pyrotechnics, shells, steel fragments, and ammunition continued exploding nonstop. *Inhale, exhale, inhale, exhale.*

"I'm trying, I'm trying!" the poor pilot yelled back. "I'm still taking you to *Honolulu.* She's closer than the *Denver.* We can board her for safety. And you can get your shells."

With herculean efforts, the pilot nudged the Higgins Boat to the highest speed it could travel. Fire and smoke in the water surrounded them, creating imminent danger. Even so, Walter could still see red, green, blue, and yellow dyes in the waters from the exploded shells.

Claude tried to stand but was so shocked his legs gave way. Walter grabbed him and propped him up. He could see his muscles contracting—his neck, his face, his arms.

"Claude, stay with us. C'mon, we're headed to another ship. We're safe so far."

Gigantic plumes of dark smoke from the explosion continued to erupt upward, encircling the barge.

Walter's eyes and nostrils burned from the acrid fumes of exploded ordinance and burning fuel oil. Coughing spells from inhalation of the fumes soon overtook him.

The oil-contaminated water splashed over the barge as she traveled at top speed to the *Honolulu*.

After the shower of debris had somewhat dissipated, only part of the exploded ammunition ship remained to be seen. When Walter and the others could finally see, they trembled in fear at the sight of the quickly sinking ship.

"Those men ... they're all gone! Walter, I tell you, they're all gone," Claude moaned. "We were just there. We just talked to them. We could have blown up with them."

The tough sailors' emotions turned raw from the sight they'd just witnessed. Walter heard someone say, "God be with them." And then he saw one of the boys lean over the edge of the barge to vomit.

An image of Alberta flickered through his mind.

Claude clutched Walter's arm. "Walter, pray for us. Now!"

Walter remained in his sitting position, but his soul was down on its knees. Trying desperately to swallow the fear that threatened to steal his breath, he pleaded in earnest between fits of coughing. "God, we've been through so much. We didn't come through all these battles only to be blasted out here on a Higgins Boat. Please God, get us to safety." He used two fingers to rub his tear ducts.

The skipper rapidly navigated the choppy waters. The seven men clutched their helmets tightly in all-consuming fear of what they'd just witnessed. Walter's whole body shook with his heart palpitations. He watched two of the gunners huddled together, trembling like shot pigeons.

Despite the chaos, smoke, and oil-slicked waters, the barge made it to the *Honolulu*.

Still hearing the wailing sirens, Walter watched with bated breath as the armor-piercing shells in crates were lowered from the starboard side of the ship. He and the gunners got them all loaded up as fast as they could. The Officer of the Deck temporarily boarded the boat.

With a shaky voice, Walter asked him to inform the *Denver* of their safety.

"Troyan, we're taking care of that now. So glad you boys are safe. No reports have come in yet as to why the *Hood* exploded. Apparently, it was not an enemy attack."

With the transfer of ammunition complete, Walter's crew headed back to the *Denver*.

But the rattled gunners kept repeating, "That could have been us, that could have been us."

"If we'd been next to that ship ten minutes longer, do you realize we wouldn't even be on this boat?" Claude asked.

No one spoke.

When the boat finally reached the *Denver*, ropes were lowered for the crates filled with the shells to be hoisted up. When the last crate was hooked on the winch, the gunners climbed the dropped ladders to reach the top of the ship.

Exhausted, Walter mustered the strength to grab the rope ladders last to get himself to the top, ever so thankful to be tethered back to his ship.

Captain Bledsoe shook Walter's hand fiercely and greeted all the gunners, thanking them for the successful mission.

"Men, you got the job done. I know that took courage with what all you went through. Well done, well done. I knew I could count on you. I'm still waiting for a report for the demise of the *Hood*."

Hugs and greetings converged upon the fraught group when Eddie, Buster, Alvin, and other crewmates ran to greet them. No one even asked about the armor-piercing shells. The sailors were just thankful to see Walter and the others alive.

Most of the *Denver* crew had witnessed the explosion of *Mt. Hood*. In shock and disbelief, they all assumed the gunners met their deaths when the ammunition ship went up in flames.

Walter, an ever-faithful and loyal gunner, made his way to his battle station to continue his watch at his assigned forty-millimeter gun, even in his filthy attire. Before he resumed his position, Chief Thornton excused him.

"Walter, you need a break and some time to clean up. I don't know that your mind is ready to be back on the guns. I've already excused Claude and the others for cleanup time and some rest. Report back at 1300."

Dazed, Walter mumbled his gratitude.

He ambled to his berth to peel off his wet and oily uniform, soggy socks, and soaked shoes. Throwing his clothes into his ditty bag, he had no strength to walk the bag to the laundry chute.

He grabbed his bed chain to pull himself up to his middle rack, but he was so weak he slipped. Trying again, he finally dropped onto his mattress, not totally sure he was alive.

When he reported back to his station a couple hours later, he heard more details about the *USS Mount Hood*. The ill-fated ammunition ship shattered with her 3,000 tons of explosives on board, not due to an enemy attack but from an unexplained accident. The explosion devastated at least thirty-six other ships nearby—along with killing her entire crew of 267. Other ships were also impacted by the explosion. As a result, forty-five others died, 327 went missing, and 371 were injured.

The force of the explosion left a trough in the harbor's floor longer than a football field, fifty feet wide, and deepening the bottom of the harbor by at least thirty feet. Fragments from the ship landed in all directions 2,000 yards out from where the main wreck of *Mount Hood* came to rest.

When Walter's next sleep shift came, his head pounded from tension. He tossed and turned, wrestling with the scene of the ammunition ship explosion right before his eyes, feeling as if his spirit had also gone underwater. His close call with death ripped his insides with violent strength.

When sleep finally overtook him, he dreamed that he exploded into a thousand pieces, with bits of him shattering throughout the ocean.

CHAPTER TWENTY-NINE

For the next couple of weeks, the *Denver* boys enjoyed a break from the normal shipboard routine while harboring at Manus for the repairs, especially using the recreational facilities. Softballs and bats traveled off the cruiser as well as basketballs for recreational activities. The turquoise waters, palm trees, and the lowlands' rain forest provided temporary tranquility for the sailors.

"I'm trying to convince myself there is no war and that I'm simply having a vacation." Walter kicked at the sand on the beach. "It always feels good to walk on solid ground."

"Let's enjoy some time off while we've got it." Eddie took off his shirt. "Come on, let's head to the waters."

The water games lifted the sailor's spirits, temporarily distracting them from guns, kamikaze attacks, typhoons, fires, and the explosion of *Mount Hood*.

Someone shouted, "Marco."

Walter yelled back, "Polo."

———————⟣∞⟢———————

"Walter, your notes are off. In fact, it sounds like you're playing a different tune. Do you have the right music sheet out?" Mr. Josef's frown infuriated Walter.

"I already finished Bach's Overture No. 4. I'm ready to play "The Dirty Dee" song. Let me show you. I'll teach everyone. Come on, cellos, play with me."

Walter stood and fiddled his ship's song in front of everyone, tapping his foot to the beat.

"Walter, put your violin back in its case and meet me after class."

"No!"

"Okay, then, let's head to the principal's office."

"I have to get back on my guns. I won't go, I won't go, I won't go … Stop shaking me, stop shaking me."

"Walter, wake up, wake up, pal. It's me, Eddie."

Rubbing his eyes with his sandy hands, Walter sat up, confused.

"I can't believe you fell asleep on the beach. That must have been some kind of dream. You kept saying, 'I won't go, I won't go.' Here, stand up." Eddie extended his hand to rouse Walter from his stupor.

"Okay, boy, that was a weird dream. Well, I'm awake now. I think I'll take a walk."

Limp arms at his sides, he walked carefree across the beach, dodging other sailors and watching the seagulls play tag with one another. He started thinking about his family and Alberta.

When will the next mail drop-off be?

What's Alberta doing now?

Is she still at the factory?

We're so far apart. I still feel so small in all of this, no matter what Eddie says. Just because we won the Empress Augusta Bay battle doesn't mean we'll win the war. God, I still see and hear the Mount Hood exploding. I don't know what I'm made of and if I can keep going.

The repair crew was efficient and completed repairing the damage quickly. As a matter of fact, the *Denver* boys agreed the patch-up was too efficient to suit them. They all wanted more liberty time. It seemed they'd barely blinked their eyes—the time to board again came too quickly. The crew had no choice but to reacclimate to the possibility and reality of more battles to be fought after enjoying the Manus beach, recreation time, and soda pop.

The good-as-new ship returned to the Leyte area in late November. Her mission was to help complete securing that area with the task force. The crew was on high alert for enemy submarines and air attacks. They kept vigil for anything above the water as well as below.

Unfortunately, on November twenty-seventh, the *Denver* endured a surprise attack by a Japanese aircraft when it dropped a bomb 200 yards off the ship's starboard side. Though it was not a direct hit, the exploding bomb fragments wounded four sailors. This close call precipitated a nerve-racking hour of attacks from Japanese kamikaze planes.

Again, on November twenty-ninth, the *Denver* crew suffered another day of torment by kamikaze aircraft. The enemy planes attempted deadly plunges right and left. The gunners constantly pounded the threatening suicide planes while combating their own fears.

A few days later, even with guns firing periodically from other ships and the enemy lurking in the sea and sky, the *USS Conner* managed to drop off fifty-seven bags of mail to the *Denver*.

As usual, the mail station crew never announced mail call until everything had been sorted through.

Walter saw the drop-off, and he was losing patience. Surely, he would hear from Alberta.

Once mail call was announced, Walter still had to wait until his watch ended at the guns, and then he had to wait his turn for his appointed time. But once the time came, he made a dash down several ladders in record time.

"Hey, where's the fire?" one man shouted when Walter nearly collided with him.

"Um, sorry."

He continued on and still knocked into a few others before he got in line at the mail station.

When he finally got to the front, he said, "Troyan." Out of breath, Walter anticipated what his hands might get.

"Sorry, nothing this time." The mail clerk looked behind Walter. "Next."

With a sunk heart, his feet couldn't take him away from the postal window. "Are you sure?"

"Oh, wait a minute," another clerk said. "Did you say Troyan? I've got a few letters here. Sorry, Walt, I hadn't gotten these to your side yet."

Walter grabbed the letters and mumbled his thanks. He found a place to get off by himself. He hit the jackpot today. He fingered letters from his parents, Chester, Arthur, and most importantly, Alberta.

Alberta's letter came first. He read it over and over, fingering her feminine handwriting, keeping her pretty face in his mind, and smelling a faint spritz of perfume on the paper edged with roses. She wrote about more women getting hired at the factory, and she especially liked her new friends, Thelma, Pauline, and twins, Mary and Sue.

> The work in our factory is hard and heavy, but our spirits are light as we join our hands together for the war effort. It's really the right thing for us to do. When I get tired, I tell myself that you're working so much harder than me. I can't wait for you to come home so we can be together again. And Mildred misses Robbie too. When will this crazy war end? I look at my beautiful ring every day.

Chester's brief letter with a couple of cutouts from censoring assured Walter that he was okay, even as the *San Francisco* battled out other Pacific engagements as his own ship did. At the end of his letter, he read, *Do you still have the cartoon picture of me? I will close with the best of luck and clear sailing.*

Mom's letter caught him up with the neighborhood news and Pop's bakery.

He opened Arthur's letter last. *Got married?* Stunned, he reread it.

> Marcia and I got married November third when I was on liberty. She looked beautiful. We got some pictures. Mom and Pop are happy for us. They say now they have a daughter. Well, brother, I guess that means you have a sister.

Walter folded his letters and meandered back to his berth in a daze. His brother got married? *Well, I will be next when this crazy war ends. I will be next. And Chester and Arthur will have another sister. A beautiful one at that.*

The *Denver* steamed ahead to the Mindoro Operation in the Philippines the next month and worked with the Carrier Escort group. The numerous enemy air attacks never let up. The fleet formation often maneuvered radically to avoid suicide crashes. One bomb dropped two hundred yards off the starboard side of the *Denver* and resulted in several wounded sailors from the fragments.

"Secure the ship!" Captain Bledsoe yelled over the 1MC on December fourteenth.

Towering walls of water kicked up ferociously as Typhoon Cobra blew into the Philippine seas. The torrential rain and winds that, at times, exceeded one hundred mph created chaos in the skies as planes went adrift, collided, and burst into flames. Salt water blew in throughout the *Denver* as the crew scrambled to batten down the ship.

In the mess hall, the kitchen crew tied the tables and benches together, scooting them to the sides, in hopes they wouldn't fly around as so many loose objects did in a typhoon.

"Why didn't we hear about these typhoons before we enlisted?" Eddie yelled through the torrential rains.

Alvin secured his jacket. "Yeah, they're almost like another enemy we're fighting. I don't know which I'm more afraid of—typhoons or torpedoes."

John Wortman, a bosun mate responsible for the ship's maintenance and equipment, yelled, "Get these hatch covers, hangar doors, portholes closed. Tie up any and all loose equipment and cover the manholes. We gotta win this battle with the waters."

"Hey, I need help over here." Walter frantically checked the drains on the deck and the scuppers for drainage of water, but he stalled as water bursts hit him head on. "The last thing we need is flooding on our ship."

Coxswain Lawrence Craig steered the ship through the storm with the bow pointed toward the waves, since a massive wave striking the ship directly amidship could cause the vessel to capsize. Keeping the engines in slow-motion idle, he maintained a speed fast enough to have adequate rudder control.

Later that evening, Walter flung his ditty bag filled with wet clothes over his shoulder to carry to the chute, thankful for the laundry crew and their never-ending work to keep clothes washed, dried, and sorted back into the ditty bags for the twelve hundred sailors aboard the ship.

Aside from the typhoon, the Mindoro Operation went according to plan with six carriers, three battleships, six cruisers, and a number of other support warships against light Japanese resistance. The Americans secured the central Philippine Island within forty-eight hours.

The *Denver* returned to Manus Island in New Guinea for replenishments, including a Christmas Day celebration.

A program was distributed, which included a Protestant Christmas Service that morning at 10:30, followed by a Catholic service. The published menu for the noon dinner made Walter's mouth water just thinking about it. A Christmas Carol Sing-Along followed by movies would come later in the evening.

When Walter, Eddie, and a number of others entered the mess hall for their dinner shift, the savory smell of cooked turkeys wafted through the whole area. Their eyes lit up when they saw the open trays of candy, fruitcake, mixed nuts, cigars, and cigarettes—all for the taking.

"I'm loading up my tray now," Eddie said.

"Not me. I'm getting food first," Walter said as he made his way to the line. "By the smell of things, the food's gotta be good. I'll check out the treats later."

The cooks filled his plate with roasted turkey, steamed rice, sage dressing, mashed potatoes with giblet gravy, cranberry jelly, peas, sweet pickles, a Parkerhouse roll, and added a bowl of creamed tomato soup and a slice of pumpkin pie.

At the end of the line, Walter grinned when he saw a makeshift Christmas tree. Someone had assembled a cut broom handle and added cigars for the branches along with red and green paper bulbs.

Sitting down, he said, "Did you fellows see our Christmas tree?"

"Yep." Alvin looked at Walter's plate full of food. "I bet you're gonna add a pound or two when you're done with this meal."

"Nah, we'll just burn it all off. You know that." Walter chowed down on his steaming turkey and dressing.

"Here it is Christmas Day, and my folks don't know if I'm dead or alive," Buster said, then slurped his coffee.

"Oh, come on, don't talk like that." Walter took a bite of his potatoes and grabbed his roll.

"Well, it's true. Do your parents know if you're dead or alive?"

Walter glared at Buster at first, then softened up. "We need to be thinking of the Christ child today."

Silence.

"Yeah, Walter's right," Claude said. "We know we're alive. It's Christmas. Let's enjoy our food."

Walter scooted over to make room for Eddie and his Christmas loot. "Yeah, we can think about the baby Jesus and be thankful. We have light duties today. Maybe we should all write a letter to home to let our folks know we're okay."

After dinner, Walter pulled the Christmas program out of his pocket and read the published message from Admiral Nimitz.

> This fourth wartime Christmas finds the fighting men of the Pacific Fleet and Pacific Ocean Areas far from homes and loved ones. But there is comfort in the knowledge that the extent of our distance from home is a measure of our success in beating back the aggressor, Japan, and that through our joint efforts, all danger to our homes and family has been removed. We may look forward to this new year assured that it will see new and more powerful blows dealt the enemy and that it will drive us closer to victory and peace. In the reestablishment of this peace, all of you brave and skilled men will have a share. That is the priceless gift you are earning for your loved ones and all future generations.

Folding the program to place back in his pocket, Walter thought about the new year coming in a few days. He hoped more than anything, the Americans would see a victory and enjoy a new peace.

Right after Christmas, the *Denver* crew was able to get ashore for a one-day liberty and do a little sight-seeing on their own. Besides watching water buffalo run around the Mindoro area, a group of sailors discovered an unexploded Japanese torpedo on the beach. With great risks, they proceeded to dismantle it with screwdrivers and pliers. All the vital portions, no longer dangerous, now lay before them like trophies. Most parts made their way into pockets to take home as souvenirs from the Pacific War.

The one-day liberty on the shore turned out rather poorly for one *Denver* lad who got lost in the jungle and wandered around all night. After near misses from potshots from the Japanese soldiers who did not want him hanging around, he climbed a tree to spend the night. The bedraggled sailor was rescued the next morning by a Marine scouting party who found him sitting perched on a high limb.

When Walter stepped foot on his ship that evening, he heard about the dismantled Japanese torpedo. He was bound and determined to find the sailors to see if he could get a part of it to take home.

CHAPTER THIRTY

JANUARY 1945

When the sailors welcomed the new year, they talked of when the war would end in most of their conversations. Weariness set in. General Douglas MacArthur's land forces had invaded the main Philippine island of Luzon. The *Denver* departed Manus in January for the Lingayen Gulf operation, and Australian ships joined the fleet.

"This war is dirty," Alvin lamented. "I don't know how much more I can take of the suicide bombers. Those pilots are our enemies, but still ..."

"Yeah, the Japs see the same sun and moon and sky that we do," Walter said. "They're following their own orders just like we are. I never cheer for their deaths. Those boys are young and have dreams, just like us."

"Well, heck, when's it all gonna be over?" Eddie asked. "Hitler and Hirohito don't care about the loss of lives. Why do they keep hanging on?"

"Your guess is as good as mine." Walter drew his eyebrows down. "I feel like all we do is look at the sky, the water, the sky, the water. We fire at the enemy to protect ourselves. We fire to get rid of 'em."

What the Denver sailors did not know was that Hirohito had given orders at the beginning of the war to his warriors to fight to the end, no matter, and to kill ten Americans before their own lives were lost. "That's an order," the emperor said. "Do not take the shame of being captured. The Americans will pay with their time and blood." The Japanese troops learned to take deprivation and hardship in stride.

The *Denver* took her place in the Lingayen Gulf in the Philippines on January sixth, operating as part of the covering group. As planned, close cooperation occurred between air, land, and the naval forces for the amphibious landing. The Navy pilots stepped up the tempo of their attacks from the skies, buzzing the enemy ships with bombs and missiles. The coordination of the combined air and water battalion was impressive.

The Army forces quickly captured the coastal towns and secured beachheads. Although the *Denver* crew defended against suicide bombers in their position, the ships closer to the gulf battled even more. Twenty-four American ships sank, and another sixty-seven were damaged by the suicide bombers.

The *Denver* took on whaleboats of survivors from sinking ships as the sailors counted their lucky stars their ship wasn't under the deep blue sea.

Walter and Eddie watched the colossal, reddish-orange, fiery glow across the entire beachfront when the combatant firing subsided on the fourth day.

"Look at that." Eddie stared ahead. "How can you describe that to anyone?"

Walter shut his eyes and lowered his head to block out the horror of the scene. "You can't, Eddie. You just can't."

When the GIs completed the Lingayen landing on January ninth, the *Denver* and other cruisers became part of mopping up of the area and consolidated their efforts with other ships. The mopping up included looking for survivors, finishing off already sinking ships, and surveillance of leftover enemy activity.

The fiery glow across the beachfront when firing was at its worse lingered in Walter's memory. He couldn't get his brain to totally grasp what he heard and saw, nor to get rid of it. Ghostly thoughts of war and death haunted his mind day and night. *How can I ever get these horrors out of my brain? They are not in my best interest.*

Although the *Denver* was not assigned to participate in the battle of Iwo Jima, the sailors nonetheless learned of the devastating results of their fellow United States Marines Corps and Navy sailors. The five-week battle, February to March, saw some of the fiercest and bloodiest fighting of the Pacific War for such a small island. When more than 7,000 Americans lost their lives with another 20,000 wounded, President Roosevelt wept. Temporary cemeteries housed the fallen.

Even with these losses, the United States pushed on, clearly winning the war in the South Pacific. But the war back home in the hearts and minds of the American citizens for the first time was on a losing streak. The Iwo Jima casualties horrified public opinion. Mothers even wrote letters asking, why are we losing all these people on this God-forsaken island?

When the Japanese believed they could exploit this discord with their enemy, they capitalized on it. They believed the Americans to be too weak mentally to deal with the losses. They bet their chips on it.

But a morale-boosting seventh-issue war bond drive, along with actual footage of the battles coming into United States theaters, swept the nation. Twenty-six billion dollars was raised for the continuing war effort, far more than any previous bond tour. The American hearts back home united once again for the war at hand. Their participation and support in the war effort on the home front forged ahead.

The *Denver* supported the operations on Palawan and Mindanao Islands until spring. As the first heavy warship to enter Manila Bay since the beginning of the Pacific War, the ship confidently entered the waters on April second like a fighter stepping into the ring to sniff out his opponent.

The gunners took their orders from Captain Bledsoe and stayed true to their sleeping and eating shifts, working as a team like no other for weeks at a time for all the Pacific engagements. The amphibious operations became routine for the crew, and the *Denver* always had her fighting gloves on. The reports about Manila's battles were grim.

"Did you say civilians? Are you serious?" Claude asked.

"It's in writing. Alvin saw it on the scuttlebutt post." Blood pounded in Walter's temples as he rubbed them. "The Japs committed mass murder against the civilians. Over 100,000 civilians died."

"We can't go back." Eddie lowered his head and shook it. "The cities and towns must be in ruin. When will this horrible war end? We're a part of this destruction, and I don't wanna be."

"We kill, or we'll be killed," Buster added. "You know that. But the civilians ... those children ... well, that's another thing."

"This is just evil, really evil." Walter walked away to look at the waters. He tried to sort out his hammering thoughts. The beauty of the deep blue waters and majestic cliffs spoke of his Creator—the slaughter of people spoke of the ugliness of mankind. He had difficulty reconciling the two.

Before leaving the area, Captain Bledsoe arranged for food donations to leave the ship for the surviving Philippine civilians. Many assigned sailors deboarded the *Denver* to help distribute the food and assist with cleanup and the civilian survivors. The Red Cross welcomed their help.

Walter's supervisor debriefed several of the gunners in preparation for their specific duties for food distribution and helping the Filipino survivors. But nothing could have prepared him for the destruction he would see.

He grimaced at the ripped-apart bodies, many dead, some clinging to life. His stomach turned when he saw survivors—adults and children—with blank stares eating rice bowls with worms. No time for raw feelings. He acted swiftly and courageously to help wherever he could by passing out food items.

When he saw plates of food infested with flies that remained on the tables the Japanese had been using, he stared. *Am I in a ghost town?* He covered his mouth to stifle a gag.

As he got further into the destruction, Eddie following behind him, he picked up a handful of Japanese invasion money scattered around the streets.

"Look what I'm taking, Eddie."

"Well, I'm gonna take some too. It feels good to take the Jap's money. It's worthless, but who cares.

"Yeah, that's my thinking too. Hey, some of this is Dutch money." Walter sorted through the bills, thinking they could be a souvenir, and he filled his pockets.

The more walking around he did, the more devastation he witnessed. Wreckage and rubble from blasted structures, including businesses and homes, lay scattered across the island. He loathed the unending scenes of the carnage and cruelty inflicted by the enemy. The Red Cross volunteers worked tirelessly, demonstrating courage. *They've been risking their own lives,* Walter thought.

His heart filled with pity and compassion as he reached out to help Filipino survivors. He worked nonstop, offering food, wrapping wounds, consoling the natives, and helping some children get to the Red Cross station. The children's bleeding wounds and lost faces tugged at his heartstrings like nothing else ever had.

His amplified thoughts toggled with anger, anxiety, and powerlessness. Walter understood the civilians' spirits had their own wreckage and rubble that could probably never be cleaned up.

Although Japan had already employed diving plane suicides for a good part of the war, the desperate country ramped up the tactic as their primary warfare in March 1945. Pilots and fuel dwindling, the Imperial forces had little resources left to hurl at the Americans. Many of Japan's experienced pilots had been killed in the last three years of the war. The younger novice pilots only had to aim their plane at an American ship and fly it into the target.

The young Japanese pilots were reminded of their duty to the emperor and the glory of self-sacrifice. They willingly gave up their lives, fitting comfortably into the Japanese warrior culture. Not a lot of training was involved, and no return fuel was required for the kamikaze pilots. Maybe the Americans would give up and agree to negotiations. *They will not fight as hard as us,* the Japanese leaders mistakenly thought. *We will tire them out.*

Japan would not blink, which only spurred on ferocity from the Americans for the remainder of the war.

Captain Thomas F. Darden came on board to relieve Captain Bledsoe on April sixth. The new captain greeted his crew from the podium at the stern, and after the formalities for the change in command, the two captains shook hands.

Captain Bledsoe bellowed out to everyone, "Okay, boys, let's sing it one more time before I head out!" He positioned his accordion straps over his shoulders and played "The Dirty Dee" song as the sailors whooped and hollered.

A couple of liberty days gave the careworn crew a much-needed respite, albeit in the ugly war-stricken area of the Philippine Islands.

"Well, at least we're off the ship," Walter said as hundreds of sailors walked down the plank onto land set aside for naval liberty time.

"What's there to do here?" Alvin asked. "I don't even see any recreation facilities."

"Well, take a look at those mango trees over there." Eddie shielded his eyes from the bright sun. "Do you suppose they're ripe yet? I might like to explore this jungle for a bit."

"Yeah, we've got free time, and we're even on a beach, but not with our friends and families from back home. I can't get too excited." Walter took off his shoes to walk in the sand.

"I can tell you're thinking about your gal," Eddie said.

"Well, yeah, maybe I am." Walter grinned and swished the sand between his toes. "Alberta is never far from my mind."

Claude started running toward the water and shouted back, "Come on! The water's gotta be warm."

Walter and the others followed.

Romping, joking, and laughing, the *Denver* sailors momentarily put the war out of their minds. The beach splattered with shirtless teen boys, some in their underwear, some in swim trunks if they'd brought them on board, and some in their work Navy pants.

Many of the young sailors had grown the looks of old men from the war trauma they'd endured for the last two years. But in these coveted liberty times with no guns firing, their childlike silliness overtook them as they splashed one another. The water fights sounded no guns, only laughter.

In the water, their only concern was sharks—a big worry in the South Pacific. But the sailors never ventured out far. The men from their Marine detachment who took post positions on the main deck, rifles in hand, during beach time were always ready to shoot a shark for their safety.

The water rippled over the sand, one wave chasing another. Shoes and shirt off, Walter waded deeper and deeper into the warm blue water until it was up to his waist. His plunge underneath took him into temporary pleasure, where he rolled over and over before coming up for air.

"He died? Did I hear this right?" Eddie frowned. "What does this mean for the war?"

"Well, I don't know." Walter rubbed his stiff shoulder, working out some pain. "In fact, I don't know a lot of things, man. I guess we'll find out more. This is worldwide news for sure."

The sailors discussed the shocking announcement of President Roosevelt's sudden passing on April twelfth when the news was announced over the 1MC.

Eddie swatted a mosquito. "So, will Vice President Truman take office now?"

"Probably. That's my guess." Walter stood straight after greasing his gun and rubbed his sore shoulder again.

"Well, so now will the Japs think America is compromised, losing our president and all?"

"Probably. That's my guess."

"Are you a broken record?"

"Probably, that's my guess."

Communication about the burial of the thirty-second president spread throughout the Navy. On April fifteen, President Franklin D. Roosevelt was laid to rest at his home, Springwood Estate in Hyde Park, New York.

Captain Darden ordered the sailors to dress in their formal whites and line up on the sides of the ship to show respect to the nation's president. He also ordered the *Denver* to stop in the waters at the precise time of the burial, which occurred at sunrise in the South Pacific at Mangarin Bay.

Walter placed his hand on his heart, as did all the sailors. He did not give much thought to his twentieth birthday. He watched the morning sun cast striking gold colors upon the *Denver* and other ships in the area, which had also stopped. With all the flags on the ships flying at half-mast, a sense of patriotism and love for his country permeated Walter's heart. He hated the war and the crushes of damage and death it brought, but he always esteemed his great leaders, starting with the president.

———————— ✦ ————————

By mid-spring, it became common knowledge within the Pacific Theater of Operations that the Germans and Hitler had finally surrendered in Europe on May seventh. The battle-weary sailors were grateful their comrades in Europe could celebrate V-E Day, Victory in Europe. But they wondered when they'd have their own victory. Thoughts of going home never left their minds, yet hopelessness prevailed.

Casualties were high in the active Pacific battles, and the stench of impending doom hung in the air. Emperor Hirohito had vowed he'd fight to the end, even on a losing streak. With all attention now turned to Japan, Allied troops continued their assaults in the Pacific.

———————— ✦ ————————

The battle of Okinawa raged for almost three months in the spring of 1945. Fortunately, the *USS Denver* did not participate directly in this amphibious battle, taking her own assignments further south. But the massacres of this interminable combat reached all the ships through posted scuttlebutts and TBS. Walter wrestled with the stories coming from other campaigns.

Japan enlisted their fourteen-year-old boys to fight, which angered the Americans. These boys are just children, they thought. When the Marines charged into the enemies' territory, the Japanese used the Okinawan population as human shields. They cried out to the Marines, if you're going to kill us, you're going to kill the civilians too.

Claims were made that Okinawan civilians were forced to wear explosive vests so that if they were picked up as POWs, they would explode and kill Americans at the same time.

Back home, American citizens were riveted by the stories from Okinawa. They were shocked at the lengths the Japanese would go to as they held fast to the bitter end. President Truman called an urgent meeting to discuss the Okinawa atrocities and how to end the war once and for all.

When the Americans finally claimed victory on Okinawa, Commander Mitsuru Ushijima committed suicide when he learned his troops were defeated.

———————⟶∞⟶———————

On June seventh, the *Denver* steamed ahead to Subic Bay in company with her old friends again. This time she wasn't taking on another task in the Philippines. Her mission was to furnish distant cover while other ships hugged the shore for the amphibious operations in the Brunei Bay area, northwest Borneo.

"You mean another cruiser division is taking on the bombardment?" Buster asked. "How did the Dirty Dee get so lucky?"

"No skin off our backs," Alvin answered.

"But we all know battles are battles, no matter our assigned position," Walter said. "None of this is good. I say we better be thinking of the others."

For several days, the gunners remained at their stations, listening for orders, always watching the water and sky. When the landing was completed successfully, word finally came to detach from the area.

When Walter's gun watches ended, he coveted his meals and sleep. But he also paid attention to what everyone else was doing aboard the ship, lending a helping hand when he was off the guns. He talked with hundreds of other sailors, solidifying more friendships. The realization that as horrible as war can be, he decided friendships gained made it more endurable.

CHAPTER THIRTY-ONE

JUNE 1945

Still in the Philippines, the *Denver's* fleet proceeded to Tawi-Tawi Island for replenishments to prepare for the Balikpapan Operation in Eastern Indonesia.

"Ya know, we're getting close to three years for living on the Dirty Dee." Claude moved over to make room for Walter at the lunch table.

Walter picked up his glass. "Pass me the moo juice. We just go from one battle to the next. Are we making any difference? I mean, we're firing these guns constantly. Balikpapan will just be another battle, but it won't win the war."

"A lot of this doesn't make sense." Eddie's spitfire spunk was all but gone. "This war just keeps draggin' on. I'm ready to get home."

"You know where this Balikpapan battle is leading us, don't you?" Alvin asked.

"Does it start with a J?" Walter asked.

The sailors knew. Mainland Japan. Details were sketchy, but the undercurrent talk of a surprise attack on Japan with a new kind of bomb floated throughout the ranks. Although Japan was in no position to win the war, her leaders remained stubbornly resistant to surrendering.

From the middle of June to July, the *Denver* remained in Condition I or II. Three Australian and one Dutch cruiser and their accompanying destroyers joined the *Denver's* fleet for the Balikpapan Operation.

"We're making our own American music with these big guns. Can you hear it? A rat-a-tat, tat and a boom-a boom, boom." Eddie shouted and mimicked a firing noise just outside of turret three. "I tell ya, these guns sound like a thousand wild men beating on drums."

"Yeah, Eddie, let's play American music when the war's over, only not with guns." Walter looked toward the conveyor belt as shells moved up.

Persistently, he kept his focus and proved his mettle when Captain Darden gave the order to fire away. As point man on one of the forty-millimeter guns, his gun shot off a barrage of fire at the enemy.

The intensity of the shore bombardment at Balikpapan could not be described on July first. No time to feel—the sailors could only react. Close hits burst in great numbers as the air, water, and land battalions coordinated their efforts. The Allied invasion fleet alone consisted of a flotilla of a hundred ships, including the *Denver,* swimming like hungry sharks toward the enemy.

In the midst of intense firing and battle-fraught sailors, the *Denver* required fueling. The *USS Chepachet* came alongside with their fueling lines, working quickly. Right then, the Japanese shore batteries opened up on the American minesweepers. The *Denver* immediately returned fire and silenced the enemy, all to the delight of the sailors on the tanker. It was not often they got to see big guns in action so close at hand.

Walter looked back to see the fuel tanker completing its job. "Well, lookee there. What in tarnation? Their crew is watching us. They're whistling and clapping and—"

Before Walter could finish, Eddie spoke up. "Hey, I bet we impressed those boys. They don't get to see these big guns firing off right before their eyes."

"Well, how often does a cruiser get fuel and fire guns at Japs at the same time?" Buster said. "I reckon we put on a show for them."

Buster's words were barely out of his mouth when Japanese bombers dropped three sticks of bombs, landing within 800 yards of the *Denver*. The explosions jarred the ship and rattled the crew's wits.

Adding insult to injury, one of the American B-24s, heading for a strike on the beach, unintentionally dropped a bomb way too close for comfort—while the *Denver* had come alongside an ammunition ship, of all things.

The explosion created two fires. One in the water and one in discussing and cussing among the seamen. Frustration and fear rose like ocean swells.

"Heck, we're not the enemy here!" Walter yelled, disgusted.

The dangerous scene whirled through his fevered brain. His paralytic grip on the elevation wheel of his forty-millimeter gun tightened. Pinching himself to make sure he hadn't dreamed this crazy situation, he prayed the captain would immediately steer their ship away from the daunting ammunition ship. Walter's horrific flashback of the *USS Hood's* explosion jolted him. *O God, keep us safe.*

———— ◦◦◦ ————

In July, leaders from the Soviet Union, the United Kingdom, and the United States met at the Potsdam Conference in Germany. The Allied powers agreed to insist upon an unconditional surrender from Japan. They warned the country that without a surrender, Japan would face "prompt and utter destruction." President Truman even hinted at the possibility of a weapon that could change the tide of war.

Atomic bomb components for that weapon were already en route to the Western Pacific aboard the *USS Indianapolis*. Aviators secretly rehearsed the atomic bombing mission, practicing flights in preparation. Right after delivery of the weapon components to Tinian Island, Japanese torpedoes struck the *Indianapolis* on July thirtieth. The sinking of the *USS Indianapolis*, which happened in twelve minutes, resulted in the greatest single loss of life at sea from a single ship in the history of the US Navy. Nevertheless, she accomplished her all-important mission.

With the completion of the Balikpapan Operation behind them, the *Denver* headed for Leyte again. The crew enjoyed a brief respite for a week. During this liberty time, Walter pulled shore patrol duty. Thankful he'd already taken the limited training in law enforcement for the purpose of patrolling the shores a few weeks earlier, he decided not to mention his assignment.

When he'd started to play his harmonica and settle down the night before, Buster jabbered, "Pssst, Walter, I saw your name on the shore patrol schedule for tomorrow. Boy, I can't wait to see my name. Lucky you."

"What? Why didn't ya tell us?" Claude cracked a crooked smile. "Hey, I woulda told you. You better let us know if you see any girls."

Alvin laughed at the barb. The men started lurid joking. Walter looked around at his buddies as if they were uninvited guests.

"Well, you'll be off the ship too. You'll see the same things I'll see. And, by the way, there's no glamour in SP duties. You should know that. Good night." Walter yawned and put the harmonica to his lips again. He continued to play softly, implying that he wanted to get some sleep.

The next day, Walter met up with his shore patrol group and the officer in charge at 0800 for an eight-hour shift.

Chief Master-at-Arms Stuckey passed out SP armbands and quickly reviewed the duties and expectations. "You each have a mandate to ensure order and discipline by our crew while we're inland. Your role as an intermediary between the locals and the *Denver* boys should a conflict arise is significant."

He passed out batons. "Bring anyone back to the ship who imbibes too much and gets belligerent. We'll determine the consequence. You've got a baton, and you've been trained how to use it. Use it if you need to."

When the group of eight men left the ship, once again, Walter savored the feel of dry land under his feet and breathed in the fresh air. After the group surveyed their surroundings, they split into pairs, spreading out. Each armed with batons, canteens, and sandwiches for lunch.

Despite the ugliness of war, Walter relished the view in the distance as the sun came crawling up the mountainsides. Not far away were trees laden with coconuts and bananas. The chirping birds and cooing pigeons added a musical touch to the scenery. Walter and Kenny Fielding, from the kitchen crew, walked and talked along the beach, getting to know each other better. He enjoyed Kenny's New York accent.

After cresting a small hill, the two edged closer to the jungle. A blue kingfisher bird swooped down from her perch right in front of them as if to show off her bright blue feathers and long beak. A couple of reddish-brown harlequin tree frogs made an astonishing appearance when they used their webbed feet as wings to slow their fall to the ground.

Startled, Walter said, "Would you look at that? I've heard about flying frogs, but I've sure never seen one."

Then he pointed west. "Hey, look over there. I think we have company."

Kenny grabbed his binoculars. "Well, we sure do. Where are their clothes?"

The shoeless and scantily clad dark natives kept their distance, seemingly fearful, yet they were curious too. They stared at the two Americans, jabbering loudly in their native tongue.

Unsure of interaction, Walter and Kenny finally offered friendly waves. The natives never came any closer while the two continued to patrol the shore for any suspicious activities that should be reported.

Walter kicked up little clouds of the warm sand. "Well, so far, it looks like our fellows are behaving themselves."

Kenny turned in a circle before answering. "Yeah, at least for now. It's still early, ya know."

They looked around at hundreds of *Denver* sailors splattered around the area, engaging in various activities.

Walter hummed aloud some arpeggios and imagined his fingers moving over the strings of his violin. He cocked his head and listened for the cellos to answer back. Enjoying his own private music, he lifted his canteen to drink some cool water.

"—and went to Hawaii. He's still doing great there for the 7th Army Airforce Team from what I hear," Kenny said.

"Uh? What did you say?" Walter, waylaid with his mental music practice, looked at Kenny, puzzled.

"You didn't hear me while you were humming? I was catching you up with the Yankees, my home state team, telling you about Joe DiMaggio's decision to enlist. Some of baseball's big names are still in Hawaii."

"Oh, yeah, right. I think I heard that too."

The two continued shore patrol duties until 1600. Thankful there were no fracases to deal with, they met up with the rest of their SP group and reported to Chief Stuckey. The warm, sultry air hung around like a best friend.

Walter stepped onto the lowered catwalk to board the ship to prepare for his supper shift, hoping to wash up a bit after a hot day in the sun. Yawning and stretching, he looked forward to sitting and chowing down in the mess hall.

With the ship at Condition III at Leyte, the seamen settled into their routine of eating, sleeping, and maintenance duties. Working in some recreation during their liberty time lifted all their spirits.

"I reckon she's a'comin' whether we like it or not," Claude yelled out when the announcement was made about Typhoon Connie's visit to the open seas. "I've never seen these kinds of storms in Kentucky. Never!"

"Well, I've had my days of hurricanes in Florida, but nothing like these typhoons," Buster replied.

"Let's get'er done, I guess," Water said. "It's Mother Nature. We have no choice."

The *Denver* crew knew the drill. As a team, they prepared the ship faster than lightning. They'd all heard that three warships and eight hundred lives had been lost the past December with Typhoon Cobra. Captain Darden turned on all the navigation lights and yelled orders to prepare emergency equipment. The sailors stowed or secured any loose equipment, secured the lifeboats, stowed the dinghies, and sealed off all external hatches to make the *Denver* as watertight as possible.

The sky cracked open, and shards of lightning pierced the clouds. When the giant storm hit, the captain navigated in such a way to maintain as much distance as possible from other ships and steered into the waves to avoid a rollover.

The pelting rain system spiraled around the *Denver* with unforgiving one-hundred-forty-miles-per-hour violent winds. With each lurch of the ship, most sailors stayed under cover to wait out the storm, fearful of the possibility of death, not due to battle firing, but from drowning. Even so, they had no choice but to surrender to the rage of the waters. The heavy waves attacked one another like sea monsters.

With Typhoon Connie behind them, the cruiser headed north for replenishments. She joined up with her bigger buddies, including the mighty battle cruisers *USS Guam* and *USS Alaska*. The ships entered Buckner Bay on July sixteenth.

The *Denver* crew said little in these hallowed waters that gently lapped against the side of their ship. The reports of close to two thousand kamikaze aircraft in large-scale attacks in this area just a few weeks ago were common knowledge.

Walter stared quietly at the sea but finally said, "I know the kamikaze attacks were awful in these waters. I wanna get outa here. How long are we supposed to be here anyway?"

"I heard all the ships are just refueling, and then we're leaving again for the China Coast," Eddie replied. "Orders will probably be coming soon."

"Well, good. I can't get out of here fast enough." Walter's mind and emotions contended with visions of kamikaze attacks he'd already witnessed—human bombs as he thought of them.

Sure enough, the entire task force continued to the China Coast for an anti-shipping sweep north of Shanghai. The Allied ships kept a keen lookout for Japan's freight and supply ships with plans to take them out should any be spotted. But Mother Nature brought forth her own battles in the skies as two more typhoons played tag with the ships in the area for four days.

Even with the drenching rain and immense winds, the gunners rotated at their stations, remaining on high alert for possible kamikaze action. Inside the turrets of the bigger guns, the windshield wipers on the small windows did little to help the gunners' vision, if any at all.

When he was off the guns and back in his berth, Walter stripped out of his drenched clothes. "I don't know how the laundry crew keeps up with this mess."

"I reckon they keep up with their jobs just like we do on the guns." Alvin looked at the puddles on the floor from their wet uniforms. "The good thing for them is those washers and dryers aren't as loud as our guns."

"They probably have a lot of fun doing the laundry for all of us, ya know, like loads of fun. Get it?" Walter cackled.

The *Denver* crew maintained their normal watches while on the China Coast. The ship sailed within her assigned grid for minesweeping endeavors, all fruitless, and watched for the enemy on water and in the air.

"This is crazy. I thought the birds were coming home to roost. Where are those insane Japs?" Buster griped, adding some choice Navy language.

"Probably up to their usual tricks of deception," Walter answered. "Most likely playing hide-and-seek. Can't you hear them calling, 'come and find us?'"

"Well, I thought hide-and-seek games were for kids," Alvin retorted. "Maybe we won't find them or their mines, and we can all go home."

"That'll be the day when I dance a jig," Buster added.

"Well, maybe you'll dance the jig soon, and I'll do a handstand," replied Walter. "The Allies have called for Japan's unconditional surrender. Hope they bite the bait."

Naval searchlight beams swept across the waters continually. The night waters glistened with the unusual designs, ever-changing like a kaleidoscope.

"Back home, people would pay money to see these light exhibitions," Walter said. "And we see it all the time."

"Yeah, but who wants to get this close to war?" Alvin shook his head.

The *Denver* had no targets but still made sweeps during the next few weeks, all fruitless. The task force decided that the Japs were either gone or were saving up for another occasion.

The *Denver* pulled out of Leyte in the middle of July to enter Buckner Bay, Okinawa Island. But right before leaving the war-stricken waters, the gunners fired a shot in anger, driving off an enemy reconnaissance plane. Little did the gunners know it would be their last battle shot.

When the *Denver* entered Buckner Bay, the guns were cleaned, primed, and ready for action. She received fuel from the *USS Celtic* and, shortly thereafter, more ammunition. Bogies appeared on the radar screen, but they were most likely only snooping, as none ever came close to the ships. With many friendly fighters hovering in the air, the sea and air brigades coordinated their enemy watches.

The *Denver* alternated between conditions I, II, and III. The gunners commenced exercises and firing drills as scheduled when circumstances allowed.

Late afternoon, August sixth, Captain Darden faced part of his crew on the main deck bow to speak openly to the divisions that could be accommodated in this area of the ship. The rest of his message would be heard through the ship's communication system. When the captain made arrangements to speak in person to a large number of the crew, rather than over the 1MC, the sailors assumed the words spoken would be significant.

His weathered face belonged to the sea and wind. The captain readied himself to release the worldwide news that a B-29 bomber had dropped the first atomic bomb, named "Little Boy." He picked up the mike and addressed the crew.

"I stand before you to report that Hiroshima was bombed this morning, resulting in tens of thousands of deaths, mostly civilians, I am sad to say. In consultation with Canada and Britain, the Americans took this foreboding action as a last resort, seeing as how Japan rejected the call to surrender. I will keep you informed of updates. Perhaps this atomic bomb explosion, the first of its kind, will end the Pacific War for all of us. Carry on my fine young men."

In seconds, Walter joined in the buzz about the ordeal. His feelings ran the gambit of shock, fear, and hope with this surprise announcement. He talked with the other sailors for hours on end when he had the chance about this startling news.

At supper, he pushed his tray mechanically through the line and grabbed his plate of food from the cooks. He looked at his steaming hot pork chop, mashed potatoes, biscuit, and corn, but his appetite dwindled. Even his bowl of ice cream didn't entice him. The image his brain created for the blown-up civilians in Japan traveled to his stomach and perched in his soul.

He made his way over to the table to join his gunner buddies. Sitting down, he played with his food a bit.

"They should have surrendered." Walter took a bite of potatoes and frowned. "They were warned that destruction was coming if they didn't. The Germans surrendered, and they were vicious."

"Heck, the Japs have been stubborn about everything since we stepped foot on this ship," Buster added. "Like I said a bunch of times, their plan was to win this war from day one."

Eddie clenched his jaw and balled his fists. "You're right, but all those civilians. You know that means mothers and children, grandmas and grandpas. They were innocent. I can't imagine this. Nope, I just can't."

Speaking around a mouth full of food, Claude muttered, "Well, I've said this a bunch of times too. This war is ugly. It's the ugliest thing I've known in my entire life."

"Well, I've already decided I'm going to church when this war's over," Alvin declared.

Walter picked up his glass of milk. "You better, Alvin. You better. It's my prayers that have carried me through this ugly war."

CHAPTER THIRTY-TWO

For the next three days, the sailors focused on their duties and stuck to their watches, still on alert for combat in Buckner Bay. Although Captain Darden's announcement continued to sting, the sailors checked their emotions under their skin—they dealt with facts, orders, and data.

When orders were given again on August ninth to gather topside for another announcement from Captain Darden, the sailors chattered like magpies.

"Well, there's no way there's another bombing," Eddie said.

"Maybe the Jap's finally surrendered." Walter's expression rang with hope.

"Should I get ready to dance my jig?" Buster hopped around a couple of times.

Captain Darden adjusted his wind-blown cap and cleared his throat.

"Men, my next announcement will be similar to the one you heard three days ago. This morning at 1100, a second atomic bomb named "Fat Man" dropped over Nagasaki, killing tens of thousands, mostly civilians, I regret to say. President Truman warned Japan to accept our terms of surrender. He informed them in advance that they could expect a rain of ruin from the air, the like of which has never before been seen upon the earth. They refused to surrender. I will keep you informed of new developments. We will remain in Condition II. Carry on."

The sailors conversed openly with one another with this news that traveled like schools of fish throughout the ship.

"I heard from Merle that this new atomic bomb was like 15,000 tons of TNT." Buster whistled through his teeth.

"What will it take for them to surrender?" Walter asked. "We've had the upper hand in this war for a long time."

"Who knows." Alvin looked out to sea. "It wouldn't surprise me at all if we go into more intense fighting. How much more can these waters take?"

Walter shook his head. "How much more can we sailors take?"

In the early morning hours of August fourteenth, the Federal Communications Commission heard an announcement accepting the terms of the Potsdam Conference was coming from Japan.

US Navy Admiral Bill Halsey immediately sent word to aircrews minutes away from their combat targets. "Cease firing unless you see any enemy planes in the air, then shoot them down in friendly fashion."

That same day, Admiral Chester Nimitz sent the following message to all Navy units: "Cease offensive operations against Japanese forces. Continue search and patrols. Maintain defense and internal security measures at highest level and beware of treachery or last moment attacks by enemy forces or individuals."

On the same evening, August fourteen, 1945, the news became official. President Truman announced the unconditional surrender of Japan.

As the broadcast spread across the United States, throngs of people took to the streets. Horns blasted, and bells tolled in nationwide celebration.

While the *Denver* traveled alongside a tanker in Buckner Bay for refueling, Captain Darden was all smiles when he addressed his crew yet again, topside, to share this latest, official newsflash.

"Japanese Emperor Hirohito has proclaimed Japan's unconditional surrender. I am sad to say we have come to realize that sixty million deaths worldwide have resulted from this long war. But V-J Day, Victory in Japan, has finally arrived, and President Truman has declared a two-day holiday for the United States."

As this news traveled, all the ships began to bob around like apples when they hoisted their general signal flags, indicating cease present exercises designating war. Horns blared in celebration. Friendly competition amongst the ships created laughter and jokes galore as women's brassieres and other strictly irregular items were also hoisted.

While Buster danced his jig, Walter did his handstand, and then he hooted and laughed like he never had before. Handshakes, slaps on the back, clapping, and cheers engulfed the ship.

Conversations flourished as this news began to sink in. Walter and the other gunners arrived for their dinner slot, almost too keyed up to eat.

"The war is over! The war is over! Well, now, tell me, is there a more beautiful word in the English language than *over*?" Walter asked.

"Pinch me, Troyan!" Eddie said. "I think I'm asleep. And when you wake me up, I need to be on the guns, right?"

"I can't pinch you, Eddie. I might be sleeping too, and I just had a dream that the war is declared over."

"What happens now?" Alvin asked. "I mean, when will the Dirty Dee head for home? I can't wait to get off this ship. It's been three years now."

"Yeah, you're right. But this ship's been our home, Al." Walter surveyed the surrounding tables filled with his *Denver* family. "She's provided well for us. Just look around. We're a lucky bunch, even if we're eating Spam and army chicken again."

Eddie got quiet and said, "Yeah, but many weren't so lucky. We all saw some of our ships go under. That's the hard thing."

Walter held up his coffee cup. "Pass the joe. Yeah, you're right. Japan thought they'd win this war, but it didn't happen. Look at us, lucky to be alive and eating supper."

When darkness engulfed the ship, Walter walked to the side railing on the upper deck, port side, and stared at the waters with indescribable relief. *Is this war really over? Maybe I dreamed Captain Darden's announcement?*

He looked up in the heavenly sky where thousands of stars twinkled like diamonds, no smoke masts from firing guns to block their beauty. For three years, he'd wrestled with uncertainties about the war. This evening, he wrestled with new uncertainties.

We won the war, but what will happen next? When will I go home? What then?

The *Denver's* "Dots and Dashes" August sixteenth newspaper issue floated throughout the ship, everyone grabbing copies to read and discuss. The main headline, "Peace," appeared in bold letters across the top of the publication.

The sailors' hands clutched the small newspaper with excitement. They read an extemporaneous speech by President Truman, including details for V-J Day. They learned that thousands took to the streets in San Francisco and staged demonstrations on Market Street with similar celebrations in Denver, Salt Lake City, and Los Angeles.

Walter grinned when he read the Filipinos were throwing tons of Japanese paper currency into the air on every street corner of Manilla. He recalled the Japanese invasion money he had collected in his pockets in the Philippines, now resting in his seabag to take home as a souvenir.

Emperor Hirohito formally accepted the Allies' terms and signed papers on the deck of the *USS Missouri* in Tokyo Bay on September second. The Pacific Theater War of World War II was officially over. The aftermath, as expected, impacted everyone throughout the world.

Although the physical war was officially declared over, the emotional and mental warfare continued on with the *Denver* sailors. What combat does to the human soul could not be described.

"You know, we're still in a hot spot," Walter lamented. "I think everyone knows we still can't trust the Japs just because they signed papers."

"Under no circumstances," Eddie added.

"I think we're gonna be here a while," Buster said. "We can dream about home sweet home, but it ain't gonna happen for a while. No siree."

By the middle of September, the *Denver* remained in Buckner Bay, and her floatplanes continued morning practices of simulated air attacks and sleeve firing. The ship engaged in simulated fueling approaches with other ships as Captain Darden gave strict orders for the crew to remain vigilant at all times and to carry on with the necessary drills and practices.

Within a few days of the signed surrender papers, the crew prepared to aid in the evacuation of ex-prisoners of war from the Wakayama area of southern Honshu, Japan. A directive was issued to fire, if needed, at enemy opposition as the ship remained in her defensive position.

Not surprised, the sailors faced another typhoon in the middle of September as they started to enter Wakanoura Wan Bay for berthing.

"At least we're not at the guns firing," Walter said.

"Yeah, we won't even have to strip down," Claude added.

Captain Darden turned the ship around to get into open waters. He would have more control of the ship with less chance of capsizing. Remaining close to shore for berthing would be too dangerous.

The boys listened to the rain pelting overhead from enclosed lower decks. The ship endured the shimmies and shakes as the rain-filled clouds let go of their waters like drapes.

Not long after the storm passed, a moldy, sharp odor set in with the lack of time for things to dry out. The humidity didn't help either.

"This ship smells like rotten mackerel!" Walter feigned puking in front of everyone, and his friends followed suit when silliness took over. "I'm not gonna miss these typhoons."

When the ship finally berthed at Wakanoura Wan Bay, Walter and the other gunners remained on status alert. They continued their scheduled watches at the guns, always listening for new orders. The ship's main task was to secure and cover Allied forces as they disembarked in case of sudden hostilities.

When the evacuations of American prisoners of war began, Walter mourned for the men as their stories unfolded. Endless days of hunger, exhausting slave labor, random beatings, filth, and illness killed many at the onset.

As the tide of the war turned against Japan, the Allied ships' flow of food and medicine declined even getting to the POW camps. Dysentery, fever, and malnutrition worsened toward the end. Water supplies ran short due to the interference of the bombing of the power plants.

On September twenty-first, soldiers from six army transports advanced into Wakanoura Wan to unload more POW troops onto the beach by the Wakayama steel mills. The soldiers remained alert for Japanese trickery, formed their units, and moved cautiously.

One morning after the *Denver* crew had completed their specific assignments, the sailors calmly made their way onto the concrete jetty a short distance away to get to the fishing village.

Instead of being armed with rifles and machine guns, the sailors swarmed ahead with cameras and plans for souvenirs. At first, the Japanese civilians were uncommunicative, bewildered, and patronizing. But when they became aware that the sailors were more interested in souvenirs than the destruction of their homes, their attitudes changed.

Hundreds of street-front stores and counters sprang up overnight, and prices were raised for the gullible Americans. The bartering began as the sailors took note of the well-stocked trays, pottery, Japanese dolls, chopsticks, cigar cases, picture scrolls, kimonos, sheer silk, and other miscellaneous oriental items.

"I'll take these two," Walter said, picking up two beautiful kimonos. He tried to convert yen to dollars to see if he was getting gypped or not. He later added a rice tray set and two wall décor hangings. Smiling, he said to no one in particular, "I hope Alberta likes these things."

He studied these new surroundings with eagle eyes and took mental pictures of the oxen-drawn carts and hordes of Japanese children crowding around sailors for chewing gum or chocolate.

The market stands of fish lined the streets, and most Japanese rode bicycles rather than cars to get around. He was surprised to not see traffic lights at the street intersections. Instead, men stood on boxes in the middle of the streets to direct traffic. Not many Japanese men were even around, but the few who were always made sure the women walked behind them, which was part of their culture.

"I'm trying to remember this so I can talk about it when I get home," Walter told Eddie.

"Yeah, me too. Look at the kimonos I bought for Emma. She'll love these."

"I bought these things for Alberta." Walter held out his purchases.

The group continued their souvenir shopping while taking in the scenes. A dinky streetcar with Japanese civilians hanging all over the outside passed by. Walter stared at the uniformed children marching to school with their name tags which included the name of the school, address, and blood type.

"Look at those." Walter pointed at the flimsy paper houses with mat floors and strange beds.

"Get a load of these monumental religious shrines," Alvin added. "Why so many?"

Claude shielded his eyes from the sunlight. "I don't know, but I can't even see where they end."

Walter waved to a group of children with toothy grins and sore-covered faces. He stooped down to smile at a scantily clad boy who was fazed and wandering aimlessly in the streets with other children like him. He offered his hand, but the boy shunned him.

"I can't even look into these kids' eyes," Alvin moaned.

"Same here," Claude added.

"It's not just the children—look at the mothers and grandmothers. They are pitiful. How did the war come to this?" Walter asked. "I mean, these children and women are innocent."

A group of rowdy older boys began to throw debris and rocks at Walter's group, yelling at them in their native tongue.

The sailors walked away to create distance, although Buster and several others walked right up to them with an approach to discipline. But with the language barrier and the sight of muscular American sailors, the boys turned and fled.

"Well, can you blame 'em?" Eddie asked. "I mean, they probably hate the Americans."

"Yeah, they think we took their dads, brothers, and uncles away from them," Walter added. "And no doubt they're all fed false propaganda."

⸺⸺⸺ ৵৵৩ ⸺⸺⸺

For the next four weeks, the *Denver* crew performed light duties on the ship while also having some time during the day to roam the beaches and backroads of Wakanoura for their remaining liberty days.

"Argh ... what's going on? I just got to sleep," Walter moaned one night as he ran his hands through tussled hair.

He raised himself on his elbow, still half asleep, when the captain started an announcement throughout the ship at midnight on October fifth.

"Attention, everyone. This is your captain. For those on your sleep shift, I hope you're awake. I think you'll be pleased to hear that I've just received orders to return this ship to the United States on October twentieth."

All the men whooped and cheered, and as the celebration grew louder, Walter laughed. "Well, no wonder he woke us up. He can wake me up any night to tell me I'm going home!"

Euphoria blanketed the entire ship.

"You've got to be kidding me," Walter groaned when news of yet another looming typhoon was reported in October. The day had been quite warm, with the humidity at an all-time high. The crew suspected a storm was brewing even before the announcement was made.

"Well, let's hope Typhoon Louise isn't too rough on us. Is that her crazy name?" Claude asked.

"I don't care what the name is," Walter grunted sarcastically. "Our sleep shift is coming up. Maybe we'll sleep right through it. Okay, that's a joke."

"Yeah, sure, can't wait for dreams of getting drowned," Eddie said.

The fury and intensity of Typhoon Louise were indescribable. With visibility less than 800 yards, the waters rose, and the rain came down in torrents. The *Denver* crew worked desperately to maintain watertight integrity and to fasten lines to anything they could find at hand. The sailors tried not to pay attention to the destruction of smaller ships—some capsizing—as they hurriedly battened down and secured the *Denver* for the storm, many thrown from their feet. Colliding ships and confusion set in as the bay was gradually engulfed in total darkness.

Walter couldn't sleep. He could hear the wail of the wind even in his berth. The intensity of the deck vibrations and the pelting rain penetrated the whole ship. The wind whipped the cruiser's masts without mercy. When his sleep shift was over, he joined the bucket brigade, emptying more containers than he could count over the side from the flood on the main deck. The ship's lurches brought on new seasickness that most men thought they had overcome.

By October eleventh, the typhoon passed to the west side of the *Denver*. The next morning, the intense sun spotlighted the damage. Masts from capsized ships dotted the waters. Debris floated all around them.

Walter sipped his coffee. "I guess we just had to have one more typhoon to send us off."

"Well, it's a good thing the war ended before Louise paid us a visit," Eddie said. "With all this mess, there's no way the invasions and the bomb attacks would've happened the way they did."

"Yeah, you're right," Walter answered. "All in God's timing."

CHAPTER THIRTY-THREE

While berthed in the war-stricken waters, the sailors chatted like a mob of sparrows as they attended to their daily duties. Laughter and jokes abounded. The ship's days were destined for home, and the sailors knew it. The countdown of days for departure even turned into silly songs.

Division officers passed around programs on October fifteenth for a Jamboree for the *Denver's* third birthday celebration. Walter and Eddie and hundreds of others gathered topside at the stern as the band cranked out music under the direction of Ensign Gilles. Three sailors imitated the Andrew sisters in a couple of songs, and the sailors went crazy with their dancing when saxophones blared out "Boogie Woogie Bugle Boy" and "Mood Indigo."

"I'm glad at least the ships get to celebrate their birthdays," Walter said, gulping a mouthful of fried chicken at supper.

"Yepper, me too." Eddie dug his spoon into the giblet gravy hole he'd made in his mashed potatoes.

"I'm heading to the cake and ice cream table," Buster said. "Who wants to trade me their piece of cake for my ice cream?"

"You got a taker," Walter answered.

The sun remained behind the clouds on October twentieth, the day of departure for the States, but the sailor's jubilant spirits made up for the dismal sky. The men bustled around, and no one took a sleep shift when the *Denver* disembarked from its berth, headed for Pearl Harbor. Everyone streamed to the main deck, stem to bow, to gather around with one another for the farewell to the Japanese Islands.

Within a few hours, still on the lookout for trouble, the gunners sank two enemy mines. Steaming ahead, the sailors resumed their daily watches of station assignments, eating, and sleeping. Always ready for orders, the gunners conducted firing and held anti-aircraft sleeve-firing practices per orders. Passing through several time zones, their schedules were adjusted.

Although the gunner crew still engaged in target practices and normal ship duties never lapsed, the atmosphere surrounding the sailors was lighthearted. The men laughed and cut up like there was no tomorrow.

After dinner one night, Buster summoned his pals for a poker game. "I've got me some do-re-mi. We might as well spend our wages. Who wants to play?"

Walter declined and took off for the mess hall for a scheduled movie time with some other friends.

Eddie hurried to catch up with him. "I guess I'm gonna join you fellows. Buster took most of my money last time I played with him. But I don't even know why I wanna see a movie. I feel like I've been in one for three years now. Ya know, like a newsreel, a documentary, or something."

Before the movie started, Walter glanced around at others cutting up.

"What's it gonna feel like?" he asked Eddie. "I mean, getting off the ship, seeing our families, picking up the pieces again."

"I dunno. I can't think too far ahead."

"Well, I haven't even finished high school, but it's not like I can just walk in the door and go back to my school. I'm too old now."

"Yeah, I know." Eddie shifted in his seat. "A lot of us quit high school. We've got to figure things out. Put that in your mess kit."

"I just hope Alberta hasn't gone back to Indiana yet," Walter said. "I plan to see her first thing. In her last letter, she wasn't sure when her factory would shut down. I just gotta say I love her, I love her. We gotta get our wedding planned."

"Well, I'm gonna grab my Emma with a hug and kiss like she's never had before. She won't know what hit her," Eddie laughed, smooching fake kisses.

The room darkened, and *The Santa Fe Trail* began to play. Walter was always up for a good western. He followed the stars' names as they scrolled across the screen—Olivia de Havilland, Raymond Massey, and Ronald Reagan.

By the middle of the movie, he was so pulled into the plot he almost forgot he was still on a fighting ship.

While en route to Pearl Harbor, Captain Darden's announcement for the rest of their itinerary came over the 1MC.

"We'll berth at Pearl Harbor for two days. From there, we'll head west to San Pedro, California, where we'll enjoy American soil for about four days. During this time, a small complement of West Coast sailors will be allowed to deboard. We'll sail south again and transit the Panama Canal and hopefully arrive at Hampton Roads by the middle of November for everyone else to head for home. We've got to get the ship back to the East Coast."

This itinerary brought much discussion among the sailors. Which West Coast sailors would be selected to leave?

"You mean to tell me we'll all be at San Pedro, but not all of us can get off the ship?" Walter fumed. "I better get picked. I'll only be one hour from home."

Eddie scratched his head. "Same here. I live in San Fran. Maybe I'll just try to get off anyway if I'm not chosen."

"Come on. It's the Navy way," Buster growled. "We should all know that by now."

"Well, I'll betcha there'll be all kinds of ships returning home," Alvin added. "There has to be a plan, I guess. For some strange reason, this ol' gal has to return to the East Coast. Let's just enjoy the ride."

"Well, that's easy for you to say." Walter frowned. "You're from Virginia. I say this is nuts."

The *Denver* steamed ahead to Pearl Harbor and arrived Sunday, October twenty-eight, for food replenishments, refueling, and more liberty time on the beaches. When she set sail for California, she proudly streamed her 1,040-foot homeward-bound pennant with aerological balloons.

The sailors performed their duties and watches as normal. Laundry, meals, mechanical checks, custodial services, deck logs, and so much more continued throughout the ship's travel on the waters, albeit with light hearts.

The sailors enjoyed more liberty time for four days when the *Denver* arrived at San Pedro on November fourth.

Captain Darden formally addressed his whole crew for the last time, expressing thanks for their safe arrival home from a terrifying war. "Men, we all know that you were just doing your jobs, but that's what heroes do. They do their jobs no matter what the odds—and you all did that in spades."

Walter swallowed hard and gripped his cap. *Am I a hero?*

At muster call on the third day, division officers announced the West Coast names who could depart the ship. Commander Wells didn't call Walter's name nor Eddie's.

Frustrated that he was so close to home, yet only a few were leaving the ship, Walter decided he would at least call home.

"Hello, Mom. I'm in California. I'm home! Well, no, not really."

"Oh, son, I'm so happy and thankful, and ... well, I hardly know what to say." His mother choked up and sniffled. "You're back, and we've already heard from Arthur and Chester. They're on their way back too. All my boys are heroes, you really are. After a pause, Mom asked, "What do you mean, 'you're home, but not really'? You're either home, or you're not."

"Our ship is at San Pedro for a couple more days. Only a limited number of the West Coast sailors received word they could depart the ship. And I say it's the lousy Troyan luck that my name wasn't called. We have to head south to the canal and get back to the East Coast. I'll get my transportation papers out there to really get back home. Alberta and I plan to marry right away."

"Oh, I can't wait to tell your father. Our family will be together again, and I'll have two daughters."

"I know, Mom, I know. It's been a long three years, that's for sure."

When Walter hung up, he stood still for a moment. Hearing his mother's voice made it all seem real—he was nearly home.

The *Denver* transited Panama Canal on the sixteenth of November. The exuberant sailors enjoyed more liberty time in Panama City and Balboa, and they weren't complaining. The remainder of the trip to the East Coast was uneventful.

On Sunday, November eighteenth, Walter made his way to Divine Service. The chaplain read some Scriptures and offered encouraging words for the sailors as they anticipated going home. He knew most wouldn't be discharged right away, even after exiting the ship, and the majority would stay in the Naval Reserve. Nevertheless, many sailors would see their families soon in various places throughout the country. He wanted his last sermon to penetrate their hearts for good. A message of hope and peace, not war and turmoil. A message of thankfulness, not bitterness. A message of faith and courage to thwart bad memories.

After the sermon, Walter sang two hymns and listened to the offered prayer. Most sailors stood and departed at the conclusion. But Walter lingered, sitting quietly on his bench. In his mind's eye, he pictured Alberta and his parents and his brothers. He thought about his neighbors who would welcome him home and wondered if there would be a celebration party.

In the midst of his reverie, he sensed God smiling down at him from above, and he was moved to pray.

God, it's me, Walter. How do I thank you? I saw a lot of enemy killings. And I witnessed lost lives on my ship, but here I am, not a war scratch on me. More than once, I thought the Denver was gonna sink. I don't want to take these horrors to my new bride. How do I put this war behind me?

Walter stood and walked to an upper deck. When he gazed upon the calm, sparkly waters, he heard a soft voice.

Walter, be still and know I am God. Trust me. I will always be with you.

The *Denver* took her boys home for good when she arrived at Hampton Roads close to Norfolk, Virginia, on November twenty-first. Captain Darden blared the ship's horn in celebration. The sailors hooted and hollered like nobody's business, throwing their caps everywhere. They demonstrated the spirit of the American Navy with zeal.

Getting closer to the port for docking, the crew had been informed that no one would depart immediately. Assignments would be given to secure the ship. Transportation orders needed to be issued. Cleanup and inspections would take place. Departure from the ship could only happen methodically, according to specific orders of the sailors' ranks.

"Holy cow, when do we get off this thing?" Buster hollered. "We ain't waitin' on the Japs, are we?"

"I'll wait all I have to." Alvin stretched out his arms into a half-circle, full length ahead of him. "See, I'm already hugging the United States, and it feels good. This ship is a prize."

"This ol' girl's been good to us. She brought us home." Claude ran both hands over the deck railing. "She was as dependable as a champion racehorse. I respect the Dirty Dee."

He added, "Someday, I'll say to my children that I was proud to be a Navy sailor. I'll tell them about this war. Walter, you're quiet. Whadaya say?" Claude placed his hand on his friend's shoulder.

"I'm taking it all in, that's all. It was just a few weeks ago we were firing the guns to save our ship, to save our lives. My brain's having a hard time."

"Yeah, I know," Alvin added. "My brain can't even sort it out."

"Well, one thing's for sure." Walter cradled his sailor's cap in his hands. "I know I'm going to build a life of peace, not war. Life's too short to waste a single minute. And yeah, I'm gonna tell my children about this war."

The sailors organized their seabags and followed orders to clean up the ship for the final inspection.

"Well, our ship is spic and span, but she's still the Dirty Dee," Walter chuckled.

"Yeah, she'll always be the Dirty Dee to us." Eddie laughed too.

The sailors talked about plans to stay in touch with each other. Friendships had formed, and close relationships had developed.

The *Denver* reduced speed, and Walter could see the port ahead. He stood on the upper deck, port side of the ship, and gazed at the blue waters. The November wind had scattered the morning mist, and the powder puff clouds formed pictures for painting. Seagulls flitting about gave him new hope. They didn't know anything about wars, Hirohito, or Hitler, and they almost made the war seem small.

Walter breathed deep, leaning against the railing. The north wind blew through his short black hair. The war had altered him in countless ways. He'd seen hard things but had grown stronger from them.

Three years ago, he'd been an untried and untested teenager, skinny and barely age seventeen. Taller now with a few added pounds, his muscles were as taut as fiddle strings. Even his posture took on a new countenance as he held his head high. He demonstrated a new maturity he didn't have when he first stepped foot on the *Denver*.

His mind began a movie reel as he recalled the sights and sounds of the war, the numerous battles, and clutches with death. Some of the frames—filled with horror. Others— with hope and laughter.

The twenty-two men who lost their lives on his ship still hammered his heart.

Jim, I'll never forget you. The sting of Jim's loss had lessened over time, yet his heart still grieved for his friend. Jim said he wished they could stay at the Panama Canal because it was the safest place in the world. Oh, if they could've only stayed.

The image of the hole on the side of the *Denver*, large enough for a truck to drive through, flashed through his mind as the next movie frame came into view. As frightening and destructive as that torpedo hit was, he smiled when he remembered the necessary repairs at Mare Island that allowed him to meet Alberta, his soon-to-be wife.

The toppling of the Angaur lighthouse with the help of his own gun held fast in his mind for a moment. He blinked away the fiery image.

Images of the Filipinos he'd helped flickered next. Children's faces bleeding, and the natives eating bowls of rice with worms. A lump formed in his throat.

He reflected on his dance with death when the *Mount Hood* exploded. *A mere ten minutes saved my life from obliteration. I didn't die. I'm still here.* Memories of the terrifying typhoons lingered in his soul. The blinding and ferocious waters that could capsize ships had enveloped him too many times with the fear of death, not with guns, but from drowning.

How long will I have these war images?

Then his mouth tipped into a grin when he remembered crossing the equator the first time, and he became a shellback after he kissed King Neptune's greasy belly.

The highs and lows, the triumphs and catastrophes aboard the *Denver* underwrote his life story from 1942 until now.

As he watched the busy seagulls circling overhead, the lasting question of what he was made of came to Walter's mind. At boot camp, he had no idea, even after his aptitude test.

But now he knew.

On the long and sometimes treacherous journey aboard the *Denver*, Walter realized that even though he'd dropped out of high school to join the war effort, he had truly been attending school all along on his ship. His life lessons and tests for noble character traits that he would use for the rest of his life were second to none.

He'd learned independence and how to be away from home for a sacrificial cause. His captains, officers, and other sailors had demonstrated the importance of perseverance to him, and he was better for it. The call for courage had come a thousand times, and he'd answered it. He'd tackled teamwork and sacrifice, all the while building confidence to face war trials with integrity.

God called him at the early age of sixteen to fight for America. He didn't contest that call nor ignore it. His allegiance to his country had grown, and his faith encircled his heart in an even greater way. He realized he could face each new wave of his life.

He stared at the waters of his homeland, now beautiful again. The waters that had transformed from nightmares to freedom.

Eddie walked up behind him and patted him on the back. "Come on, Walter, it's time to go."

Walter turned around to join his friends, whistling the Dirty Dee song.

EPILOGUE

On a sunny but chilly day on December second, 1945, Walter walked into the sanctuary of the Southport Methodist Church in Indianapolis, Indiana. Taking his place, heart in his throat, he stared at his beautiful bride, Alberta. Mildred Brown, Alberta's friend from the Mare Island Shipyard factory who introduced her to Walter on the blind date in 1944, stood next to the bride. The happy couple stood side by side facing Alberta's uncle, Pastor Ferman Taylor, and exchanged their marriage vows.

Climbing up the steps to board their train, the honeymooners took off for Norfolk, Virginia, for Walter to fulfill Navy duties before his formal discharge from active duty in April 1946. Meeting up with Eddie and Emma, the two couples found housing together on the East Coast as Walter and Eddie completed their final Naval World War II duties.

Settling in Indianapolis, Walter enrolled in night classes to complete his high school education. Within twelve years, the couple welcomed four daughters to complete their family. Eddie and Emma and their son and two daughters settled in Santa Rosa. The friendship between the two couples continued. Walter and Alberta were grief-stricken when Eddie passed away in 1959.

Arthur and Marcia made their home in Carmichael, California, with their two sons and two daughters. They embraced their Japanese American son-in-law with love in 1981.

Chester and his new bride, Beverly, established their home in Alameda, California. Chester became a member of the Pearl Harbor Survivor Association, and he and Beverly attended their meetings and dinners for many years. The horrors of Pearl Harbor stuck with him the rest of his life.

As a Navy reservist, Walter was called upon to serve his country again in the Korean Conflict in 1951. Per orders, he was stationed at White Sands, New Mexico, for a short time.

In the years following both wars, Walter continued to play his violin and harmonica on special occasions, much to his family's delight.

Their third daughter, Becky, the author, remembers helping her mother prepare ham salad sandwiches for the family. Alberta would say, "Throw that Spam can away quickly, Becky. Your dad grew tired of Spam on the *Denver*, and he vowed he'd never eat it again. He loves my ham salad, but he doesn't know he's eating Spam!"

As he told his buddies on the *Denver*, Walter built a life of peace. He stepped into the roles of deacon and song leader at his church and headed up the benevolence ministry. Until their deaths, Walter and Alberta devoted themselves to their faith and family.

Walter with neighbors Dick and LaVerne Adams; Pop and Arthur run over to their neighbors' home in chapter one.

Walter, front right, Thanksgiving dinner aboard the *USS Denver.*

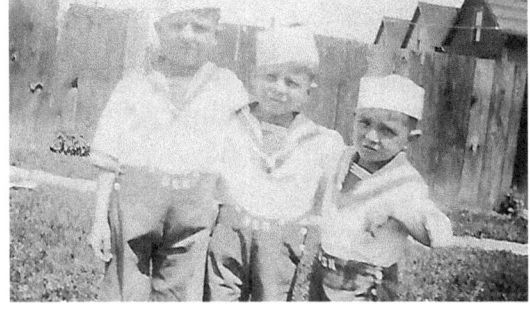

Walter and his brothers, 1928, in sailor outfits Elizabeth refers to in chapter fourteen when she is visiting with neighbor Betty Adams.

Elizabeth looks at this picture with worry in chapter fourteen, taken in 1941, of her three sons.

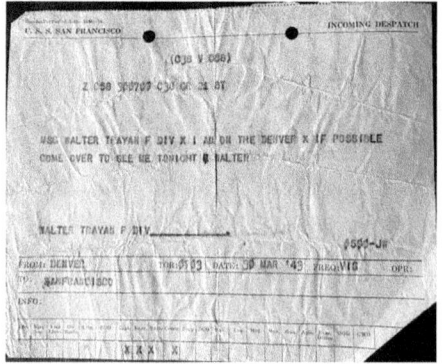

Walter's telegram to the *USS San Francisco* to invite Chester to come over to his ship, chapter eighteen.

Chester's cartoon drawing he gives to Walter, chapter eighteen.

The *Denver* Showboat Program.

The USS Denver gunners, Walter third row back, far left.

Walter, Alberta, Emma, Eddie, 1944 on liberty in San Francisco, chapter twenty-four.

Captain Bledsoe plays his accordion, chapter twenty-four.

Arthur, a radioman flying in reconnaissance planes on the East Coast, chapter twenty-four.

Japanese Invasion money Walter picked up at the Philippines in chapter twenty-nine.

USS Denver, left, getting oil from tanker, January 12, 1945.

The last issue of the *Denver's* "Dots & Dashes," chapter thirty-one.

Japanese souvenirs Walter brings back from Wakanaura Wan, Japan, chapter thirty-one.

The *Denver* crew celebrates the ship's birthday, chapter thirty-two.

Elizabeth in front of the family car with dog, Jacky, at her side.

Walter and Alberta marry on December 2, 1945, nine days after Walter steps off the ship.

The honeymooners, Walter and Alberta, Norfolk, Virginia, December 1945.

"If I had a close friend at all, it was Eddie Page."
—Walter Troyan, March 19, 1990

"Our Naval power in the western Pacific was such that we could have challenged the combined fleets of the world."
—Admiral Bull Halsey

"Let us pray that peace be now restored to the world, and that God will preserve it always. These proceedings are closed."
—General Douglas MacArthur

ACKNOWLEDGMENTS

I owe a debt of thanks to many precious people who helped bring this book together:

My wonderful Elk Lake Publishing team: Deb Haggerty, Cristel Phelps, Steve Mathisen, Derinda Babcock, and Jeff Gifford, all of whom made this book happen.

Jeanne Leach, my excellent freelance editor, who held my hand, sentence by sentence and prayed with me for the success of this book.

Barbara Curtis, my special writing mentor and friend, who encouraged me to write this story, answered countless questions, provided all kinds of resources, and would never let me give up when faced with challenges.

Terry Page, son of Eddie Page, who took me into his family to confirm and expand the facts surrounding our fathers' very special friendship aboard the *USS Denver* and beyond.

Elroy Voet, a *USS Intrepid* WWII veteran, who answered countless questions as he shared his own boot camp and ship experiences. His anecdotal accounts enriched my writing.

Connie Burdine Ballou, a fabulous researcher who found the name of my father's orchestra director at Santa Rosa High School as well as finding Eddie Page's children.

Judee Troyan Maye, my cousin, who provided military records for her father, Arthur Troyan, Walter's brother.

Pam Troyan, Arthur's daughter-in-law, who gave me a letter my father wrote to Arthur during the war about the *USS Denver* landing support in Tinian and Saipan.

Daryll Tsujihara, Arthur's Japanese American son-in-law, who provided rich insight for the Japanese Americans who were whisked away to internment camps.

Tessa Troyan Siegfried, Arthur's granddaughter, who jumped right in to help me with details for the extended Troyan family.

William Rodney Davis, son of Nelson Davis, a *USS Denver* Fireman 1C, worked in the M Division in the boiler room, who provided resources and photographs.

Regina Craig and Mary Reisert, daughters of Lawrence A. Craig, Coxswain on the *USS Denver*, who provided their father's recollections of his time on the ship.

Merle Van Vleet, my father-in-law and WWII fighter pilot veteran, who shared general information about serving in the war.

My sisters, Nancy, Jincy, and Libby, whose love for our parents, Walter and Alberta, encouraged me to write their story.

My daughters, Amanda, Hannah, Liz, and Tavia, and their husbands, who cheered me on from the sidelines.

Troy, my husband and best friend, who gave me unending support and encouragement in the writing of this book from start to finish. Thank you for your many hours of research to help me out and stepping in for extra housecleaning and cooking when I was writing.

God, my Heavenly Father, who has showered me with unending love and guided my writing path every step of the way.

NAVY SHIP TERMS

Aft—Toward the direction of the back, the stern

Amphibious Landing—Military action of coordinated land, sea, and air forces organized for an invasion

Anti-Submarine Screen—An arrangement of ships and/or aircraft for the protection of a screened unit against attack by a submarine

AWOL—Absent without leave

Berth—A bed or sleeping area on a ship; can also mean the place in a port or harbor for a ship to moor, sometimes called berthing

Bogey—An aircraft suspected to be hostile

Bow—The forward part of the ship

CIC (Combat Information Center)—A room on a warship that contains the radar, charts, plotting, and communications equipment necessary for the efficient operation of a ship in battle.

Exec—The ship's Executive Officer. He is second in command to the captain.

Heads—Navy ship toilets

Higgins Boat—Landing craft used for amphibious warfare and many other tasks in both theaters of war.

Knots—One nautical mile per hour (1 knot = 1.15 miles per hour)

Listing—A nautical term to describe when a vessel tilts to one side, noted by degrees

Magazines—Holds shells under spring presser in preparation for feeding into the firearm's chamber

Minesweeper—A small warship designed to remove or detonate naval mines to keep waterways clear for fighting ships in times of battle

Moored—Attaching a vessel by cable or rope to the shore or to an anchor

Muster call—Taking attendance, holding sailors accountable for assignments

Port—Refers to the left side of the ship when facing forward

POW—Prisoners of war

Projectiles—A missile designed to be fired from a rocket or gun

Quartermaster—The quartermaster is the enlisted member in charge of the watch-to-watch navigation and the maintenance, correction, and preparation of nautical charts, clocks, and navigation publications.

R&R—Rest and Relaxation

Scuppers—An opening in the side walls of a vessel or an open-air structure which allows water to drain

Scuttlebutt sheets—Posted dispatch sheets, usually in the mess hall, providing general information such as other aspects of the war

Seabees—Navy construction crew

Shakedown Cruise—A nautical term in which the performance of a ship is tested, generally before a ship enters service or after major changes such as a repair, simulates working conditions for the vessel

Sortied—A sudden issuing of troops from a defensive position against the enemy

Starboard—The right-hand side of a vessel, facing forward

Stern—The back or aft-most part of the ship

Swabby (swabbies)—Slang for sailor

TBS—Talk between ships. A VHF radiotelephone system for contact between ships in close proximity.

Topside—That part of the hull between the waterline and the deck

Turrets—Weapon mounts designed to protect the crew and mechanism of the artillery piece and with the capability of being aimed and fired in many directions as a rotating weapon platform

Wake—A trace on the water surface generated by a moving ship

Zigzagging—A ship's practice of frequently altering direction, usually employed to disguise the true course and confuse the enemy convoy

NAVY COLLOQUIALISMS

Ammo—Ammunition

Blanket Drill—A nap

Cast-Iron Bathtub—A battleship

Chatterbox—A machine gun

Do-Re-Mi—Money

Hashburner—Cook

Joe—Coffee

Mickey Mouse Rules—Petty rules and regulations

Moo juice—milk

Nip—Japanese person

Put that in your mess kit—Think it over

Side Arms—cream and sugar for coffee

Thousand-Yard Stare—Look of a man with a combat harrowed psyche

SHIP CONDITIONS

Condition I—General Quarters, all hands at battle stations

Condition II—Modified General Quarters, used in large ships to permit some relaxation among personnel

Condition III—Wartime Cruising, generally one-third of the crew is on watch, and strategic stations are manned

Condition IV—Optimum Peacetime Cruising, provides adequate watch manning and personnel economy for normal peacetime cruising condition

12:00 AM	0000	12:00 PM	1200
1:00 AM	0100	1:00 PM	1300
2:00 AM	0200	2:00 PM	1400
3:00 AM	0300	3:00 PM	1500
4:00 AM	0400	4:00 PM	1600
5:00 AM	0500	5:00 PM	1700
6:00 AM	0600	6:00 PM	1800
7:00 AM	0700	7:00 PM	1900
8:00 AM	0800	8:00 PM	2000
9:00 AM	0900	9:00 PM	2100
10:00 AM	1000	10:00 PM	2200

WORLD WAR II AMERICAN NAVY SHIPS

Battleships – Battleships, typically with a length of 887 feet, served mainly to bombard enemy coastal defenses in preparation for amphibious assault and as part of the air-defense screen protecting carrier task forces.

Carriers – Aircraft carriers in World War II were like floating islands. They allowed planes to be launched from a distance to attack other warships. With a length of 872 feet, they were also used to spot enemy ships from far away.

Light Cruisers – The World War II light cruisers stayed closer to the battle line to help defend against torpedo attacks by enemy destroyers. Walter's ship, a Cleveland Class light cruiser, was 608 feet in length.

Heavy Cruisers – Chester's ship, the *USS San Francisco,* was a New Orleans class heavy cruiser with a length of 588 feet. The heavy cruisers were designed for long range hits, high speed, and heavy caliber Naval guns.

Destroyers – The *USS Aulick,* the destroyer that accompanied the *Denver* for her inaugural entrance into the Panama Canal, was 376 feet in length. Destroyers required significant seaworthiness and endurance to operate with the battle fleet. They came to be known as torpedo boat destroyers. Two destroyers, *USS Eaton* and *USS* Stanly, stayed by the *Denver's* side when she was dead in the water.

PT boats (Patrol Torpedo) – These vessels were small, fast, and expendable for short range scouting, armed with torpedoes and machine guns for cutting enemy supply lines and harassing enemy forces. Walter told the author the PT boats went crazy when the *Denver* was hit on November 13, 1943, and this firsthand fact, he saw with his own eyes, is in chapter twenty-one. President John F. Kennedy was the commanding officer of PT-109 with skirmishes in the South Pacific during World War II.

THE *USS DENVER'S* WAR RECORD

Under the direction of the four captains, Robert B. Carney, Robert P. Briscoe, Albert M. Bledsoe, and Thomas F. Darden, the *Denver's* gunners fired 18,249 rounds of six-inch, 22,746 rounds of five-inch, 65,993 rounds of forty-millimeter, and 32,074 rounds of twenty-millimeter projectiles. The ship got around. She steamed slightly over 150,000 wartime miles. At the conclusion of the war, the ship's official score of victories was impressive.

She earned the nickname of "Razor" for her gunnery effectiveness and "Lighthouse Buster" for dismantling two lighthouses during shore bombardments against Palau and Suluan over the course of her career.

The *USS Denver* was sold on February 29, 1960 to Union Minerals & Alloy Corporation in New York City for more than $260,000. She underwent final demilitarization and scrapping for recycling later in the year.

Along with her sister cruiser ships from Cruiser Division Twelve, the *Denver* received the Navy Unit Commendation, signed by US Secretary of the Navy James Forrestal, for the Battle of Empress August Bay. She also received the Navy Occupation Service Medal for the duties she performed in late 1945 off Wakayama, Japan, as well as eleven battle stars for her World War II service.

"Life aboard the *USS Denver* was the most traumatic part of my life."—Walter Troyan, March 19, 1990

In Memory of the Twenty-Two lives Lost on the *USS Denver*

(Some have been memorialized as fictional characters in this book to honor them.)

Olin Francis Beebe

Peter Charles Chaido

Louis Frederick Cotaling

Rivet John Daigre

Justus John Drefs

Buster Eli Fanning

Harold Earl Fielding

Joseph James Geraci

Jacob Martin Grace

Joseph Peter Gulas

Alvin Perry Hiett

William Horak

Clyde Bradley Jackson

Charles Francis Jurovich

George Frank Kasper

Thames Frederick Norris

Lieutenant E. M Post

Norbert Joseph Reeder

Claude Francis Tarkington

James William Thompson

Joseph Garland Via

Charles Edwin White

ABOUT THE AUTHOR

Becky Van Vleet is a wife, mother, grandmother, swimmer, gardener, oil painter, power walker, and writer who loves God. She and her husband, Troy, make their home in Colorado Springs where they both share a passion for all things World War II. Becky especially enjoys getting together with friends and family and reading books to her grandchildren. Her website is devoted to preserving family stories and memories, believing it's important to tell our stories to the next generations. By writing *Unintended Hero*, Becky's World War II story will always be preserved for her father and for others to read.

BECKY'S WEBSITE

We all have a story to tell! For sure this is nothing new, as storytelling has been around since the beginning of time. If you like family stories and preserving memories,

Becky invites you to sign up for her newsletter and blog. Go to www.beckyvanvleet.com and look for the link on the homepage. You're in for a treat, as you will receive a gift from Becky, another true family story. Not only does Becky share her own family stories, she likes to share her readers' and other guest authors' stories as well. Maybe the time has come to tell your story for others to enjoy.

BECKY'S OTHER BOOKS

Becky is the author of the "Traveling Series" children's picture books. Inspired by true family stories, young children will delight in the inanimate objects that come to life when they travel through three generations.

Talitha, the Traveling Skirt

Harvey, the Traveling Harmonica

Roxie, the Traveling Rocker

Wally, the Traveling Watch (coming soon)